When Stars Have Teeth

Dani Trujillo

Cover Design by Marcus Trujillo

Editing by Alexis Richoux, Bear Lee and Nancy Juarros

Interior Artwork by Dani Trujillo

Also By Dani Trujillo

Lizards Hold the Sun

When Stars Have Teeth

Dani Trujillo

For the slayer within.

CONTENTS

1. Chapter 1 1
2. Chapter 2 7
3. Chapter 3 13
4. Chapter 4 26
5. Chapter 5 38
6. Chapter 6 56
7. Chapter 7 66
8. Chapter 8 74
9. Chapter 9 81
10. Chapter 10 86
11. Chapter 11 94
12. Chapter 12 111
13. Chapter 13 121
14. Chapter 14 134
15. Chapter 15 143
16. Chapter 16 152
17. Chapter 17 159
18. Chapter 18 164
19. Chapter 19 168
20. Chapter 20 175
21. Chapter 21 180

22. Chapter 22 191
23. Chapter 23 197
24. Chapter 24 204
25. Chapter 25 211
EPILOGUE 216
Acknowledgements 220
About the Author 221

Chapter 1

These meetings were really starting to get on her nerves. Buffy felt like she was on exhibition. *See Modern Indian Struggles Today*! No matter what she said, pain won grants. Not success. Buffy hated it, but more money meant more programming. So, she sold pain.

It made her feel dirty.

College Buffy had dreamed of a job like this, but she hadn't known what all it would require of her. Back home, she could strike the fear of Creator into someone spouting harmful comments. If she did that now, she risked losing her job. Buffy was already on thin ice after walking out of the last board meeting.

Setting her bag on her desk, Buffy removed her high heels. She stretched her toes in the cool air before slipping on a pair of black leather moccasins. Freeing her red hair from the bun at the nape of her neck, she attempted to massage the tension from her muscles. Her neck cracked.

Alcatraz Island loomed outside her window, a constant reminder of why she did this job. After spending a few weeks helping Rosebud, her best friend and Director of Curation, expand the Bunchberry Tribal Museum, Buffy saw the city differently. She imagined what it would've looked like six hundred years ago, when their people lived peacefully on the land. It kept her going, even when clammy pink hands slid across her back or into the crook of her neck.

Inhaling through her nose, Buffy forced the air out slowly through her mouth. The people needed this money. As many resources as the center offered, there was always a demand for more. The housing initiative was on the slaughtering line, and she was determined to keep it from being cut. The unhoused population in San Francisco continued to grow with rising rent prices and Natives needed places to fall back on. This program *had* to happen.

Pinching the bridge of her nose, she breathed deeply again.

Time to get yourself together, Buffy.

Everything would work out. She always got what she fought for. This grant would be no different.

"Are you ready?" Veronica, Buffy's assistant, poked her head inside the open office door. "Everyone's lined up."

Buffy sprang from her chair and followed Veronica down to the ground floor. The gathering room was the entire expanse of their building thanks to the knocked down walls from when they first opened a decade ago. Now, the room was wide, with plenty of space for community activities and events. Decorated with tribal flags from across Turtle Island, the gathering space felt like it was located on the rez instead of one of the largest cities in the country.

Tonight was an Elder dinner, free hot meals for all of the older Natives in the city. It was the only evening event Buffy worked religiously. She was worried that at their advanced age, an Elder might disappear between one week and the next. It was for the same reason that her dad, Muskwa, received a call every Tuesday afternoon while she shopped for fish at the wharf. Her excuse was that she needed his advice on purchasing fresh fish, but they both knew she missed him.

Buffy noted multiple new faces in the crowd tonight. She washed her hands and pulled on a pair of white latex gloves. The ladle handle was warm in her palm. Stirring the venison and mushroom stew, she spooned it onto plate after plate. Along with acorn bread and crispy oven-baked sage leaves, the meal celebrated local Indigenous food while providing hearty and healthy meals for their aging population.

A young man came through the line, free of gray hairs and deep wrinkles. Buffy narrowed her eyes. She hadn't seen this man before. His ink-black hair was cropped short to his ears, thicker than a forest on his head. His blue flannel shirt hugged tight to his lean body, dark brown skin peeking from his sleeve.

Buffy spooned the stew into a bowl and placed it on his tray. "This for you?"

"For her." He pointed to an old woman seated alone at one of the tables. A cane hung on the back of her chair, long salt and pepper hair wound into a braid in the center of her back.

"You're new," Buffy said, watching him gather utensils.

"Santiago." He extended a hand towards her, black ink peeking from under the sleeve.

"Buffy." She waved a gloved hand at him, watching while he pulled back.

"Nice to meet you, Buffy." Santiago nodded at her and turned back towards the old woman.

Buffy watched him from the corner of her eye while she served the long line. Soon the seats were full and she couldn't find the stranger in the sea of Elders and their family members. She put her curiosity to the side; there were plenty of regulars that deserved her full attention.

She started with Mr. Norman, an old Tlingit man from Alaska. He had taken a fishing job in the bay one summer and never left. His children vacated the city for cheaper towns but Mr. Norman remained. Buffy had been trying to convince him to join the Elder Drum Circle but he was obstinate. This was only his third Elder dinner and she still found him silent more often than not. The only reason Mr. Norman stayed around at the center was because he was the guardian for one of his grandchildren, and the center's classes, free meals, and access to computers and internet were his saving grace.

"How's the stew?" Buffy greeted the men seated at the table with Mr. Norman, starting with the Eldest and ending beside the only slightly younger Mr. Norman.

She garnered only appreciative grunts and stuffed-mouth mumblings. Buffy brought them all fresh water bottles before pulling a chair up beside Mr. Norman.

He eyed her warily, offering only a grunt at her cheery greeting.

"The drum circle is having a beginners' class next Wednesday," Buffy said. "Can I sign you up?"

"Will you ever stop asking me to?" Mr. Norman grumbled around a bite of acorn bread.

"Nope." Buffy smiled wide. "I'm stubborn."

"Like a bull." Mr. Norman ignored her and continued eating. Buffy sat silently beside him. Mr. Norman huffed under her gaze. "Fine. Can you get me a ride voucher so I can skip the bus?"

"I'll see what I can do." Buffy kissed his cheek and moved on to her next victim.

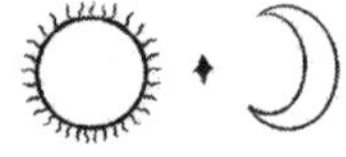

Santiago watched as she moved around the room. Buffy was tall, strength evident in the roundness of her shoulders. Her figure was full and Santiago guessed she was an athlete of some kind. She moved through the packed room easily, twisting and turning herself through open spaces between people and tables. Her smile stole the breath from his chest and he watched her intently, hoping for her to do it again.

"Santiago." His grandmother's voice pulled him from his thoughts. "Can you get me a tea?"

When he found the table again, the redheaded enigma was in his seat, chatting animatedly with his grandmother, that smile wide on her open mouth. Someone was blessing him today.

Santiago set the tea in front of his grandmother, grasping the back of her chair.

"Did you get a plate?" Buffy turned her umber eyes on him, concern in her gaze.

"No." He shook his head, staring straight back at her. Santiago tried to think of something to say, but his heart was hammering too hard for him to focus.

"Family members are welcome once Elders are fed." The redhead pointed back towards the food table. "You should get a plate."

"I don't need any."

"We usually have leftovers." She narrowed her eyes at him. "It's your first visit. Humor me and get a plate. Promise I'll be out of your seat by the time you come back." Her voice was firm and Santiago could tell she was a woman used to being in control. He hated to admit it, but he liked being bossed around by the women he dated.

"You're welcome to keep it." Santiago dragged his eyes over her seated figure, from her moccasins up to her dyed red eyebrows. She didn't grace him with a second glance, bringing his grandmother back into conversation again.

By the time he returned with a full plate, Buffy was gone.

"Abuela," Santiago said as he took his seat, offering his plate to her. "¿Quieres más?"

"No, estoy llena, mijo." She patted his hand and watched as he devoured the food. "¿Te gusta?"

"Yeah." Santiago swallowed another bite of the venison stew, mushrooms catching on the roof of his mouth. "It's different, but good."

"The young lady was telling me about all of the events they have here." His grandmother's eyes were bright, her voice excited. "They even have a shuttle so that I could come here during the day."

"Que bien, abuelita." Santiago squeezed her hand, relief finally settling into his heart.

Santiago worried for his grandmother in her old age. His father, Alberto, visited shortly after her eightieth birthday, and found her frail and malnourished. With no family in the area and living in a rapidly gentrifying neighborhood, his grandmother had fallen into a depression. The demons pulled her into the darkness and whittled away at her body, stealing her sun and energy.

Abuela Paulina was strong but stubborn as an ox. She had refused for months to see a doctor or even consider an antidepressant. Outdated beliefs took time to remove from the mind. It wasn't until Santiago quit his job and booked a flight that she was finally willing to see a professional. Santiago spent the first three months of his new life in San Francisco taking his grandmother to a myriad of appointments, watching as she blossomed once again.

Finding this urban Indian center was the cherry on top. If Santiago was ever going to be able to move back to Colorado, he needed to find her a community. He needed to surround her with a family that would keep her in the sunlight and remind her how brightly she could glow.

"There is a quilting session tomorrow night," Abuela said with wide brown eyes. "Can you drive me?"

"Por supuesto."

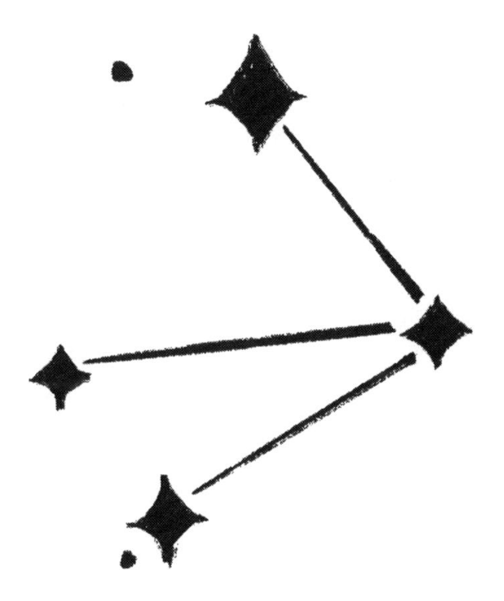

Chapter 2

Buffy was exhausted. This grant application was running her into the ground and she needed a vacation. Rolling her shoulders back, she felt her bones crack and pop from their computer-stiff positions. Maybe a visit to her elder brother in sunny Spain was on the cards. Now that Xiomara had moved across the pond too, Calehan finally upgraded his studio apartment to a home with real doors.

"Visit any time!" Xiomara had yelled across their new home, voice breaking up over video chat.

How long ago had that call been? Buffy couldn't remember the last time she spoke more than five words to her eldest brother.

Maybe it was time to take up Xiomara's offer to visit. She couldn't avoid the entire family forever, especially now that they were moving to exotic vacation destinations with cheap shrimp.

Since leaving Bunchberry, Canada and the tiny isolated reservation she grew up on, Buffy had let distance grow between her and her siblings. Their family had survived so much and she couldn't bear to bring them into the darkness that owned her. Shame flooded her body at the thought.

Calehan's departure to Spain hadn't been too much of a surprise, but Buffy's move to the US had shocked the entire family. The guilt had been eating away at her for months, and she was certain that if she was split down the middle, only acidic green ooze would come from her bones to burn her alive.

Sliding her fingers across the phone screen, she navigated to the family group chat.

Frankie was smiling at her from Juniper's latest photo update, his growing hair in two little braids on each shoulder. Calehan followed up with a photo of Xiomara laying between his legs and Anubis on the couch beside them. Nataani replied with a photo of him and Joy mucking the stalls on their ranch. Her family had their own perfect little families, and she couldn't bear to bring them down.

Buffy was the negative sibling, the pessimist, the glass-half-empty, negative Nancy. In her eyes, it looked as though her departure had alleviated some of the dark clouds following her family and to go back would be to subject them to the darkness once again. Sorrow and grief followed her, and it was her duty to keep it as far away from the others as she could.

Her moving away had been the best choice for everyone.

The center was less than thirty minutes from her apartment, so Buffy chose to walk home. The winter chill was harsh against her skin and Buffy relished in the numbness that enveloped her body. Soon, the hilly street brought a burn to her thighs and she sucked in a cold breath. Oyster sauce and garlic permeated her nose and Buffy had to remind herself that she had food at home. The draw to waste all her money on take-out was overwhelming in San Francisco. Her freshman fifteen turned into twenty once she moved from Bunchberry to Winnipeg and discovered take out was walking distance from her dorm. She had a regular order at both restaurants by the end of first semester.

Camila was in the kitchen when Buffy got home, a frozen pizza in the oven and a bottle of white wine open on the counter. Buffy untied her moccasins and hung her sweater beside the door, sighing heavily. She shook off the chill from outside and wiggled her numb toes.

"A glass of wine for your thoughts?" Camila brandished the red wine. Buffy took it gratefully and slid onto the countertop.

"I'm too tired to have thoughts." Groaning, Buffy leaned against the wall behind her. Her skin was tingling all over, the heat of the apartment and roaring oven forcing feeling back into her extremities. "This grant application is way more complicated than it was supposed to be."

"You should quit." Camila waggled her eyebrows up and down.

Buffy rolled her eyes at her roommate. "I can't quit every time it gets hard."

"I'm just saying you could get a job anywhere." Camila pulled the pizza out of the oven. The cheese was bubbling, tomato-tainted steam bursting through the layers of cheese. "You're so skilled, Buffy. Any company would be lucky to have you."

"Thanks, M*om*." Buffy tapped Camila on the back pocket with her bare toes, hopping off the counter to pull plates from the cabinet behind her. "I love working at the center. It's my dream job. I just hate selling our souls for funding."

"Who hasn't sold their soul for work at this point?" Camila swallowed the remainder of her wine in one gulp, following it with a particularly cheesy slice of pizza.

"It would just be nice to get funding for our successes rather than our traumas."

"You will." Camila held her eye. "One day."

"One day." Refilling their glasses, Buffy clinked hers against Camila's. The sun was setting at the edge of their windows, the western horizon shimmering in the golden light. Plants adorned the windowsill in shades of green, dotted with the dark black and red leaves of the plants Camila said "screamed Buffy". She'd never tell Camila, but Buffy loved the dark-leaved little plants. If they could stay alive within darkness, so could she.

In front of the plants was the bright, hot-pink couch Buffy had fought against for days. Ultimately, Buffy cared significantly less than Camila about the color of the couch and eventually let Camila have what she wanted. Buffy didn't hate it as much as she thought she would.

"How's Miguel?" Buffy asked, watching her roommate from the corner of her eye. She had put off asking, but Camila had worn her tight curls in a bun for four days straight.

Something was up and her brother was a frequent source of stress. Buffy was taking an educated guess.

"He's okay. The transition has been really difficult." Camila paused, eyes glued to the sunset. "On all of us."

"The adjustment takes time. He's still so young." Buffy felt for Camila and her family. Her younger brother, Miguel, had spent time with kids who eventually landed him in the middle of a robbery that quickly went south. Despite being unarmed, Miguel was tried as an adult at age fifteen. Now twenty-seven and fresh out on parole, Miguel was struggling to find his footing in the world. "Did he find a job yet?"

"No." Camila sighed; her eyes fixed on a spot by the sink. "He's been making all of his therapy appointments, parole meetings, everything. But they keep passing on him whether it's through the temp agency or online. He can't even get an interview at the gas station, Buffy." Camila kept her voice steady, but Buffy knew her well enough to hear the strain in her throat.

"It isn't fair." Buffy watched Camila wring her hands until her knuckles turned white. Though she wasn't one for physical affection, Buffy knew Camila thrived on physical comfort. Buffy did her best and bumped their socked feet together. "Why don't you send him to the center?"

"What do you mean?" Camila squinted. "He's a felon and we don't even belong to anyone." Camila and Miguel were unenrolled Indigenous Mexicans who lived in the in-between of being Native and being an immigrant. Buffy accepted them both with open arms, however they wanted to participate, but Camila struggled with feeling as though they belonged. It was one of Buffy's many missions to get her roommate involved with the Chicano group at the center. She hoped Miguel could be the bridge Camila needed.

"Camila." Buffy waited until her friend met her gaze. "He's family."

"Are you sure?" Camila chewed her bottom lip. Her gaze darted around the room, avoiding Buffy like she was the naked sun.

Buffy glared at Camila over the top of her wine glass. "Have him come in next week."

"Thank you, Buffy." Camila squeezed her arms tight around Buffy's neck. "He really is trying his best. The world isn't made for people like him. He just needs a chance."

"He's got one." Buffy nodded firmly and wiggled out of Camila's grip. "Now, what about you giving Elena a chance?"

"Ay dios mío. I knew you were going to bring that up." Camila waved her off like a petulant mosquito.

"Of course I'm going to bring it up. You two are perfect for each other." Buffy followed Camila to the couch.

"She has a twin brother. What if he's my soulmate?"

"Oh my God, Camila, you're so dramatic." Buffy huffed. "No one is saying you have to marry her, but she could be more than a once-a-month booty call. It's been a decade."

"I'm pretty comfortable with our current arrangement."

"Elena isn't." Buffy said.

"I know." Camila whispered.

"Invite her over for takeout night next week. We can hang out here and watch a movie or something." Buffy shrugged.

"You really want to subject yourself to the torture of dinner and a movie with me and my ten-year situationship?" Camila raised one lone brow.

"Not at all." Buffy grimaced. "But I'll do anything for you." She shivered as though the statement had icy claws running down her back. Buffy preferred to demonstrate her love in other ways, and saying it out loud was typically her last resort. Camila was much more direct and Buffy knew she had to be the same to show Camila that she was serious.

"Aw, it's like you love me or something." Camila smiled devilishly.

"Shut up," Buffy grumbled.

Camila wrapped her arms around Buffy's shoulders and squeezed tightly, pressing rapid-fire kisses to her cheek. Squealing, Buffy wrestled herself free of the tiny woman's grip and sprung up from the couch.

"I love you, Buffy!" Camila dragged the words out long, like she was talking to a baby. Buffy ignored her and stomped to the kitchen to refill her glass of wine. "You're such a loving best friend, Buffy!" Camila continued antagonizing her from the pile of blankets on the couch. "You love me so much!"

"Do you think they'd send me back to Bunchberry for murder, or would I have to stay here?" Buffy pointed the empty wine bottle at her.

"I think you should just stay here forever, murder or not!" Camila called out to Buffy's retreating back.

Taking the wine into the bathroom with her, Buffy showered quickly and finished her wine. She brushed her teeth, using the now-empty wine glass to collect water and rinse her mouth. Buffy turned the water cold and filled the wine glass all the way to the top.

Buffy climbed into bed. Setting her glass of water on the nightstand, she closed her eyes and let her head thunk back against her headboard. She took a deep breath and fought to relax the tension in her body. One by one, she tensed each muscle group starting with her head and finished with a wiggle to her toes. Buffy opened her eyes.

She swallowed.

Grabbing her phone, she unlocked it, bright red notifications littering the screen. She opened the call log.

Juniper ... 11:23

Winona ... 2:15

Juniper ... 2:45

Juniper ... 5:37

No voicemails.

37 unread text messages

Buffy locked her phone and turned off the lights. She swallowed the guilt like acid.

Chapter 3

Santiago found himself on the sixth floor of the center, beneath a painting of a poppy-covered hill. He originally intended to drop Abuela off and take himself for a fish sandwich, but the desire to see the mysterious redhead again pulled him deeper into the building. And then he had looked at photos, then the murals, and before he knew it, he was so far inside the building he might as well act like he was meant to be here.

Enamored by the painting, Santiago was lost in his thoughts, when a woman's voice broke through the haze. He spun toward the voice.

"Can I help you?"

The redhead from the night before stood to his side, narrowed eyes glaring into him in the dark hallway. She looked irritated. He smiled.

"Hi." Santiago turned to face her, white teeth shining in the low light.

Buffy shook her head, perplexed at his lack of answer. "Are you lost?"

"No." He took a step closer to her, moving into the glow of the streetlamp outside. "Just exploring."

"Explore during the day," Buffy scoffed and stalked towards the elevators, slapping the button. "When the offices are open."

"If the offices aren't open, what are you still doing up here?"

"Working." Buffy stood to the side as the elevator opened. Stretching her arm across the open doors, she gestured at him. "After you."

Santiago slid through the door, hiding his grin at her brusque behavior. She was feisty. He leaned into the back corner to watch the woman in front of him. Buffy pressed the button for the ground floor, turning to face him so that her back was flush against the elevator wall. For a moment, they stared at each other in silence.

"You know," she said, crossing her long legs at the ankle and eyeing him dubiously. "Caregivers are welcome to participate in workshops and events."

"I'm less of a caregiver and more of a part-time chauffeur." Santiago wrinkled his nose at her, dismissing the idea. Abuela would balk to hear him called her caretaker.

"You can call yourself whatever you want." Buffy held the door for him again when they reached the bottom floor. "But no more wandering around the building. I thought you were a ghost at first."

"Don't tell me I spooked you." Santiago paused in the hall, looking at her over his shoulder.

"Me?" Buffy scrunched her nose, looking offended. "No, but I'm not the only one who works late."

Santiago simply nodded at her with a kind smile, a slow deep movement of his chin dipping to his chest. Buffy glared at him, his curious gaze bringing a blush to her skin. A drum sounded behind them, followed by loud and raucous laughter. A signal the quilting class was coming to an end.

Buffy leaned her back into the door, the hinge groaning as she cracked it open. Cold ocean air snuck into the building, biting Santiago's exposed ankles.

"You should head back in there." Buffy jerked her chin towards the gathering room. "They'll be finished soon."

"I'd rather talk to you." Santiago glanced over his shoulder, stretching to hear the voices behind him..

When he turned back, Buffy was gone.

He stopped himself from calling her name with a bite of his bottom lip. Something about this tall, brusque woman caused a stir in his heart. He wanted to see her again.

Santiago found his grandmother seated amongst the other quilters, tucked between an auntie with giant red glasses and another auntie wearing a hijab with the Zia symbol patterning it. Santiago smiled, Abuela Paulina looked right at home.

"How was quilting class, Abuela?" Santiago took the bag of fabric remnants from her hand and led her outside.

"Wonderful, mijo." Abuela Paulina patted Santiago's arm and climbed into the car. She settled the bag of fabric on her lap and turned on her seat warmer. "Thank you for finding this place."

Santiago kissed her cheek and rounded the car. He climbed in beside her and cranked the heat, hoping the cold hadn't reached Abuela's joints just yet.

"You're too good to me." She patted his hand where it sat on the gearshift.

"Nah." Santiago clicked his tongue disapprovingly. "You treat me too well, Abuela."

"¡Basta ya!" Abuela Paulina waved him off.

Their short drive home was heavily obscured by fog, the purple house barely coming into view as they pulled up.

Pear, Santiago's cousin and partner of their law firm, was waiting for them on the front porch, spread out on the bench swing while he played on his phone. The glowing porch lights haloed Pear in gold and Santiago rolled his eyes.

"What are you doing here?" Santiago held the door open for Abuela Paulina.

Pear pressed a kiss to her cheek as she walked through the door.

"You're taking me out for a beer to celebrate." Pear stood and smoothed over his button-down shirt. He must've come straight here from the courthouse.

"Did you win?" Santiago asked, following Abuela Paulina into the house.

"Obviously. I'm our best lawyer." Pear rolled his eyes and punched Santiago in the shoulder. "Get dressed."

Buffy adjusted the straps of her corset, tying the red satin ribbons tighter against her skin. She slid Camila's leather jacket over her arms, unhooking the wrist strap on the sleeve so that her arms could move freely. This jacket was oversized on Camila's tiny frame but looked cropped on Buffy.

Camila shouted Buffy's name from the living room.

"I'm coming!" Buffy screamed back. Taking one last look in the mirror, Buffy slid into her heels and joined Camila in the living room.

"Car is downstairs," Camila fussed over the red on her lips in the hall mirror before they were out the door.

The bar was packed, music thumping in time with her heartbeat. Buffy held tight to Camila's hand while they wound their way to a table at the back. Camila ordered two beers from the passing waitress while Buffy surveyed the crowd. Thanks to her heels and nearly six-foot figure, she was a head above most of the bar patrons. She still hadn't adjusted to the diversity here. San Francisco was the perfect example of the American melting pot she'd heard so much about. Hair of all colors and textures filled the bar, each one telling the story of a thousand ancestors. Buffy rubbed lines into the condensation on her beer bottle. Thinking about her ancestors transported her right back home to Bunchberry.

It had been almost three years since she left Winnipeg for San Francisco and she still dreamed of her forested home. San Francisco wasn't that different from Winnipeg but it was a completely different planet compared to the four hundred-person rez she grew up on. California was warmer and significantly more humid, but the sea salt air and fog reminded her of her island home. The humidity had been a shock to her, leading to an unfortunate breakout of heat rash during her first summer. But the nighttime chill always reminded her of home. The sun took her warmth with her in both of these places, turning summer night into winter without warning.

Buffy was lost in her thoughts of home when Camila waved a hand in front of her face.

"Earth to Buffy." Camila snapped a few times, finally drawing Buffy's gaze. "We're talking about my thing right now. Pay attention."

"You're right." Buffy focused herself on her friend. "I'm listening."

"Did my brother come in for his interview?"

"He did, and he accepted the position we offered. He starts next week." Buffy said.

Camila squealed and clapped her hands in excitement, throwing her arms around Buffy's neck. "Thank you! You're the best roommate ever." Squeezing Buffy tightly once more, Camila released her and leveled her with a serious gaze. "If he fucks up, you just let me know, okay? I'll set him straight right away."

"He's going to do fine, Cami," Buffy reassured her friend with a hand on her shoulder. "How's Elena?"

"I do not want to talk about Elena." Camila glared at Buffy this time, her gaze sharp enough to cut glass. "No grant talk, no Elena talk."

Buffy raised her palms in defense. "Aye aye, captain." She tapped her beer bottle to her forehead and winked.

Camila stuffed a handful of onion rings onto her small plate and covered them in ketchup.

"Don't look now," Camila spoke around the fried onions in her mouth. "But there's a guy staring at you."

"Hot?"

"Extremely. So is the other guy with him."

Buffy chanced a glance over her shoulder, miming a hair flip to cover the movement. It didn't hide her gaze because the stranger's eyes never wavered, watching her through each moment. She shook her head immediately, closing her eyes to save herself from the fire of Santiago's flaming gaze.

"Fuck." Keeping her eyes closed, Buffy turned back to Camila. "He's a new client at the Indian Center."

"What type of client?" Camila raised one thin black eyebrow.

Buffy shrugged. "The new kind."

"They're coming this way."

Santiago materialized behind her, the smell of eucalyptus reaching her before he did.

"Hi again." His smile was warm, eyes clear as he stared at her.

"Hi." Buffy let him brush against her, crowding close to their bar top table.

Camila smiled wide and stuck her hand out. "I'm Camila."

"I'm John." Santiago's companion grasped Camila's outstretched hand. With hair cropped close to his head and his beige skin clean shaven, he looked older than Santiago.

Though he looked remarkably like him, if she had to guess, the men were related. "But I go by Pear."

"Pear?" The women questioned, the same furrowed brow on both of their foreheads.

"That's a story for another day, trust me." Pear shook Buffy's hand.

"Buffy." She told him.

"Like the slayer?" Pear questioned, a broad smile on his face.

"Something like that."

"Deadly." Pear knocked their knuckles together.

Santiago ordered another round of beers while Camila started her interrogation. Camila was well known in their group of friends for being the resident FBI agent. If anyone had questions, Camila would hunt down the answer.

"Do you work together?" Camila pointed between the men.

"Yes," Santiago answered, offering no elaboration while he stared at Buffy.

Buffy rolled her eyes and Camila turned to Pear. "What exactly does your work entail?"

"Lots of arguing, mostly." Pear and Santiago shared a laugh while Buffy sent a look of annoyance to her friend.

"We're immigration lawyers," Santiago explained, casting a sideways glance at Buffy.

Camila's eyes went wide, empathy taking over her expression. "Rough."

"Incredibly," Santiago muttered, swigging his beer, darkness in his eyes.

Buffy stared at him. She hadn't expected Santiago to be a lawman. She had assumed he was unemployed at first glance, the beard shadow and scruffiness of his overall appearance suggesting so. Well, maybe that was her own prejudice, but what kind of lawyer was allowed to look so...unkempt?

"You look surprised." Pear snickered at the shock on Buffy's face.

"Just didn't strike me as the lawyer-types." She shrugged him off.

"What do I look like?" Santiago rested his arm across the back of her bar chair, his knee on the outside of hers.

"With hands like that, I figured you worked with them. That's all." Buffy rolled her eyes and set her eyes back on her friend.

"Well, with legs like that, I figured you rode horses," Santiago nodded down at her heavily muscled thighs. "But instead, you work at the center doing...what exactly?"

"Grants." Buffy narrowed her eyes at him. How dare he correctly guess where she grew her muscles. Without daily ranch work on Bunchberry, she lifted weights three days a week to keep her ass perky. Evidently, her minimal commitment was paying off.

"You secure funding for the center?" Santiago questioned.

Buffy nodded.

"Sounds important."

"It is." Buffy took her time to gaze at his faze. Black stubble adorned his chin, longer than it had been the first time she saw him. His rose-colored lips parted around his red tongue, quickly, before it disappeared again. An image of his scruff against her thighs flashed through her mind. It had been three weeks since she'd had someone in her bed and she had an itch that needed scratching.

"Buffy is working on this huge grant right now." Camila tapped her nails along the glass in her hand. "But no shop talk tonight! I mean it!" Camila made a point of glaring at each of them in turn, hammering in her point. "This is a work-free zone."

"Yes ma'am." Pear mock saluted and zipped his lips shut with a twist of his fingers.

Santiago made the same motion when Camila turned her sharp gaze on him.

"Great. Now let's dance." Grabbing Buffy and Pear by the hand, Camila dragged them toward the dance floor. Santiago followed leisurely behind them. Buffy tried to pull her arm from her tiny friend's grip but it was ironclad. Camila was frighteningly strong for her size and Buffy was certain if they ever had a break-in, Camila would be more than enough to scare them away. No guard dog needed.

Sweat started to bubble along Buffy's red-dyed eyebrows. She had never been to a Mexican country music club and the dance floor was extremely intimidating. Camila had described the music as *banda*, but Buffy wouldn't be able to tell banda music from cumbia, anyway. The couples were in pairs, legs interwoven as they turned in circles under the multicolored lights. Some couples moved so quickly, she didn't understand how they stayed upright. Legs blurred together and snaked around each other like vines.

The music was playing louder than most concerts she had been to. Dragging her feet, she let Camila grab her by both hands and turn them around in a circle. Pear let Camila use his hand to spin herself, pulling her into his arms and whisking her into a fast-paced dance.

"Dance with me." Santiago held his hand out to her, his face even and cool.

"I'm okay." Buffy leaned onto the empty table at the edge of the dance floor. Just the thought of dancing amongst all these expert couples made her stomach turn.

Intimacy darkened the room, the dancing couples had hands everywhere, bodies woven into each other like clouds after a storm. She didn't consider herself much of a dancer and this looked *complicated*.

The problem was Santiago was looking at her like he might eat her alive. He came closer to her, their shoulders brushing. He was also meltingly hot, his lean muscled frame hidden behind another flannel button down. Santiago stood almost as tall as her, quite a feat considering she was wearing heels. Small heels, but they added height, nonetheless.

Santiago gazed at her confidently, a slight smile on his lips. Buffy stared right back at him. She dragged her gaze pointedly over his form, from his black sneakers to the blue flannel and the small black plug sitting in his gauged ear. Santiago took his time roving over her, lingering at the dip of her chest. She felt his eyes on her like sweaty palms in the dark. Buffy swallowed.

"You want another?" Santiago nodded at her mostly empty beer.

Buffy nodded, thankful for the excuse. She breathed a sigh of relief when Santiago wandered towards the bar. The temperature of the room dropped at least ten degrees with his retreat. Alone at last, she checked the time on her phone and shifted on her feet. The heels were starting to dig into her skin.

Buffy watched as Camila danced through the crowd of people, changing partners every few turns. Pear joined her at the table, glancing back at Camila.

"She's full of energy," Pear commented.

"You should see her after an espresso." Buffy laughed.

Santiago returned with two beers clutched in one hand, his fingers wrapped around their glass necks. Buffy licked her lips at the sight.

"Thanks, primo." Pear took a beer from Santiago before the other man could react. Buffy plucked the other one from his grasp and took a sip.

Santiago stood there confused, glancing down at his suddenly empty hands. Looking back up at Buffy, Santiago smiled wide and Buffy blushed under his watchful gaze. The urge to throw herself into his arms and let him whisk her away overwhelmed her. No harm could come from a little dancing. Santiago offered his hand once again, soft russet skin beckoning her.

Buffy placed her hand in Santiago's warm palm.

Santiago grasped her firmly and spun her into his arms. Losing her footing, he dragged her through a few steps and turns before she righted herself and instantly stiffened up. Her knee bonked against his when she tripped over his foot, the steps too quick and the turns too frequent for her to follow. She felt like a newborn giraffe.

Laughing, Santiago caught her eye. "Relax." He guided both of her hands around his neck and wrapped his arms around her waist. Meeting her hips with his, his thighs pushed into her legs, moving her backwards and around.

Buffy was finding it hard to relax. Giving up control wasn't exactly her forte, and she despised giving it up to a strange man she barely knew. Being hot didn't mean he was trustworthy. Buffy glared at Camila's laughing back and brainstormed ways she could get her back for this embarrassment. How dare she force her to come out instead of leaving Buffy home alone with her book and vibrating friend. If she had stayed home, she never would've been tempted by Santiago. And her resolve was thinning more and more by the minute.

His breath was warm against her neck. Buffy felt his nose against her temple and stiffened. Santiago turned them a few times around the floor until they were in a darker corner. Instantly, she felt less eyes on them and let out a sigh.

Buffy wrapped her arms around his neck and relaxed into his movements. Hips together, he swayed them to the beat, adding small steps to the side here and there. Buffy leaned back to meet his eyes. The lights danced like stars in his nearly black gaze and Buffy couldn't bring herself to look away. The music switched to a slower, deeper breath and she felt her mouth go dry as heat stirred between them.

Santiago slowed their steps, rooting his feet and bringing her hips to the slower rhythm. Buffy paused and tried to pull from his grip, leading him back towards their friends. His grip on her waist tightened and he twisted her under his arm. Santiago settled her back to his chest. His fingers wrapped around the edge of her hip, rubbing the bare skin between her jeans and top. Buffy gulped. Her heart was beating as fast as the reggaetón drums pounding in her head. She and Santiago were glued together, legs and feet intertwined while their hips swung to the music.

Buffy's skin hummed under his touch, flames licking between them. His nose tickled the skin behind her ear and she nearly snapped. Turning in his arms, she faced him and slotted their legs together. She could feel his excitement against her stomach. Santiago groaned and trailed his hand up her back, gripping around the nape of her neck with his forearm nestled along her spine. Foreheads together, Buffy's resistance thinned further. What harm could come from a little one-night stand? Technically, he wasn't a client of the center, his grandmother was. She probably wouldn't even see Santiago again after this. No harm, no foul.

Buffy searched the crowd for her roommate. Camila was wrapped in the arms of a short man in a cowboy hat, twirling her across the floor like a feather.

Camila winked exaggeratedly at her from around the white cowboy hat, sticking her tongue out and wagging it furiously. This, of course, backfired for her and resulted in some very intense evasive maneuvers to escape a sloppy drunk kiss from Cowboy Hat.

Reassurance from her roommate was all she needed, and Buffy made the decision to take Santiago home with her. Tickling her fingers up his arm, she wove her fingers into the hair at the nape of his neck, nails scratching along his scalp she pulled him in closer.

Santiago pulled her hips into his. Biting into the exposed skin of her neck, Santiago pulled back to gaze at her. Buffy eyed his lips, wondering how long he was planning to torture her.

She watched a smirk settle onto Santiago's mouth, desire unmasked across his face. He raised his hand to wrap around the edge of her jaw and pulled her mouth to his.

Bass thrummed in the floor, vibrating up her legs and through their connected lips. Fire flamed in her belly and she tipped her head further back, nuzzling into his shoulder. Santiago dropped his hand to her throat, rubbing his thumb over her drumming pulse. Buffy squeezed her thighs together as heat raced across her skin. Buffy grabbed his hand and nodded towards the door. Santiago followed wordlessly. He nodded at Pear, who was dancing with a curvy brunette, and disappeared out the door.

They didn't exchange any words as they wove through the crowd to the street. Frigid night air turned to steam when it met their sweat-slick skin. Buffy took his hand and led him towards her apartment. Attempting to quicken her steps, Buffy tried to pull Santiago along faster but he resisted. She let him pull her to a stop, turning to face him.

"Come here." Santiago tugged the hand grasped in his, urging her closer.

Buffy stood rooted to the spot. "It's cold. We're almost there anyway."

"Come here," Santiago repeated himself, holding her gaze. "I wasn't done kissing you." His voice was gravelly and Buffy twitched her thighs together. Kissing felt like a waste of time when they were twenty steps from a warm bed.

Defiance played in her gaze as she studied him. What was the game here?

"If you're into some kinky domination stuff, that's fine but it's not my thing." Buffy tried to pull her hand from his grip but he held her tight.

Instead, he came to her. Their nearly identical height allowed him to stand toe to toe with her, their eyes level. Buffy's brown eyes flicked back and forth, confusion and irritation brewing. He put her out of her misery and drew her into a deep kiss.

Buffy felt his tongue slide into her mouth.

The earth stopped spinning around them.

Buffy dissolved in his embrace like cotton candy on her tongue. The smell of pan dulce and eucalyptus surrounded her, sugar dancing into her veins. His lips were tender on hers and she wondered who had crafted this man from stone, softened his edges to the point that even she could not crack him sharp. She was shocked to find herself leaning into his touch, gentleness seeming to pour out of her and into his arms. It felt like he had turned her into putty.

She was breathless when Santiago finally pulled away, chasing him down for another slow meeting of lips. Buffy tried to hide her embarrassment at the obvious effect he had on her, but Santiago didn't give her the chance. Pulling her by the hand he still held in his, they crossed the street hastily. Buffy led him to her doorstep and brought him inside.

The tiny San Franciscan elevator squeezed them in together, stoking the fire blazing between them. Buffy sent a prayer to her building manager, hoping that the elevator was more maintained than it appeared. Santiago was crushing her against the dirty walls, metal creaking around them as they rose. Buffy was pretty sure there was a smudge in the shape of her bare left ass cheek right beside the buttons, but she wasn't sticking around to check.

Leading him down the hallway, Buffy stumbled over her own feet, distracted by Santiago's warm grip inside the back of her corset. His fingers danced over the flesh of her hip, dipping over her hipbone before pulling away again.

What a tease.

Two could play that game. Buffy turned in his arms and gripped him by the collar, holding his face to hers while she ravished his lips with hers. Sliding her tongue against his, Buffy pressed her hips into his. He groaned as she rolled her hips into his. She could feel him hardening beneath her. Turning, she pulled out her key and threw open the door.

Buffy was biting into his flannel-covered arm when they finally stepped across the threshold. Now that they were in private, they were wearing far too many clothes. Her fingers flew to his belt and she trapped him up against the front door. She didn't bother pulling his belt through the loops, instead tugging the zipper and shoving them down to his thighs with his briefs.

Buffy dropped to her knees in front of him, an audible groan escaping Santiago at the sight. Before she could take him in her mouth, he was on top of her. Her bare shoulders rubbed against the hall rug. She didn't have time to argue, shocked by his easy manhandling of her. Unbuttoning her jeans, he pulled them down her legs and tossed them behind him.

Santiago's face was between her breasts and she thanked herself for wearing a corset. She wasn't particularly well endowed, but the corset gave the illusion that she was. Her heartbeat thrummed in anticipation, the throbbing between her legs bordering on painful. Closing his mouth around her nipple, Buffy could feel his erection against her thigh, hot where it rubbed against her.

She was going to die from this.

"Any STDs?" Buffy whispered, her voice breathless.

Santiago looked up at her from beneath his thick black eyebrows, speaking with her nipple still in his mouth. "I'm negative."

Her thighs clenched around his waist at his words, her body burning with his touch. His mouth wasn't enough. She needed more. Buffy wanted all of him.

Reaching between them, she pulled her thong to the side and guided him inside her. His teeth bit into her reddened nipple and Santiago struggled to suppress the groan in his throat.

Fuck.

Buffy squeezed him inside her greedily, her eyes heavy with lust. His gaze never wavered from hers, even after he released her nipple and rose to her face. Santiago stole her lips in a wicked embrace, grinding into her while his tongue ravished her mouth, pulling a whimper from somewhere deep inside her.

Buffy watched his brows furrow, sweat forming on his upper lip. She could tell he was fighting to keep his climax at bay. A smirk settled onto her lips. There was a special kind of power in making a man finish early. But ladies always came first.

Buffy reached towards him and scratched her nails down his chest. She felt as though she had been running a marathon the entire night and, with the finish line right in front of her, she was scared to complete the run. Santiago caught her mouth in a kiss, grinding his hips deeper into hers. He was kissing her like she was the only water source in thousands of miles.

It felt terrifying.

Even more so because she liked it. She could taste the desire and desperation on his tongue and it only turned her on more.

When was the last time someone had desired her like this? She was no stranger to casual sex. In fact, that's really all she had ever been interested in. But even the hottest of her hook-ups hadn't set her on fire like this. No one, man or woman, had looked at her like he did. No one had groaned for her like Santiago. It had come from deep within him, a wanton and unguarded vocalization of emotion.

Distracted with her surprise, she didn't notice when he kissed his way down her neck and pulled her other nipple into his wet mouth. Combined with his torturous movement against her core, Buffy let go as soon as his teeth closed over her skin.

Santiago didn't hide his smirk of satisfaction when Buffy lost herself around him. She closed her eyes, his intimate gaze still staring at her in her mind.

Sitting back on his knees, Santiago pulled Buffy up and into his lap. He guided her arms around his neck. Exhausted from her powerful trip to the clouds, she let him kiss her, slowly, tenderly, sharing breath with each other. Blinking, Buffy looked at him and could feel his heart thrumming in time with hers.

It was too intimate. They needed to get back to *fucking*.

Buffy pulled his hand from her hip and took his middle finger in her mouth, holding his eye as the tip touched the back of her throat. With a growl, Santiago pulled his hand from her grasp and stood, holding her thighs to keep himself inside her.

"Which way?"

"Last door on the left." Buffy attached her lips to his neck, secretly hoping to leave a mark or two behind. A reminder of the night she jumped from this cliff.

Chapter 4

The sunlight blazed in her eyes, rousing Buffy from a dreamless slumber. Sweat beaded on her upper lip despite her bare feet dangling out of the sheets. Buffy struggled to take in a deep breath, her chest compressed under a crushing weight. Heat surrounded her and stifled the air she attempted to suck in. She felt like she was wrapped in a straitjacket and locked inside of a sauna.

Santiago's ink-covered arm was laying across her torso, the weight heavy despite his lean frame. He was facing her, rose-colored lips parted while he slept on his belly. Panic flooded her and sweat rose across her body.

Staring at him in shock, Buffy recalled last night and distinctly remembered falling asleep beside him. Why was he still here? Hadn't she told him to leave? She couldn't remember.

Damn it, Buffy. Distracted by the dick, once again.

Normally, she never let hookups stay the night, and now she was trapped under the thick arm of her hottest hookup in years. Swallowing down the acid rising in her chest, Buffy squirmed. Santiago was deceptively heavy and she was stuck beneath him.

Maybe she did need more than three days a week in the gym.

Buffy groaned softly, squeezing her eyes shut to block out reality. Having sex was one thing but sleeping together...there was nothing more vulnerable than that. She hoped he hadn't seen her fall asleep before him. Thankfully though, she was awake before he was. Nerves crawled across her skin as she imagined Santiago waking up and never leaving.

Buffy needed to get him out of her apartment, but she was quickly distracted by the tattoos stretched across his sunbaked skin. Her focus had mainly been between his legs last night and the artful designs had escaped her attention.

Thick black lines twisted over his arm, intricate scenes and symbols decorating nearly every inch of him. Some of the images were shaded in a way that made the design jump off his golden skin. Buffy couldn't stop herself from reaching out, trailing her fingers over the designs decorating his body. She traced over the largest one with her nails. It was a panther crawling over his shoulder and extending down his arm and back. More ink spots poked out over the top of his boxers and Buffy faintly remembered lines of ink covering his legs too. She needed to give him a full-body inspection.

Santiago's hand flexed against her hip, once, twice. Groaning in her mind, Buffy looked up to meet open glossy brown eyes. She hoped he would make this easy on her.

"Breakfast?" Santiago's voice was deep and raspy with sleep and her thighs clenched at the sound.

Her libido needed to behave.

"I don't really do breakfast." Buffy tried to slide away from Santiago, his face precariously close to hers. She tucked her chin toward her chest, hoping the smell of her morning breath hadn't reached his nose.

"I can do a burger." Santiago shrugged, palm smoothing over her thigh.

"Listen." Buffy was trying to let him down easily. "I'm not looking for something serious-"

Santiago interrupted her with a kiss, an all-consuming, soul-sucking kiss. He pulled away before she was finished. "I'll see you later."

Kissing her tenderly on the forehead, he dressed easily, pulling his clothes on piece by piece. He moved with such ease and coolness that Buffy wondered if he was always like this. Maybe his personal brand of fuckboy was the romantic one. This was probably how he treated everyone he fucked. Kill them with kindness and your roster never thins out. Smart. Buffy glared at his back.

Santiago rounded the bedside and kissed her once more, lips featherlight against her own. Within seconds, he was gone. Santiago strode through her bedroom and let himself out the front door as though he had done it a thousand times before.

What the fuck just happened?

Buffy was frozen in her spot. Mouth hanging open, her eyes darted around the room in silence, half expecting Santiago to walk back in and announce that it was all a prank. She kept the thin sheet tight to her chest, bewilderment clouding her thoughts and ringing her ears. She didn't hear Camila padding to her room over the storm raging in her head.

"Well, you look thoroughly ravished." Camila tucked herself into the covers at Buffy's feet. "Tell me when to stop." Holding her hands parallel with each other, palms facing in, she drew them apart slowly. Her eyes widened with each inch her hands separated but Buffy wasn't paying attention.

"That was the best sex of my life." Buffy muttered, mostly to herself.

"You should marry him." Camila said.

"Are you insane, Camila?" Buffy scoffed. "I don't have time for a relationship."

"One day, you're going to have to let someone in." Camila patted Buffy's bare ankle twice and waltzed from the room like some kind of therapy fairy.

Buffy stuck her tongue out at her curly-haired friend.

"I saw that!" Camila flipped her off without turning back.

Buffy sank face-first into her blankets. What had come over her last night? She couldn't even blame the alcohol, considering she only had two beers before she was ready to leave with Santiago. Something about the way he touched her and gazed at her set a fire in her belly that only he could extinguish. Dancing with them had been her downfall. Camila was the one to blame here, really. She had invited them onto the dance floor and practically thrown Buffy and Santiago together.

Camila had forced her to smell his delicious scent and feel the heat of his burning palms through the thin fabric of her dress. And it had definitely been Camila who had slid him inside herself unprotected.

Fuck.

Grabbing her phone from the side table, Buffy logged into her health app and scheduled a new appointment. STD screening, obviously. It would be a cold day in Hell before she blindly took a man at his word. She needed to make sure that she was still testing negative after her sex-crazed stupidity.

Buffy sent a quick prayer to the gods that she wouldn't run into Santiago at the center any time soon. She worried her will was weak against his thought-obliterating penis. Heat flushed her skin at the memory, as though she could still feel his touch across her body. No, she couldn't see him again. She knew this feeling and she knew it quite well.

The beginning throes of emotions.

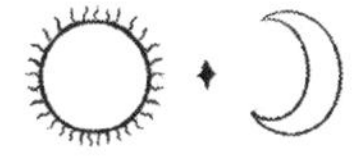

Running late for her health screening, Buffy stopped by the taco truck across the street from her apartment. Normally, they didn't serve before ten in the morning, but the owners had developed a soft spot for Buffy over the years and often catered events at the center for a significant discount. Buffy waved as she crossed the street.

"Bufita." Myra's blonde braids swung down her back while she chopped onions. Part-owner of the truck, Myra was constantly refusing to accept Buffy's money. This meant that Buffy was often stuffing twenties into the tip jar. "I have a friend who needs some help. She is an Indian like you. She's stuck in a shelter right now. Immigration issues." Myra rolled her eyes in annoyance.

"Absolutely." Buffy pulled a business card from her wallet and wrote her extension on the back. "Give her my card and I will get her set up as soon as she can come in."

"You're the best." Myra blew her a kiss and handed over the steaming carne asada breakfast burrito. "Burrito on the house." The slip of her tongue over the *rr* brought a smile to Buffy's mouth, reminding her of the new sister Calehan had brought home only a few years ago. They hadn't married yet, but Xiomara became a member of the family in no time.

Stuffing the tip jar with a twenty-dollar bill, Buffy caught the bus towards her health appointment. Luckily, it was down the street from the center and wouldn't make her too late for work. She would've walked if not for the fog making it ten degrees colder outside and chilling her to the bone.

In the summer, she enjoyed the thirty-minute walk, but her ability to handle the cold had grown weak with all the years away from Bunchberry. Its frozen tendrils reached into her skin now, deep into her bones, and settled into her blood, icing her body from the inside out. Now was as good a time as any to feel terrible about herself. Sighing, she pulled out her phone and thumbed to the family group chat.

Juniper: Buffy, have you bought a plane ticket yet?
Winona: When do you land? I'll pick you up on the way north.
Calehan: What day are you flying in? We land on the 23rd.
Clyde: Can I bring this girl I've been seeing?
Joy: No.
Nataani: The more the merrier
Winona: Juni's house is packed enough already. No plus ones.
Calehan: Xiomara is coming with me.
Joy: She doesn't count as a plus one, Cally.
Juniper: Buffy, send me your flight info ASAP!!!

Buffy silenced her phone and shoved it to the bottom of her bag in hopes it wouldn't resurface for at least a few hours. Thoughts swirled in her mind, tugging nausea up her throat and turning her belly. She could feel the darkness tugging at her, looping her thoughts back to black again and again. Taking a deep breath, she got off the bus a stop early, beelining to a neighborhood coffee shop.

With a cinnamon latte in hand, she sipped her drink and worked through her anxious thoughts. In her mind, she wrote her thoughts along the windows and doors of the shops lining the street. Once the words were etched into the building and she walked past, she left the thought behind. Easier said than done, truthfully, but there were no rules about repeating your thoughts.

By the time she arrived at the health center, her coffee was gone and the black hole in her brain was no longer sucking her in. Resisting the negative spiral had gotten easier over the years, but it never failed to rattle her for the remainder of the day. She peed in a cup and gave them three vials of blood before she was back in the cold. Work was waiting for her.

Half asleep from her wasna and cornbread lunch, Buffy was slugging away at a tiny, last-minute grant proposal to fund one specific project; recovering the center's hand drums with new leather. The proposal was going to a Mixtec-owned leather company and Buffy was confident they would win the grant. This was the part of her job that she loved, pitching small grants to reasonable partners. Unfortunately for her, this aspect only made up for about ten percent of her time.

A knock on the door brought her back to the present, crumbs of cornbread still stuck to her concentration-dry lips.

"A client downstairs is asking for you." Veronica stuck her head in the crack of her office door.

Buffy groaned, dropping her head into her hands. "The day is almost over."

"She said someone named Myra sent her," Veronica elaborated.

"Oh!" Buffy furiously saved her document before locking the desktop and pushing away from the computer. "Yes, Myra is a friend of mine. Is she doing her intake now?"

"Yup!" Veronica waved her off while Buffy waited for an elevator. "Some hot lawyer is with her."

The smell reached her before the elevator doors opened. Sticky sweet, the air was heavy with the earth scent of sweetgrass. Buffy breathed in deeply, letting the scent fill her lungs and mind. Every morning, one of the interns cleansed the building. Sometimes they burned sage, sometimes tobacco, sometimes palo santo. Buffy loved it when they chose to burn sweetgrass. The familiar scent instantly transported her home to Bunchberry.

Chatter was minimal today, the ground floor comfortably quiet. Buffy headed toward the intake area, a corner of the building set aside with comfy chairs and couches. Meant to resemble a living room, the space felt intimate and safe away from the ruckus of the rest of the center.

A young boy was on the floor pushing a yellow dump truck over the carpet. Buffy waved to the doe-eyed boy before a voice said her name. She recognized the voice instantly.

Stopping in her tracks, she turned to the couch beside the boy, just barely hidden from her view. Irritation flamed in her gut.

Santiago was smiling like he had pulled off the most difficult heist of the year. Admittedly, he had. He was certainly the last person she expected to see right now. Buffy couldn't escape him. She had made promises to Myra and intended to keep them all. Buffy felt her cheeks betray her and begin to burn under his gaze. The same gaze he had used on her when she fell to her knees before him.

Fuck. Snapping out of her shock quickly, Buffy focused her attention on the client in front of them.

"Hola." Buffy waved to the dark-haired woman sitting across from Santiago. "Soy Buffy, la amiga de Myra." Buffy hoped Myra had mentioned her to the woman.

"Soy Clara." Her voice was deep and soft, brown eyes wide while they gazed at Buffy.

"I didn't know you spoke Spanish," Santiago murmured, just loud enough for Buffy to hear.

"I don't." Fighting to restrain herself from rolling her eyes in front of a client, she handed Clara the Spanish-language informational packet. Pointing out a few upcoming events, she made sure to note free food was always provided at the events. "We also keep dry snacks around all the time, so if you ever need pasta or chips or anything, feel free to swing by."

Santiago translated for her, ensuring Clara could understand everything. Buffy chided herself for not learning Spanish. Now Santiago had a reason to be here as a translator on top of being Clara's lawyer.

"I'm sure you're in great hands with Mr. Morales over here." Buffy's smile was wide, genuine, as she gestured to him. She was sure he was good at his job, if the tailored Italian three-piece suit had anything to say about him. "We also have legal aid, so if you have other questions, please utilize our legal team as well."

"I'm not translating that." Santiago smiled.

Buffy fought the urge to roll her eyes and shot him a slicing look.

"Why are you here?" Buffy whispered harshly under her breath.

"I'm supporting my client." Santiago laughed at her look of annoyance. "I promise not to get lost in the building after dark again." Buffy ignored him and went back to helping Clara fill out paperwork. "I was hoping to connect with your legal team. Clara is Maya from Guatemala and I wanted to see if they had any insight with Indigenous immigration cases. I'm trying to keep her and Poncho here in the Bay."

Buffy blinked. Maybe she was a little self-centered. Santiago really was here for work. She narrowed her eyes at him to hide her surprise. "We have a few people on the legal team with immigration experience. I can get you their phone numbers."

"Thank you." Santiago flashed a warm smile at her and Buffy squeezed her thighs tighter together. A vivid memory of those white teeth around her nipple flashed through her mind.

Buffy cleared her throat.

By the time Clara had finished filling out the paperwork and her son had devoured a bowl of stew, the center was closed and the moon had risen. Buffy organized a shuttle for Clara and Poncho to drive them home. Santiago translated the conversation between Buffy and the driver, keeping Clara in the loop and letting her know she was heading home. The driver, a fifty-something Uncle named Tony, spoke Spanish and Clara visibly relaxed in front of him.

Buffy once again felt like an idiot for not learning Spanish. Camila spoke the language, for Creator's sake. She felt stupid for not learning the language in her few years in the city.

Waving goodbye to Uncle Tony and the little family, Buffy locked the center door behind them and strode toward the elevators. Santiago piled the signed forms in his arms and followed her. Silently, he handed her the stack of paper and watched as she filed them in the cabinets to the side of her office.

"You can go." Buffy spoke without turning around, her back solid in front of him.

"Everyone's gone." Santiago gestured to the dark and quiet building. "I'll drive you home."

"No thanks." Buffy switched her wedges for a pair of running shoes. "I'm just up the road."

"I remember." Santiago held her eye.

Fuck. Buffy was caught.

Santiago clearly knew 'up the road' was an embellishment. "I'll drive you home. It's on my way." He smiled at her again and Buffy felt the fight drain out of her.

Begrudgingly, Buffy took him up on his offer. The wind was howling, the fog heavy over the Bay, and she knew the walk home would be brutal. It would be ridiculous to deny a ride from someone she trusted.

Together, they exited the building in silence. Santiago held doors open for Buffy to walk through, waiting behind her while she locked each one they passed. She did her best to ignore his delicious gaze on her form.

Santiago opened the passenger door before she could get to it, offering a hand to help her inside the low car. Buffy ignored it, throwing her things in the back seat and crouching awkwardly to pull her long legs inside the vehicle without stumbling like a baby giraffe.

Santiago climbed inside beside her and pulled out onto the dark street. Buffy rode silently beside him, her eyes trained out the window to ensure he didn't kidnap her.

"When can I see you again?" Santiago looked at her with intent plain on his face. He wanted her again too.

"I told you that I don't date." Buffy opened the car door as soon as he came to a stop.

"That's fine." Santiago followed her out of the car and held her eye across the hood. He stalked over to her slowly. With a warm hand on her back, he guided her up the stairs to her building door. "I want to fuck you again." He spoke softly, his voice only for her.

Before Buffy could react, his mouth was on hers. She gasped in surprise and Santiago took the chance to deepen their kiss. Santiago slid his hand into the hair at the nape of her neck, tilting her head to the side to bring their bodies closer together.

Buffy gripped his waist, the soft fabric of his sweater sliding through her clammy hands. Pulling a moan from her mouth, his lips moved over hers while his tongue stroked her slowly, like melted honey on her tongue. The kiss was over before she could kiss him back or invite him in. Pressing a kiss to the back of her hand, Santiago walked down her steps and stood beside his car. Buffy stood frozen on the doorstep, the taste of sugar still on her lips.

He watched her from the road, waiting for her to unlock the main door and step inside. Buffy couldn't resist waving to him when she looked back over her shoulder, touched by the intensity with which he watched her enter the building. She could still feel his gaze as she disappeared up the stairs.

Taking a deep breath, she tried to banish the flush from her skin before Camila saw her and launched into relentless teasing. Hands shaking, Buffy fought to get the key into the lock. She hoped Camila couldn't hear her fumbling at the door. Pushing inside, the scent of cinnamon filled her nose. A pitcher of creamy horchata sat on the counter. Buffy helped herself to a glass, hoping to slow her heart rate and banish the taste of Santiago from her mouth. His kiss was playing on a loop in her head, and it was taking everything in her not to call him back up to her bed. The sugary rice drink only intensified the taste of him on her tongue. Buffy cursed herself.

Camila was on a yoga mat in front of the TV when she caught sight of Buffy in the kitchen.

"There you are!" Camila sprang up out of warrior pose and followed Buffy. "Why aren't you drenched? I thought you were walking home."

"I got a ride." Buffy shrugged dismissively.

"From who?" Camila crooked her head to the side, reminiscent of a curious puppy.

Buffy sighed heavily; evading her intuitive roommate was useless. "Santiago drove me."

"The guy from the other night?" Camila wiggled her shoulders. "Why didn't you bring him up?"

"He drove me home because his client is the woman Myra asked me to help."

"Oh wow. Small world, huh?" Camila smirked at the coincidence. "Maybe you're meant to be."

Buffy shot Camila a look that could slice steel.

Camila pushed further. "Buffy and Santi, sitting in a tree."

"Go back to your yoga." Buffy waved her friend off and tried to escape to her bedroom. Camila simply followed her.

"K-I-S-S-I-N-G." Camila plopped onto Buffy's bed. "Are you going to see him again?"

"Well, since we're working together, I assume so." Buffy padded around her room, getting ready for bed in an effort to distract herself from this conversation.

"Are you going to fuck him again?" Camila waggled her eyebrows.

"Probably not."

"But he's so hot!" Camila threw herself down on Buffy's bed in dramatic fashion. "You said he's good in bed. Why not?"

"He asked me on a date."

"Oh, so scary. A date." Camila pushed her bottom lip out in a pout. Buffy smacked the skin of her pouting lip with a finger.

"You know I'm not interested in a relationship," Buffy argued.

"That doesn't mean you can't go out with him. It's just fun." Camila shrugged.

"Dating equals feelings. I don't have feelings for him."

"Yet." Camila held her pointer finger in the air.

"Ever." Buffy waved her off and pulled at her sheets, pushing Camila off the bed and onto the floor. "How's Elena, by the way?"

The smile fell from Camila's lips and was replaced by a dark scowl.

"I'm going to throw you off the balcony," Camila muttered, returning to the living room and her virtual yoga class.

"Will you teach me Spanish?" Buffy called.

"No!" Camila screeched back, her voice echoing through their apartment. Laughing at her roommate's hot temper, Buffy shut the door.

Buffy showered and attempted to clean herself of Santiago's heady touch. She scrubbed at her skin but still felt his arm around her waist, his fingers in her hair. Huffing, she threw the shower curtain open, nearly ripping it from the rings. Buffy ran a brush angrily through her wet hair, forcing her thoughts on anything other than how Santiago spoke to her on the porch.

I want to fuck you again.

She could hear him repeating the words in her mind. Buffy wanted to fuck him too. But she knew better than sleeping with him again, especially if they were going to be working together. Buffy climbed into bed, the scent of eucalyptus enveloping her as soon as she hit the sheets.

Santiago might as well have been in the bed beside her.

Buffy lurched from the bed as if it was on fire, tearing the sheets off behind her. Shoving the old sheets into the bottom of her laundry basket, Buffy pulled out her extra set and remade the bed. Holding her extra pillow to her face, she inhaled.

Santiago was still there.

Irritated that her plan hadn't worked, Buffy threw the offending pillow to the floor and climbed in bed. Thankfully, her pillow smelled only of her shampoo since her shower. Snuggling under her quilt and tucking her toes into the bottom of her sheets, Buffy waited for sleep to overtake her.

It didn't.

Instead, vivid memories of Santiago plagued her. Wetness pooled on the sheets beneath her and Buffy cursed herself.

Closing her eyes, Buffy employed every trick she had ever learned to aid sleep. She counted sheep into the hundreds, wrote Santiago's name on the falling leaves of her mind over and over again, even tried to count the tiles on her ceiling, but sleep still refused to take her.

Santiago plagued her mind and body until he was all she could think of. Buffy reached inside her nightstand and took out her final sleep trick. A while later, she tossed the vibrator to the side and finally fell asleep, the tattooed man still on her mind.

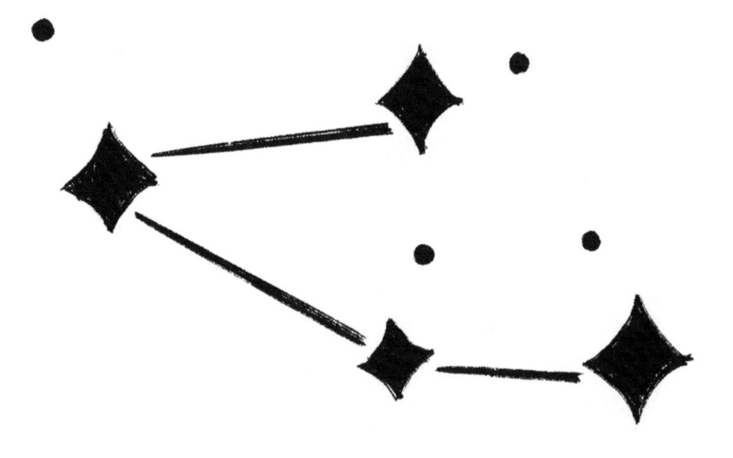

CHAPTER 5

Buffy was filling her third cup of coffee when she ran into Camila's brother.

"Good morning, Miguel." Buffy offered him a clean mug from the cabinet.

"Morning." Miguel met her eyes only for a glance, before shifting his gaze to his hands. Incarceration affected everyone differently and it was clear that Miguel's confidence had been decimated. Buffy mentally cursed the American justice system.

"How are you enjoying the center so far? Everything going well? I hope Armando isn't teasing you too much. Sometimes he takes the head chef title a little too seriously." Buffy leaned against the counter, attempting to make herself shorter and less intimidating.

Miguel nodded. "Armando is nice." He didn't offer anything further.

Buffy saw his hand shake while he filled his coffee mug. Nerves.

Despite being twenty-seven, Miguel had the shyness of a teenager. She supposed he kind of still was a teen, having lost those years in prison. A thought popped into Buffy's head. Many of the center members had asked for donated prom dresses last year and the Elders had even made some of the donated gowns. A community prom would be the perfect way to fundraise for the center and give the members a fun event to host together. Buffy could count at least ten Elders that she knew for a fact had never attended a prom or homecoming. She made a mental note to speak with Veronica and smiled back at Miguel.

"If you need anything," Buffy said as she placed her hand on his shoulder, "you know where to find me." She squeezed him gently, hoping he had a love for physical touch like his sister did.

Miguel scurried away to the back of the kitchen, turning on the water and filling the deep sink. Buffy watched him load the sink with dirty dishes and soap, setting his coffee on the shelf beside his head. His shoulders were rounded, shrinking his already slender body even more. A sigh fell from her mouth, splashing the coffee inside her mug.

Camila's constant worrying was starting to rub off on her. Miguel had shown up for his interview and for his first two weeks of work. So far, so good. All they could do was support him and wait for him to blossom. Patience was the key here. Imprisonment had made holes in his heart and they would take time to heal. She hoped his job at the center could be part of that healing.

Buffy turned, her knees knocking into a gaggle of thin, wiry limbs. A squeal sounded under her, and Buffy jumped in surprise.

"Poncho!" Buffy recognized Clara's son, wearing the same tattered jacket from the other day. Poncho had three granola bars clutched in his tiny right hand. Redness bloomed up his neck as he peered up at Buffy, locking his hands behind his back. She fought the frown that pulled at her lips. There was no need to hide his hunger here at the center. That was what the center was here for: to take care of its people.

"¿Tienes hambre?" Buffy asked, dropping to a knee to meet his eye.

Poncho nodded slowly, his big brown eyes like glassy moons. Leading him into the kitchen and to the large steel fridge, Buffy opened the door and evaluated the contents.

"Here we go." Balancing a heavy covered plate, Buffy removed the foil and warmed it in the kitchen microwave. The food steamed as she placed it in Poncho's hands: beans and rice mixed with mushrooms, pork, corn and cilantro. Leftovers didn't often make it to the center fridge, but most of the kids hated mushrooms, and thus one lone plate remained. Opening a hidden drawer under the counter, Buffy removed a packet of hot sauce and handed it to Poncho.

"Gracias." Poncho said, turning and running off toward his mother.

"Buffy." Veronica leaned into the open door of the kitchen. "They're asking for you upstairs."

Fighting back a sigh, Buffy followed Veronica to the elevator. Chatter filled the center and grated against her already raw nerves. The original 1920s elevator arrived with a sharp ring, the sound piercing through her skull.

"What do they want now?" Buffy guzzled her coffee while the elevator began to rise. She avoided board meetings like the plague. If they were asking for her, the issue had to be serious. Mediation for a bunch of old rich people was the absolute last thing she wanted to do today.

"They're arguing about the food budget." Veronica said.

"Not again." Buffy sighed, flicking her hair behind her shoulder. She was tired of this argument. The white members of the board wanted to put a limit on the amount of food the center provided for free. The entire team at the center was against this, but the truth was that those board members held the purse strings. Their hands were tied if those strings pulled shut. Buffy would be damned if she didn't put up a good fight though.

Veronica ran to her desk and pulled a folder out of the drawer. She handed it to Buffy.

"Wait." Buffy flipped through the pages in front of her. "They're still discussing the proposal from last quarter?"

Veronica shrugged.

Buffy squeezed her eyes shut and pinched the highest point on the bridge of her tall nose. This food budget proposal had been on deck at the last three board meetings, making this meeting the fourth. An entire year had gone by with no resolution. Anger roiled in her belly and Buffy fought to control her expression.

If she went in with a full bitch face, the proposal would never be approved. She had to go in firm enough to convince them to approve it today without turning the entire board against her. It had taken six months for Sandi, the director of the center, to allow her back into board meetings after her first one. Though Buffy still believed she had the right to yell, considering everyone was screaming at her.

Use your inside voice, Buffy reminded herself. She followed Veronica down the hall.

"Good morning." Buffy slid through the open glass door. Standing at the head of the room, she held her coffee in front of her and addressed the room. "Shall I shed some light on the food necessities of the community we serve?"

"The issue isn't their needs," a thin man with white hair and eyebrows said. "The issue is that some of your members are taking more than their fair share."

"Explain what you mean by 'fair share' to me." Buffy sipped her coffee and waited. "Who determines the fair share?"

"Are you insinuating that some people should be allowed to take four or five packages of free food?" A platinum blonde woman with pale green eyes glared at Buffy.

"That is exactly what I'm saying." Buffy replied.

"So, you want us to pay the grocery bill for every Indian in the county?"

"If that was what we were proposing, absolutely." Buffy pulled a chair over and took a seat at the head of the table. "Sadly, we'd need far more than the current food budget to adequately feed all of our members. As it stands, the center is the only source of food for at least seven families in the city alone, and thirty-five within the Bay. I know of three foster youths who come here for breakfast and dinner because their halfway house never has things that are safe to eat, if there is even anything at all. One of our interns takes the train in from Hayward and eats breakfast and lunch for free here at the center instead of paying fifteen dollars twice a day *on top* of the fee for the train card that you all vetoed for non-tenure employees last year."

The newest board member, an investor from England, spoke up. "The money for your homeless kids is going to have to come from somewhere."

"Trust me, I'll find more than enough." Buffy smiled and downed her cup of coffee. "Any more questions?"

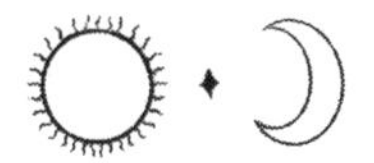

Buffy didn't know what she was thinking. She was already tucked into bed when Camila convinced her that a night at the country bar was exactly what she needed. Rounding up a group of their girlfriends, they set out for the new line dancing bar across the bridge. Boy, did she have regrets now. Two of the brownest people in the building, Buffy and Camila stuck out amongst a sea of cowboy hats and white-blonde hair.

There was no shortage of strangers arriving at their table, inviting them to dance with a plethora of cringey pickup lines. Buffy was currently in the arms of an amply freckled ginger man a few inches shorter than her. He bought a plate of nachos for their table and asked her to dance upon delivery. She couldn't say no to him after that. His arms were strong around her, fingers pressing all the way to her hip bones while he twirled and dipped her to the beat of the music.

"Andrew," he said against her ear, breath smelling like whiskey. Camila had regarded him as Canelo, after the redhead Mexican boxer. Andrew danced well, his thighs heavy where they pushed into hers. The desire in his eyes wasn't doused out when she stood at her full height, at least three inches taller than him. If anything, his gaze seemed to darken. Confident short men had an energy unlike anyone else. His breath was damp against her neck, the skin cold when he pulled away to look her in the eye.

Buffy watched his eyes shift to her mouth, gazing at her cherry-stained lips. She let him kiss her then, their legs still moving to the music. Andrew was timid against her mouth, the skin of his lips rough against hers. Control shifted easily to her when she nipped sharply at his lower lip. Buffy broke away from him to sip her drink, searching for a face in the crowd.

Andrew's hands wandered and Buffy found herself dreaming of the last man she danced with. She could see his face in the shadows of the bargoers, someone wearing his eyes, another sharing the slope of his nose. Tricks played in her mind, the smell of Santiago's cologne enveloping her. The smell was so real, she stopped moving in the middle of the dance floor, turning in circles to look for him.

"You want to get out of here?" Andrew interpreted her sudden freeze differently than she intended. His arm wrapped around her waist, his lips open against her neck.

Making wide eyes at Camila, Buffy attempted to telepathically beg her roommate to break up this moment. Mercifully, Camila pushed between Buffy and her ginger barnacle, pulling Buffy away quickly. "Bathroom break!"

Hand in hand, the two women found their way to the back of the club. A pink neon sign with the word *cowgirl* welcomed them.

"Redheads don't do it for you?" Camila teased as they entered the bathroom.

Buffy rolled her eyes. "I'm just not in the mood tonight."

"Are you okay?" Camila's brows furrowed in the center of her forehead, nearly touching with concern. She rested the back of her hand against Buffy's forehead. "When are you ever not in the mood?"

Shrugging her off, Buffy washed her hands under the cool water, letting it drip down the back of her neck instead of drying her hands with paper. Buffy fanned herself with her clutch. The air of the tiny bathroom was stifling. "He just was too soft."

Camila touched up her brown lipstick, the darker line along the edge popping her lips forward as if they were 4D. "You know what I think you should do?"

"I know exactly what you want me to do and no." Buffy wagged her finger between them. "I'm not doing that."

"You deserve a few orgasms," Camila argued. "Besides, you've been downright grouchy this week. You could use a little stress relief." Smoothing her hair in the mirror, Camila winked at her. "You can have the apartment to yourself tonight, I'm staying with Elena so we can leave early tomorrow. We can't arrive late again, or her mother will make us spend the night. That might actually kill me." Camila shivered as though the idea made her physically disgusted. She faced Buffy and gripped her by the shoulders. "Do us both a favor and relax, okay?"

Irritation flamed in Buffy's gut as Camila walked away. She hated that her friend was right and hated her even more for suggesting she call the man who brought fire to her belly. Buffy chewed on her thumb, lost in her warring thoughts.

Two women stumbled out of the back stall, not a hair or hemline out of place despite their wandering hands. Red flushed cheeks mirrored each other while they smiled bashfully.

Now Buffy was jealous. Against her wishes, that was the one emotion that could always control her. Her phone rang twice before the familiar voice teased her ear.

"Hi, Buffy." Santiago was smiling; she could hear it in his voice.

"Hi." She shoved the warmth in her chest away, scowling to sour her own mood. "How are you?"

"I'm well, debating if I want late night pizza or tacos. Care to cast a vote?"

"I'm a pizza girl," Buffy said. "Just don't tell my sister, I think she would consider it a betrayal."

"Pizza it is. Do you have a favorite?"

"I don't want to tell you." Buffy chewed her lip.

"Well now you have to." Santiago argued.

"Hawaiian with olives." Buffy mumbled.

"Hawaiian with olives?!" Santiago's laugh came from deep within his chest, the rumbling heavy in her ear.

"See, this is why I didn't want to tell you."

"Come on, Buffy, you can tell me anything. Care to share your disgusting pizza with me? I can pick it up on the way to your place."

"I'm not home." Buffy kept her voice flat, cool, unimpressed. Santiago was just a man. That was all. She didn't want him to think she was sitting around dreaming of him. "I'm at this bar all the way across the bridge."

"I'll be there in twenty." Santiago's voice was clear through the speaker of his phone, footsteps and closing doors sounding in the back of their call. She could hear his engine roar to life behind his smoke-like voice.

"No!" Buffy scrambled for words. "You don't need to pick me up, I can take the BART just fine. I can meet you at my place in like an hour."

"I'll see you in a few, Buffy." Santiago's voice was firm, high and twisting on her name but stoic in his statement. He left no room for argument. "Send me your location."

"Okay." Buffy chewed her lip as she ended the phone call.

Was he really going to drive all the way across the bridge to pick her up at midnight? Tapping her toes against the tile floor, she wondered if calling a ride would be a better shot. At least she could probably get a share to split the cost between Oakland and home.

Swiping open her home screen, she clicked her ride-sharing app as a message rang through. She touched the banner on the top of the screen, bringing her into the empty text conversation between her and Santiago. He sent her a pin. Opening the link, she could see him on the map, already turning onto the bridge.

Buffy couldn't help the blush rushing up her neck or the butterflies kicking up a storm in her belly. No one had ever been willing to pick her up from a night out before, much less excited to do so. Though, to be fair, she couldn't remember asking anyone who wasn't related to her for a favor like this.

It was an odd feeling. This anticipation of seeing him again, coupled with the knowledge he was coming all this way just for her.

Santiago was driving here, to see her. She let herself smile then, wide, clear, full of teeth. Bouncing on the balls of her feet, Buffy chewed her lip in an effort to staunch the bubble of air floating her up off the ground.

"Buffy!" Camila's voice was shrill where it came from the open bathroom door. "You can't hide in here all night!"

"No need." Buffy told her as she squeezed back into the crowded country bar. "Santiago is coming to pick me up."

Camila didn't hide the smug smile of satisfaction at Buffy's confession.

"I'm not going to fuck him." Buffy argued.

"Whatever you say, Buffy." Camila smiled, reading Buffy like a book.

"Stop looking at me like that." Buffy grumbled. Her phone vibrated against her skin. Buffy squinted at the bright screen.

Santiago's little blue dot was blinking right on top of hers. Butterflies stirred in her belly. Heat crawled up her neck at the thought of seeing Santiago. Her skin began to tingle in anticipation.

Kissing Camila and their friends goodbye, Buffy excused herself thanks to an invented blinding migraine. She put on her best mask of pain and ducked out of the club. Searching for his car, butterflies swam in her belly. Santiago had been an incredible partner last time and she had high hopes for the number of orgasms she would receive tonight. He was a giver, that much was clear.

Santiago stood from the car when he saw her, waving her toward him. Opening the passenger door, he held his hand out to help her climb in. Buffy placed her palm in his and he pulled her into his chest. Knocked off balance, she gripped his shoulders and let his embrace guide her. Buffy felt his lips against the edge of her mouth and she turned into him. She let him kiss her senseless, drinking him in with all of the eagerness that built while she waited for him to arrive. Knowing he was coming all this way just for her lit a fire between her legs.

Whoops and cheers sounded from behind them and they pulled apart. Santiago set her feet on the ground and they turned to find Buffy's group of friends winking and hollering at them. Buffy rolled her eyes, climbing into the passenger seat. She let Santiago press a kiss to her cheek before shutting the door. Folding four of her fingers down on each hand, Buffy flipped her friends off through the car window.

Buffy watched Santiago chuckle at her as he pulled away from the thrumming bass.

"Are you as drunk as your friends?" He glanced at her from the corner of his eye.

"Almost." Buffy answered, snickering behind her clutch.

Santiago smiled, reaching over to pull the clutch away from her face. "You out here being a lightweight on me?"

"Of course not," Buffy scoffed defensively. "Just had a lot of free drinks tonight."

"Found yourself a good dance partner?"

Buffy shrugged, looking out the window. "Or five."

"No one caught your eye?"

"I didn't say that." Buffy defended. Her knee pulsed against the car door. Why was he asking her about other men when she was in his car? Maybe calling him had been a mistake.

"Camila didn't need a ride home too?" They stopped at a red light, his face bathed in the deep color. Buffy followed the red light across the high planes of his cheekbones and nose. Her mouth watered.

"She's staying with her friend tonight."

"Friend?"

"Her word, not mine." Buffy dramatically waggled her eyebrows at Santiago.

"Is Elena her girlfriend?"

"It's complicated." Buffy laughed. "Camila isn't really the relationship type either. They're more than friends but less than a couple, I guess." Buffy shrugged noncommittally.

"Did you and Camila ever..." Santiago let the sentence trail off, his eyes roving over her face for answers.

"God, no." Buffy shivered at the thought. "Her brother and my cousin were in jail here together, and when I moved to the city for work, I stayed with her for a few weeks. We hit it off and I just never left." Buffy shrugged. "I didn't even know she liked girls too until I found Elena wearing her clothes in the kitchen one morning."

Santiago laughed. "Pear did that to me once. Except it was two older women and we were only nineteen. Think I popped a boner right there in the kitchen."

Buffy howled with laughter, imagining two grown women watching a young Santiago be so affected by their presence. Before she knew it, they were turning down her street.

"That was quick." Buffy said, directing Santiago to a parking space.

"Time flies when you're laughing at me." Santiago kissed her cheek and stood from the car.

Buffy chuckled again, watching from the rearview mirror as Santiago rounded the car to her side.

Santiago pulled Buffy from her seat, keeping her hand in his as they climbed into the elevator. The levitating box was cramped while it rose, humidity weighing the air down around them. Buffy could feel Santiago's eyes on her. They were as heavy as hands on her back, her face, the tops of her thighs. She was throbbing by the time the elevator released them onto the top floor, memories dancing across her skin.

Santiago followed her inside the dark apartment. Buffy locked the door behind them and flipped on the hall lamp.

"Something to drink?" Buffy slipped the heels from her feet, padding barefoot into her kitchen. "Red wine?"

"Perfect." Santiago followed her lead and removed his shoes. Instead of sitting at the counter across from her, he followed Buffy into the kitchen. He slid the pizza box onto the counter and came closer to her. Grabbing the bottle of wine from her hands, he filled each glass generously, dribbling the last bits into her glass for a bigger pour. He handed the full glass to her, brushing his hand gently down her arm when she took it from him.

Distrust simmered in her gut. Buffy narrowed her eyes at him as she took a sip of the dry red. Santiago narrowed his eyes back at her, watching her cheeks flush.

"Stop looking at me like that," Buffy told him.

"Like what?" His voice had dropped a few octaves and Buffy felt her heart beat faster.

"Like you want to eat me," she said.

"I do want to eat you." Santiago stared at her, not a chuckle teasing his throat. He was dead serious. Downing the rest of the wine in his glass, Santiago set it in the sink and lifted Buffy onto the counter beside him. Placing her wine glass back in her hand, he pulled her legs around his waist. "Finish your wine."

Buffy rolled her eyes and put the glass to her lips, watching Santiago over the rim of her glass. His hands wandered across her bare thighs, leaving fire burning in his wake. She lowered the glass and Santiago stepped closer. The wine burned down her throat at the same time he leaned forward, licking up the curve of her neck.

Breath escaped her as Santiago kissed down her torso. Dropping to his knees before her, he quickly pulled her underwear off and pushed her skirt up over his head.

His chin was wet when he met her eyes again. Santiago ran his tongue over his lips and groaned. Buffy squirmed at the lewd act. Drawing her leg up, she pressed her heel into his back and encouraged him closer. His gaze was making her nervous. He was spending too much time just gazing at her.

Santiago pulled her to the edge of the counter, wrapping his arms firmly around her waist. He balanced her precariously on the edge of the stone. Deep brown eyes gazed at her, evaluating every inch of her face. She hoped he couldn't see the anxious thoughts racing through her mind. The effect he had on her had to remain a secret only she knew.

Buffy met his lips with hers.

The stubble of black scruff scratched against her face. Santiago had velvet soft lips, but the roughness of his half-grown beard was distracting her. Buffy pulled away. The skin of her chin felt raw.

"I think you should grow this out." She rubbed her thumbs along his cheeks and over his jaw.

"Yeah? You like the beard?" Santiago rubbed his nose against hers.

"I like it better than whatever this is." Buffy chided, scratching her nails down his cheeks.

"I'll think about it." Santiago claimed her mouth again, silencing her argument. His tongue tickled across her bottom lip, and she opened for him enthusiastically.

"Fuck me already," Buffy complained, unbuttoning his pants and tugging at the zipper.

Santiago kissed her, trapping her wrists in his hand to stop her from completely disrobing him. He broke their kiss and pulled away. Buffy whimpered before she could stop herself. Santiago ripped her dress up and over her head.

Buffy avoided his gaze, hoping he wouldn't tease her. Santiago caught her around the chin, bringing her gaze to his. Gently, he rubbed his nose against hers.

"Have you slept with anyone since?" Santiago whispered.

"No," she answered.

"Good," Santiago said, sheathing himself inside her in one thrust. Uncovered.

Still dressed in his T-shirt and jeans, Buffy flooded with desire. Santiago wanted her so badly he couldn't even bother to undress himself. That thought heartily fueled her confidence.

Buffy shivered as he moved, feeling him everywhere. He was eclipsing her, overwhelming her body and mind. Something in the depths of her brain whispered hesitancies, warnings. But Buffy couldn't hear them over the sound of Santiago's heartbeat in her ear. She smiled when their eyes met, foreheads pressed together while they shared breath.

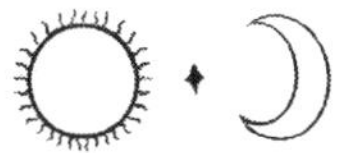

Buffy was *supposed* to kick him out again.

What was wrong with her lately?

Rolling over, Buffy watched Santiago's sleeping form. The two weren't touching when she woke, save for the bottom of her foot resting on his warm calf. She pulled the traitorous limb away gently, hoping he wouldn't wake.

They were naked under the duvet, each of Santiago's midnight black tattoos on display. His arm was outstretched on the bed between them, as though he had been reaching for her in his sleep.

Ew.

Buffy outlined his tattoos with her eyes, admiring them in the daylight. She recognized a few images; a hummingbird, corn, nopales. A black jaguar prowled his shoulder blade, the claws clamping into the flesh where his neck met his shoulder. Moving on to his face, she was almost certain he didn't have any tattoos up there, but she needed to be sure. Leaning her chin in her hand, she popped up on her side to evaluate his sleeping form.

Buffy met Santiago's open brown eyes.

Lucky for her, she wore the perfect aloof mask. "Hi."

"Checking for a teardrop tattoo?" Santiago smiled at her as though they woke up beside each other every day.

Buffy blinked back at him and shook her head no.

Santiago pushed the red hair from her exposed shoulder, "How long have you lived in California again?" His fingers trailed down her arm, settling on the bare skin of her thigh.

"Two years." Buffy didn't ask where he was from. She didn't want to know. This was uncharted territory as it was.

Peeling herself from his embrace, she padded into the attached bathroom and started the shower.

Santiago watched her from the bed. Buffy had neglected to cover her naked form, not out of a desire to enthrall but simply because she was used to being alone. She never allowed sexual partners to stay the night and hadn't thought to cover herself with a robe or discarded shirt. She could feel Santiago admiring the view, his legs spread wide as he watched her shamelessly. She felt his gaze on her like warm hands. Desire grew in her belly and she considered climbing back in bed with him.

He needed to get the hell out.

Buffy paused beside the bed. She needed to say something, but her mind was blank. Santiago caught her thin wrist in his grasp, pulling her down onto the bed beside him.

"Breakfast or lunch?" Santiago posed it as a question, though he should've known what her response would be. Hadn't he listened to anything she said?

"I fast on Saturdays." Buffy lied. Santiago needed to take a hint. There was no changing her mind.

"Your eyes tell me when you lie." He smiled softly at her, rubbing the center of her palm with his thumb. Buffy hated how quickly it eased her anxiety. She pulled her hand from his grasp.

Narrowing her eyes at him, she thought over her next words carefully. Typically, her partners were easy to dissuade. Buffy would simply miss a few phone calls, have some inconvenient plans, and usually they disappeared on their own.

That wasn't going to work this time. Santiago was too addicting.

"I told you, I don't date." Buffy met his eye before she lurched from the bed and hurried into the shower. Locking the door behind her, she stomped the butterflies down in her belly. For some reason, locking the door behind her felt extreme. She bit her lip, hoping that Santiago wasn't hurt by the action.

It doesn't matter what he thinks, Buffy told herself.

He's just a guy.

Acid churned in her belly and Buffy felt the claws of guilt sinking into her spine. Buffy knew she had a mean streak and she usually gave it her all to keep it in check around others. Santiago threw her off kilter and caused her to lose her grip on the red monster. He was going to make her crazy. She should've never taken him home the first time. She knew better than to sleep with clients and now she had screwed herself.

They needed to end it.

Buffy tiptoed out of the shower and listened at the door.

Nothing but silence.

Unlocking the door, Buffy pulled it open and stepped out. She held her head high, feigning nonchalance.

Her show wasn't necessary. The bedroom was empty.

The smell of coffee reached her nose and Buffy followed the scent without another thought. She found Santiago barefoot in her kitchen, coffee pot in hand.

"Don't worry," Santiago laughed at the uneasy look on her face. "I drank mine already." He placed a mug on the bar top in front of her. "Milk?"

Buffy nodded.

Santiago poured a dash of oat milk into her mug. Stirring it with a spoon, he placed the warm mug in front of her.

"Thank you." Buffy said, sipping down the bitter drink.

Santiago just smiled, putting the milk back in the fridge and washing his mug in the sink. He reached up and placed his mug back in the cabinet. Rounding the counter, he sauntered up to Buffy, peering down at her with a slight quirk to his plush mouth.

"I'll see you Monday." Santiago said, kissing her softly. Without another word, he was gone.

The door clicked shut behind him. Buffy remained frozen in place, lips still pursed, the scent of him surrounding her. His time in her kitchen had left his evergreen scent hanging in the air.

What the fuck had just happened?

Sipping her coffee, Buffy tumbled through ideas about where to go from here. Santiago was the best fuck she'd had in years, but he seemed to want more than a quick lay. If they were going to keep this going, she needed to set some ground rules before the man started calling her his girlfriend.

Draining the coffee quickly, she got up to clean the kitchen before Camlia came home. Last thing she needed was Camila asking why the kitchen counters were sticky. Eyes tracking the countertops, Buffy looked for their dirty wine glasses. Opening the cabinet, she found their wine glasses clean and stacked with the others.

The only item out of place was her now-empty coffee mug. Santiago had even straightened the rug they bunched up the night before. Buffy squatted so that her eyes were level with the countertop he had ravished her on. It was streak-free, completely dry, and smelled vaguely of the mandarin cleaning agent Camila bought from the corner store.

God dammit, Buffy thought.

She rushed to her bedroom, switching out her now soaked thong for a fresh one. Santiago was going to be the death of her.

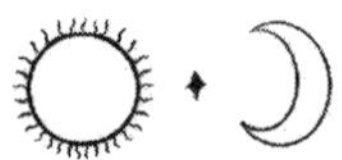

"Someone got laid." Pear whistled as Santiago walked into the kitchen. "Doing a nice little walk of shame, eh primo?"

"What are you doing here so early on a Saturday?" Santiago pressed a kiss to Abuela's cheek where she stood over spitting hot oil.

"Need to pick your brain about a case," Pear said through the food in his mouth.

"On a weekend?" Santiago questioned. His cousin was an incredible lawyer but he wasn't one to work on a Saturday.

"I know Abuela makes tostones on Saturdays." Pear smiled and followed Abuela to the kitchen table. He kissed her cheek and pulled more fried plantains onto Abuela's plate, then his own.

"Who got your dick wet?" Pear jutted his chin towards Santiago.

Santiago hissed, "cállate", at his idiot cousin, praying Abuela Paulina hadn't heard.

Abuela clicked her tongue disapprovingly in her cheek and smacked Pear on the back of the head. "Have some respect." She glared at him and took his plate, placing it in front of Santiago instead.

"Wow." Pear placed a hand over his heart. He feigned a deep frown before snapping back to his cheerful self. "Anyway, back to my case." Pear stood and grabbed a new plate from the cabinet beside the stove. "They pulled a ticket from when she first came to the country back in '97 and drove a dirt bike without a license through Jamul."

Abuela Paulina rolled her eyes and began to straighten the dining table, muttering grievances under her breath. One of Abuela's closest friends as a child had been undocumented, and together they had gone for a joy ride in their aunt's old Volvo. A week later,

Abuela's best friend and her entire family had been deported. The guilt had never left her. Add on three decades of higher and higher rates of deportation, and Abuela had too many friends sent away to count. She was rightfully angry.

Santiago glanced at his grandmother, seeing the shake of her hands while she fiddled with the salt and pepper shakers.

"Jamul was barely a town in the '90's." Santiago scoffed, anger flaring in him too.

Abuela Paulina stood and clattered dishes in the sink.

"Abuela, leave the dishes for me. Go enjoy your coffee." Santiago spoke gently, hoping that Abuela's stubbornness would fail to rear its head this morning. With a huff, Abuela Paulina refilled her coffee mug and disappeared into the sunshine of the backyard.

Pear offered apologetic eyes to his cousin. "I forgot."

"We should keep work at the office," Santiago reminded his cousin.

"You're right." Pear nodded.

"I had a case a few years ago in Texas." Santiago washed his tostones down with a long gulp of coffee. "I can pull it for you on Monday."

"You're the best." Pear dried while Santiago washed the dishes. "How is she?"

Santiago glanced at the open back door. He could see Abuela Paulina's feet hanging from the porch swing across the yard.

"She's good." Santiago dried his hands. "High energy, she's been eating, laughing, she seems herself."

"Good." Pear let out a breath. Abuela Paulina had raised him after both of his parents passed during their incarcerations. She was his mother, and the fear of losing her scared him even more than Santiago. Pear would never show it though.

"I'm sure she wouldn't mind if you wanted to move back in." Crossing his arms over his chest, Santiago leaned against the kitchen counter and peered at his cousin.

Stubbornness truly ran in the family. Pear was currently wearing the same iron gaze their Abuela wore when she stood her ground.

"I can't live with my grandmother forever," Pear whispered.

"Why not?" Santiago shrugged. He was thirty-two and living with his grandmother and he didn't consider it a problem. It was their job to care for Abuela and living with her was part of that.

Pear glared at Santiago.

"Besides, it would be more like she was living with you, than you living with her." Santiago chuckled and leaned around his cousin to peek outside again. Her feet were still swinging gently in the air.

"I can't," Pear grumbled, peering down at his feet. "I've got to get going. See you in the office on Monday?"

Santiago nodded and hugged his cousin before turning back to the kitchen. Pear walked outside to say his goodbyes to Abuela Paulina. He would never leave without a goodbye. Pear loved Abuela more than himself, but he didn't trust himself to care for her. Pear was still a party boy, and in his mind, he wasn't good enough for their grandmother. Santiago wished Pear knew just how wrong that was.

"Abuela!" A scream sounded from outside. Santiago took off running, ice seizing his heart.

Santiago found Pear on his knees beside a slumped-over figure. Pear shouted Santiago's name, his entire body shaking. Pushing Pear behind him, Santiago crouched in front of his grandmother. He rested his hand against her chest, feeling it rise and fall with her breath. She was alive. Santiago let out a heavy sigh.

He pulled the coffee-soaked blanket from her lap, dropping it to the grass under him. The mug shattered against the ground, jolting Abuela out of her spell.

Blinking, Abuela Paulina began to shiver.

"Give me your jacket." Santiago held his hand out, taking Pear's thin jacket and wrapping it around Abuela's shaking shoulders.

Grumbles of confusion fell from her mouth. Santiago reminded himself to stay calm. Freaking out wouldn't help anything.

It took a few minutes before she was able to form words.

"What are you doing?" Abuela Paulina squinted at them, pushing their hands from her body. "Alberto, I can sit up by myself."

Pear froze, his mouth open, gaze darting across Abuela's fallen form. Santiago hadn't mentioned that Abuela Paulina had taken to calling him Alberto, his father's name. He didn't blame her really; he was the spitting image of his father and his own mother called him the wrong name half of the time. Even without her health issues, Abuela Paulina was old and loss of memory was to be expected.

"Quiero ayudarte." Santiago kept his voice low and even, channeling the smooth calmness of his father. Gripping her hand in his, Santiago pulled Abuela to her feet and guided her back inside the house. He tucked her into her favorite chair and wrapped her up in a knitted blanket. By the time she was settled in front of an old rerun of her favorite trivia show, Pear had finished disposing of the broken mug and cleaned up the coffee-stained white blanket.

"You didn't tell me she's getting worse," Pear spit, venom coating his voice.

"She isn't getting worse." Santiago attempted to remain calm.

"She thinks you're her son!" Pear hissed.

Santiago rolled his eyes. "She's eighty-seven," Santiago argued. "Even if she had never been sick before, confusion and memory loss is not uncommon at her age."

"It's uncommon for her."

"Abuela isn't superhuman!" Santiago threw his hands up in frustration. "I'm scared to lose her too, Johnny, okay? But she's a human being. She can't be strong and perfect forever."

"I'm not ready," Pear whispered.

"Neither am I." Santiago sighed and glanced behind him, listening to Abuela Paulina shout out answers at the television. "We still have time. Abuela is just old, not sick."

Pear nodded but Santiago could tell his cousin wasn't absorbing the words. He felt his heart tug in his chest. Santiago couldn't imagine losing either of his parents anytime soon and now Pear was being faced with the loss of the only one he had left. Of course he was scared.

"She has a quilting class tonight. Can you take her?" Santiago waited for his cousin to meet his gaze.

Pear nodded.

Santiago knew that Pear kept a distance in an effort to protect himself from hurting in the future. But he didn't want his cousin to regret not spending time with their grandmother, especially if she only had a few years left. Abuela Paulina had beaten breast cancer once, survived a car accident and derailed train as a teenager, and successfully gave birth to five children. She had lived a long life and old age was the one thing she couldn't outrun. Santiago knew Pear needed to spend time with their grandma before her memories were completely gone.

The air didn't return to Santiago's lungs until he heard the front door click shut. He returned to Abuela in the living room, handing her a glass of cold water.

"Mijo, mira este programa conmigo." Abuela reached for Santiago, her palm open and waiting.

Santiago took her hand in his, squeezing it tight.

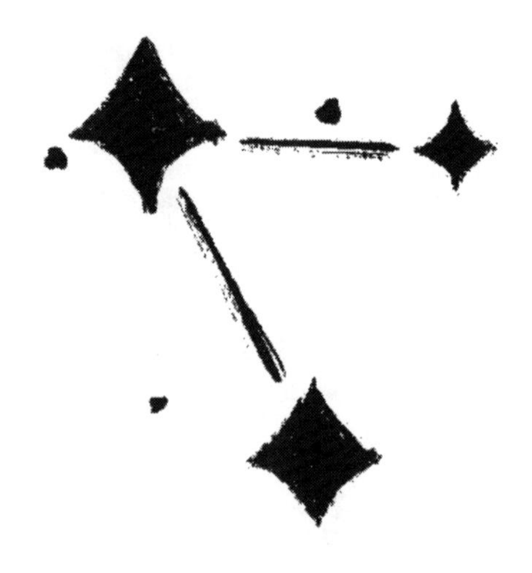

Chapter 6

Buffy forced her thoughts to stay on work, though she found herself replaying the same scenes over and over again. Santiago, making her coffee and doing her dishes. Santiago, opening the door for her and insisting on walking her up the steps even if he wasn't coming in. Santiago, head between her thighs while he worshiped her like a goddess.

Santiago.

Santiago.

Santiago.

Buffy dropped her head onto the cold wood of her desk. She needed to clear her mind, free her spirit from the infection caused by him.

Veronica knocked on her open door, curls haloed by the fluorescent lights. "Lunch is up, you coming?"

Nodding furiously, Buffy followed Veronica downstairs.

She regretted her decision to eat as soon as she entered the room. Santiago's grandma was sitting at a table alone, a full plate of food in front of her. Buffy ducked behind one of the people, but he wasn't tall enough to obscure her from view.

"Buffy?" His voice was familiar.

Buffy straightened and faced Mr. Norman with a fake smile. "Good morning, Mr. Norman. I'm happy to see you here. Is the shuttle treating you well?"

Mr. Norman grumbled his grievances about the traffic in the city while Buffy prayed that Abuela Paulina would not turn around.

Shit.

Abuela Paulina waved to her from across the room.

"Mr. Norman, why don't you take a seat and let me get lunch for you?" Buffy looped her arm through the old man's and led him towards Abuela Paulina's table.

"Nice to see you again." Buffy gripped the seat beside Abuela Paulina, pulling it out for Mr. Norman. "This is Mr. Norman, he rides the shuttle often as well. I thought he might be able to explain the ropes to you."

Abuela's warm brown eyes fell on Mr. Norman. "Well, I would certainly appreciate that."

Buffy prayed to the gods that Abuela Paulina had no knowledge of the relationship Buffy had with her grandson. The last thing she needed was to become part of the gossip at the center.

Mr. Norman shook Abuela's hand gently, avoiding direct eye contact. Buffy could see a flush creeping up the back of his neck.

Well, well, well. Mr. Norman did have feelings after all.

"I will go get your lunch, Mr. Norman." Buffy excused herself quickly, darting away from the table.

She watched them as she made a plate of lunch, their heads leaning close while they spoke. Mr. Norman laughed at something Abuela Paulina said and Buffy realized it was the first time she had ever seen his teeth. Buffy smiled.

She set the plate of food on the table in front of Mr. Norman. He thanked her offhandedly and immediately returned his attention back to Abuela Paulina. Buffy felt like Cupid.

Turning to scan the room, she searched for familiar faces.

Clara and her son were seated at a table of Chicano families. The parents were laughing loudly, voices around the table speaking in both English and Spanish. The boys were racing to finish their apple juice boxes while the girls had moved off to jump rope with the older kids. Buffy watched until she saw Clara speak, light flooding her eyes when she was understood by the group—and understood their response. Satisfied, Buffy moved on to the next group.

By the time Buffy had made her rounds saying hello to everyone in the room, Abuela Paulina's laughter was bouncing through the rafters. Every person at the table wore a smile on their face, and Abuela Paulina was playing peekaboo with a baby nestled into another Auntie's arms. Buffy nodded and returned to her office.

The biannual grant meeting was only two hours away and she could feel the disdain spreading through her bones already. Nerves had begun to swirl in her belly and Buffy left her stew untouched, instead settling for a few nibbles of corn bread.

The Arizona tobacco company was their largest funder and Buffy absolutely could not fuck it up. Despite being located within twenty miles of the largest reservation in the country, none of their upper management were Indigenous. Unless you counted the mythical Cherokee grandmother one of them claimed to have.

Flipping through the slide deck again, Buffy ran through her notes in her head. This was her chance to save the housing program. She had to convince a table of rich white men that a housing program was worth the investment. Rationale and logic weren't enough with them. They wanted tears. They wanted pain, something people could make movies about. They wanted a story that could sell them as the best ally to Indian Country since Lincoln. Money. They wanted money.

Buffy wanted the housing program because San Francisco had a huge unhoused population— both Native and non-Native. Solving this problem for their people could impact all unhoused people in a positive way. There was more to her decision than making the news and frankly, she didn't care about their investment. A financial return wasn't her goal. Helping people was.

"Are you almost ready?" Veronica joined her at the front of the conference room, hot coffee in her hands.

"After this coffee, I will be." Buffy took the cup and guzzled a long swig.

"It's tea." Veronica grimaced as Buffy immediately recoiled from the cup.

Buffy grunted in disgust.

"I'm worried about your blood pressure," Veronica mumbled.

"Well, don't." Buffy waved her away and turned off the projection screen. "Send them in."

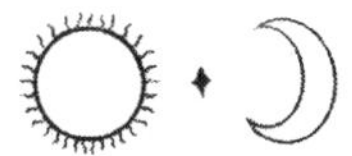

Santiago ignored Pear's pleading for what felt like the twenty-seventh time that morning.

"I said no."

"You're saying no but I'm hearing yes." Pear pointed both his index fingers at Santiago and wiggled his thumbs.

"That's because you ruined your hearing at all those car meets." Santiago had been a faithful SUV driver growing up in Colorado. But for Cali-raised Pear, a lowrider was the only vehicle he would drive.

"Rude." Pear narrowed his eyes and strode to his cousin's desk. "Are you sure you don't want to go out tonight?" Pear did his best imitation of puppy dog eyes but ended up looking like an aged-out frat boy.

Santiago looked at Pear with a blank expression.

"Fine!" Pear threw his palms up in surrender. "I give up."

"Thank God," Santiago muttered, standing and gathering his things. "I have a lunch meeting."

"You have time for a lunch date but can't come to boys' night?" Pear glared at him.

"It's a meeting for Clara's case." Santiago flipped Pear off and let the wind shut the door behind him.

Truthfully, Santiago loved boys' night when it was actually about the boys. Now, boys' night was mainly about picking up women. But he wasn't on the hunt for ladies like the rest of their group was. If he could be assured they wouldn't all ditch him before the middle of the night, he would happily accompany his cousin. But he knew which head ruled their brains, and it wasn't the one *with* a brain..

Santiago was nearing the middle of his thirties, and he was ready for a family. He wanted to arrive at the bar and leave it with the same person. He wanted that same person to sleep beside him every night and join him in the quest to have a grandpa lifestyle minus all the kids. In short, he wanted a soulmate.

Buffy made his heart thrum in a way it hadn't since he was a teenager. She had a mean streak that inexplicably turned him on. Even when she was attempting to push him away, he found himself drawn further under her spell. Despite her hard demeanor, she was soft and caring on the inside. He craved her softness like a drug.

The first time he saw her, stink-eyeing him in the food line, he was done for. She dominated his thoughts daily and he had faith that he was in hers. At least somewhat.

Santiago opened the center door, sliding through in hopes of going unnoticed. Burning palo santo hit his nose immediately, instantly lowering his heart rate. He walked briskly to the elevators, keeping his head turned away from the community room. Abuela Paulina had taken the shuttle in earlier that morning and he figured she was still here. His grandmother could spend an entire day at the center now that Buffy had introduced her to Mr. Norman and a few other Elders. Speaking of Mr. Norman, he needed to question Buffy about his intentions with calling his grandmother every night at eight p.m..

The elevator arrived empty and took him directly to the top floor. Exiting, he took a quick glance around before turning toward her office. Buffy was inside of an all-glass conference room. Filled with people in suits and updos, Buffy stuck out in her high-waisted blood red slacks and the solid black top covering her ample chest. Her hair was tied in a simple braid, white leather wrapped around the end of the strand. A golden yellow bird dangled from her ears.

Santiago couldn't tear his eyes away from the image of her at work. She stood proudly at the front of the room. Shoulders squared, she faced the group of people head on, unwavering. He watched as she answered questions, pointed to her slides, and silenced unnecessary comments with a sharp glare.

Buffy Yellowbird was an enigma he couldn't get past.

"Can I help you?" A voice startled him from his staring.

Santiago turned, a young woman staring at him with a brow raised, her lips outlined in a darker brown than the rest. He smiled.

"You must be Veronica." Santiago offered his hand. Veronica shook it, recognition dawning in her gaze.

"Eres el *hot lawyer*?" Veronica trailed her gaze up and down his body.

Santiago tried not to blush.

"You can wait in her office. Como unos diez minutos." Veronica pointed to the open door at the end of the hall.

Santiago nodded and headed for her office immediately.

The hot lawyer, huh?

An ego boost was exactly what he needed this morning.

Buffy's office was quiet, far enough from the drumming class downstairs to muffle the noise.

Santiago set the foil-wrapped pupusas on her desk, beside a cold bowl of stew and barely-touched cornbread. Santiago turned, taking a quick scan of the pictures that faced Buffy while she worked. Buffy was secretive, and his only chance to learn about her friends and family was right now. He couldn't waste it.

There were only three photos, all tucked into a corner beside her computer. One of a man and woman holding four children. Another was an image of a man and woman with long brown hair holding a baby beside Buffy, a woman with short blue hair, and a third woman with a shaved head. The last image was of a huge group of people, all standing tall, broad, and strong in front of a pasture of horses. One of the girls in the image had bright red hair. Santiago leaned closer to the image, attempting to decipher who he was looking at.

The photo was weathered and old, so he couldn't make her face out clearly, but those strong thick thighs and muscular shoulders told him that was his Buffy. Santiago grinned at the image, the smile she wore bigger than any he had seen on her face yet. He was determined to cause Buffy to smile like that.

Sitting in the chair before her desk, Santiago took an analyzing scan around the office. The whole place was overwhelmingly black, save for the white walls. Buffy worked at a black desk, with a black chair, a black computer, a black area rug, and a black built-in bookcase.

Black must be her favorite color, he thought.

Her home had been different from her office. There was black throughout, but not as much. Her house screamed soft, sweet Buffy while her office was the spitting image of the in-control Buffy he'd witnessed in the conference room. He almost felt like a voyeur, like he was spying on the side of Buffy that she hadn't yet shared with him.

Santiago wanted to see more of her. He wanted to watch her guard come down and free the sweet woman inside. Every time a bit of that soft heart shone through, it wrapped around his heart like a vice and *squeezed*. If she was like that every day, he would've proposed marriage already.

The only problem was that she rarely ever let her guard down. It was only in the afterglow of an orgasm, when she fell apart and let him put her back together, that she let him in. Her eyes would be clear and open, a smile across her face while she peppered kisses along his skin and clung to him like her life force. Just as quickly as she came, the guard would reappear.

Santiago wanted more. He wanted the sweet Buffy all the time, just for him.

All he had to do was show her that it was safe to be soft around him. That he wouldn't hurt her, that he would protect her. That he could love her the way she deserved. She just had to let him.

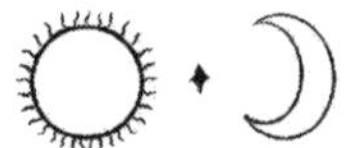

Buffy huffed as she shut the glass door behind the last board member.

"I can't wait until we have an all-Native board." Buffy wiped nonexistent sweat from her brow. She was tired of fighting partners and her own organization for money.

"They're *so* out of touch," Veronica agreed, gathering the dirty cups while Buffy packed up the leftover snacks. She tucked her pink glasses on top of her head, giving the illusion of pink cat ears popping out of her thick black curls. Veronica was full of personality that never waned, no matter how hard things got. Buffy appreciated this as one of her greatest strengths.

"Take the rest of the day off, V." Buffy nodded to her assistant and headed to her office. She couldn't wait to close the door and sit in the beautiful silence. Irritation flamed in her gut and she gritted her teeth. She wondered if installing a punching bag in her office could count as a business expense. Then she could work off all this anger in a healthy way, all alone in her office.

That dream was crushed as soon as she stepped through the door.

Santiago was sitting in front of her desk.

"What are you doing here?" Buffy snapped. The meeting had *not* gone well and speaking to another man, even one as hot as Santiago, sounded like hell. Grant presentations bookended by a plethora of inappropriate questions from non-Natives left her blood burning. She was still simmering in her rage and Santiago was straight in the line of fire.

Santiago turned, a warm smile on his face despite her harsh voice. "Nice to see you too." Rising from the chair, he palmed her elbow and pressed a kiss to her cheek.

Buffy hated how her body flushed at his touch and how she leaned into his kiss, craving his calming presence. Her heart slowed when he touched her, and Buffy wanted him to touch her forever. Snapping herself out of it, she tensed in his arms and pulled away.

Buffy narrowed her eyes, annoyed with his jovial behavior. He was seemingly unaffected by her touch. Unfair. "Are you here to distract me or what?"

Undisturbed, Santiago took his seat and waited for her to sit down. "I came to see you." He gestured to the foil wrapped package on her desk. "Have you eaten yet?"

"Yes," Buffy lied. She could smell the meat and spices in the foil and her mouth began to water. Bringing lunch to work was not part of having sex. Unwrapping the foil, she pulled out two pupusas. Santiago reached forward and placed a small cup of red salsa on the desk between them. She was punched in the nose with the smell of the salsa and knew instantly it would be too spicy for her.

"They're chorizo and cheese," he explained. "Salsa on the side."

"I love chorizo," Buffy muttered, eyes glued to the dough in her hand. Tucking it back into the foil, she set the pupusa to the side. "I'm on the clock."

"You're salaried." Santiago raised an eyebrow at her.

"I already took my lunch hour."

"I can hear your stomach growling from over here." Santiago called her bluff, gesturing towards the bowl of cold stew. "We can talk about work. How is your grant going?" He smiled, cheek distended with meat and cheese. He looked like a chipmunk and Buffy wanted to laugh. How dare he make her laugh right now?

If eyes could spit venom, she would've burned him with only a look.

"I'll give you an update on Clara then." Dipping his pupusa in the red sauce, he chewed through a bite while Buffy watched him. "Her refugee status should be approved within the week. I'm trying to help her find work. They won't approve a work visa without a job offer on the table. Does the center help people find employment?"

"Yes," Buffy answered, peering at the food he brought her. The smell of chorizo was everywhere, each bite he took wafting the scent further up her nose. Dipping her finger into the cup of red salsa, Buffy tasted it. Smoke filled her mouth and she could taste the warmness from the roasted garlic and onion. Spice hit her at the end, burning down her throat and leaving the edges of her tongue on fire.

Santiago was watching her with a knowing look. Rolling her eyes, she ripped the top off the pupusa and poured a heavy amount inside. She wouldn't let him think she was weak. "Tell her to swing by this week and I will get her set up with our employment team."

Buffy bit into the pupusa and felt her tongue set immediately alight. Fire danced through her mouth and Buffy took another bite, hoping the heat would wash down. It didn't.

She felt sweat break out on her brow. Hopefully Santiago couldn't see that closely.

"I can do that." Santiago crumpled the foil in his hands and tossed it into the trash can. "How do you like it?"

Buffy thumbed the corner of her mouth, where cheese and salsa threatened to escape her pink painted lips. "It's delicious. Where are they from?"

"My house." Santiago smiled while she choked briefly, swallowing harshly before looking at him. "My grandma made them."

"You live with her?"

Santiago nodded. "She's lived in the same house for sixty years." Santiago laughed at the surprise on her face. "They came during urban Indian removal programs. My mom is from Colorado and my dad loved it there almost as much as she did. Abuelita refused to leave San Fran, even as things got harder, so I came back to stay with her."

"You're from Colorado?"

Santiago nodded.

"I've always wanted to go there," Buffy said without looking at him. "See how different the Rockies look."

"You a fan?"

"Of the mountains," Buffy said. "Not the team."

"I'll take you sometime." Santiago smiled in earnest.

"I'm sure you say that to all your ladies." Buffy rolled her eyes, twisting the foil around her napkin until it was shaped like a ball. "Are you here in San Francisco temporarily, then?"

Santiago shrugged. "I miss Colorado. But the Bay has its advantages."

Buffy stared at him.

Santiago was undisturbed. "Come on, Buffy." Standing, he walked around to her side of the desk, taking the garbage from her hand. "You know you're my only one. Call me later." Leaning down, he kissed her cheek and disappeared out the door, tossing her trash in the basket on his way out.

"Don't make this a habit!" Buffy shouted after him.

Chapter 7

Camila had half a shoe on when Buffy got home.

"Going out?" Buffy asked, filling her bottle with cold water and taking a long gulp.

"Elena has a show." Camila threaded a gold hoop through her ear. The hoop hung low, brushing the golden skin of her collarbone.

"Tell her I said to break a leg."

"She'll think you might want to break her leg." Camila attempted to divert Buffy's attention.

"If I was going to break either of your legs, it would be yours, Cami." Buffy smiled menacingly. She had been trying to convince Camila to take Elena seriously as a girlfriend for more than a year now. They both knew her heart belonged with Elena. Camila was simply too stubborn to admit it.

Camila huffed and tiptoed away from Buffy.

"What are you doing tonight?" Camila called from her bedroom, emerging with a red lip gloss in hand. "Vas conmigo? They're covering Selena y Jenni Rivera tonight. I know you like them." Camila wiggled her shoulder against Buffy until she squirmed away.

Buffy's mother, Hozho, grew up in Arizona where toeing the line of Latina and Native was the majority culture. A lover of dancing and banda, Hozho raised all of the Yellowbird siblings on Mexican-American classics like "Bidi Bidi Bom Bom" and "La Bamba".

"No, thank you." Buffy opened the fridge, browsing the lackluster contents. "I'm not interested in being your buffer tonight."

"Rude." Camila rolled her eyes. "You got plans?"

"No," Buffy said. She was not going to call Santiago just because he requested it. In fact, that was exactly why she wasn't going to do it.

"Oh. You look nervous like you do right before a date." Camila looked Buffy up and down.

"No, I don't," Buffy said defensively.

"Okay." Camila raised her eyebrows in disbelief.

The two women eyed each other stubbornly, neither willing to bend.

"I won't be home tonight." Camila grabbed her tote bag from the couch. "Utilize this alone time, okay? You need to relax."

"You need to tighten up." Buffy clipped back.

"Do I need to call you a dick appointment myself or are you—"

"Leave already." Buffy cut Camila off before she could finish her sentence.

"I love you!"

"Me too," Buffy muttered.

"You're going to call Santiago, right?" Camila paused in the hallway. "I just think you're well suited—"

"He brought me lunch today," Buffy admitted, casting her gaze down to her feet.

"Like to work?"

Buffy nodded. "Homemade pupusas."

Camila's mouth dropped open in shock.

"He's down bad for you."

"That's exactly why I won't be calling him," Buffy snapped.

"Buffy! Why not?" Camila rose her voice, the shrillness bouncing off the high ceilings.

"He's getting too attached already."

Camila sighed, opening her mouth then closing it again.

"Give him a chance," Camila said. "He might be open to something casual. I mean, do you really want to go through a few bad dates and another STD test? At least with Santiago, you know exactly what you're getting." Camila kissed her cheek and disappeared out the front door.

Throwing herself down on the couch, Buffy heaved out a sigh. Her mind was racing, spiraling around and around, her thoughts darkening each moment she spent in silence. A buzz sounded from the coffee table beside her head. Buffy turned to look at her phone without sitting up.

Incoming Call: Juniper

Her older sister did have the habit of calling her at her worst moments. It was as though Juniper had some kind of Buffy radar and her spine tingled whenever Buffy felt an emotion. Letting the call roll through, Buffy played the message on speaker.

"*Buffy! Call me back. We need to discuss Christmas. What time do you land? Frankie has a choir performance on the 22nd, do you think you'll make it to that? Also, what are you buying Joy this year? Is she still into skateboards? Nataani wants to start doing gel polish on their nails but I'm afraid the house will explode. What are you getting them?*"

Buffy let the phone slip through her hand and fall to the floor. Her stomach sank to her feet and began to leak acid into her veins. The hammer of her heart pumped the acid through her entire body until she was consumed by guilt. She wished her family could just forget about her. It would be easier that way. She could come back as a happy surprise rather than a teeth-pulling disappointment.

People needed to stop requesting phone calls from her. Didn't her own family know she hated talking on the phone? It was going to burn her inside out with anxiety. Thoughts of Santiago plagued her mind and she recalled the easy smile he had for her. Great. Now she felt guilty for failing to call two people.

What did he have to talk to her about anyway?

They were simply fucking. They had nothing to discuss other than STD screenings and birth control types. What did he want from her?

Buffy paced across the living room, staring out the window as the fog rolled into the bay.

Call me.

His voice echoed through the room as though he was standing beside her.

Why would she call him? What did he mean by that? Squeezing her phone in her palm, she pivoted, tracing her steps on the hardwood floor.

Maybe she should call him. She needed to set him straight. Sure, they slept together a few times, but that was it. Santiago was treating her like a date, and he needed to stop.

Buffy put the phone to her ear, listening to the ring.

"Buffy." He said her name like he had been waiting for her call. "Did you have dinner yet?"

"No." Buffy kept her voice short. "I told you I don't eat dinner. Listen, Santiago—"

"I had a meeting next to the sushi bar you like." Santiago's voice carried through the phone, wind and horns honking in the background. "Care to split a few plates with me?"

"I don't." Buffy stopped, her stomach growling in hunger. In fact, she did want sushi. Their fridge was woefully empty, and she was at the edge of prolonged hunger that turned into pure rage. "Fine, you can bring me sushi. But then you have to fuck me. This is not just dinner."

Santiago couldn't hold back his laugh of surprise. "I think that can be arranged. I'll be there in fifteen minutes."

Ending the call, Buffy stood in silence for a few seconds.

She began to pace. Had she made a mistake? Santiago handled her moods with ease and seemed to bounce back no matter how often she shut him down. She would have to be firm with him when he arrived. He couldn't have any hope for her. That was how people got hurt.

Buffy needed to drive home the point of their relationship.

Sex.

That was it.

Hurriedly, Buffy changed into a black lace bra with a matching thong. The lace stretched across her curves, the dark pink of her areola on display against the curling flowers.

She was shouldering her robe when the knock sounded on her door. Buffy took a deep breath. She could do this. She just had to set him straight and then let him fuck her brains out.

Easy.

Gripping two beers by the neck, she threw the door open.

Santiago whistled lowly, trailing his gaze across her legs and chest. Buffy ushered him into the living room, locking the door behind him. He caught her by the waist, pulling her close for a kiss to her lips.

Buffy almost dropped the beers as his embrace devoured her. His lips were demanding, coaxing her mouth to open under his. The smell of eucalyptus surrounded her and she melted under his affection. He pulled away suddenly, kissing her lips one last time.

"Hungry?" Santiago asked.

Buffy blinked. Her thoughts had been thoroughly erased thanks to his kiss and she couldn't think of anything but him. He pushed her hair behind her ear.

"I know you like Sushi House." Santiago smiled and nudged her shoulder with his.

Oh yeah, Buffy remembered. *Sushi*.

"We can eat on the coffee table." Buffy pointed toward the table with her lips, turning abruptly from him. She hoped he couldn't see how easily he affected her with just a kiss. With a heavy sigh, she set the beers on the dense wood table.

Santiago followed her, reaching under the table for a floor cushion. He threw it on the floor beside her before grabbing one for himself. Buffy sat down eagerly, hoping the solid ground would grant her racing mind some stability.

Handing her a napkin, Santiago popped open the containers. The scent of fresh rice and nori flooded her senses. He flipped the lids over, so they could use them as plates. Picking up a volcano roll with his chopsticks, he placed it in the container in front of Buffy.

Santiago looked up at her with a soft smile, his eyes gliding across her face. Now was the time. She had to set him straight.

Buffy narrowed her eyes at him. "This is not a date."

"Whatever you say." Santiago took one of the volcano rolls for himself. Smiling with his mouth closed, the sushi poked out the skin of his cheek like a hamster. He was always smiling with a mouth full of food. Buffy fought the smile that tickled her lips. He was *not* cute.

"I already sent you money for my half anyway," Buffy quipped.

Santiago simply shrugged and kissed her cheek. Flames licked across her cheek where his lips touched her skin. He dipped his avocado roll into a mix of wasabi and soy sauce and placed it in her mouth.

"You wear this for me?" Santiago asked, using the clean end of his chopsticks to push her fallen robe open. Buffy straightened her shoulders. Cold air enveloped her chest and hardened her nipples under the black lace.

"Easy access." Buffy winked at him, settling her feet into his lap. Black slacks stretched across his lean thighs and her mouth watered. "Do you ever go to work at your actual office?"

Santiago laughed, a piece of nori stuck to his bottom lip. Without thinking, Buffy reached forward and peeled it from his dark lip. She licked it from her thumb. Santiago watched her with rapt attention. Buffy suckled on her thumb, dragging her teeth over the sensitive skin.

Santiago gulped. She smirked. At least she had an equal effect on him.

"Sometimes." He rubbed his hands over her calves, working the thick muscles. "I work from home as much as I can."

"I bet your grandma likes that." Buffy let herself smile this time. Elders would forever be her sweet spot. Abuela Paulina had already wormed her way into Buffy's heart herself, and her grandson wasn't too far behind. That was exactly why she needed to set him straight.

"She does." Santiago gathered their trash and put it in the paper bag. "But she makes me lunch when I work from home, so I'm the one reaping the benefits."

"She's lucky to have you." Buffy watched him walk across her moonlit living room.

Throwing the bag out under the sink, Santiago returned and pulled Buffy from the floor. Bringing his arms around her waist, Santiago swayed gently, moving to the rhythm of her breath. Buffy pushed him off, her heart racing in her chest. The cloud of arousal was starting to fog the rational part of her brain. She needed to set boundaries with him before she got distracted.

"Listen, this thing between me and you?" Buffy used her pointer finger to gesture between their chests. "This is a sex-only situation, okay?"

Santiago didn't nod, didn't speak, didn't react. He blinked at her, once, twice. Kissing her with the third. Buffy pulled back, putting her palms up on his chest to stop his advances.

"Look, the thing is that I kind of like..." she trailed off, breaking eye contact and looking around the room. His gaze made her feel naked. "I don't want to use condoms, so can you just keep your dick away from other people or whatever?"

Santiago stopped his slow swaying, his hands flexing on her hips. He stood straight to look at her. "Sex-only or not—I don't fuck multiple people at once. It's you or nothing." His voice was firm, final.

It set her on fire.

Buffy hid her surprise well, but she suspected he saw the twitch of her jaw at his words. "Good." She shook her head, crossing her arms over her bare chest to keep from touching him.

"Just to be clear." She looked away from him again, peering at the starry sky out the window. "I am only sleeping with you as well."

She could see him smile in her peripheral vision. Averting her eyes from his, she unbuttoned his shirt and pulled it open.

"No feelings," Buffy reiterated. She didn't want any blurry lines or miscommunications. Hurting him was the last thing she wanted to do.

"Whatever you say," Santiago whispered against her skin.

"I don't do feelings," Buffy said again.

"Stop talking." Santiago molded their lips together.

Taking advantage of her barefooted stature, Santiago folded himself over her. Her nails dug into his lower back, pulling at the belt of his pants. Lips moving against hers, he guided them to her bedroom and kicked the door shut behind them.

"Sit." Santiago nodded at the bed.

"Get naked," Buffy argued.

"Not yet." Santiago kept his eyes on her as she sat, her open robe masking the curves and rolls of her soft skin. She moved to pull the robe off. "Leave it on." He gripped the silk fabric and used it to pull her into him for a blinding kiss.

Buffy still had her eyes closed and her lips pursed when she felt herself falling backward. Santiago pushed her to her back and pulled her legs around his head. A groan left his mouth at the sight of her, and Buffy felt herself clench under his gaze.

"You're beautiful." Santiago spoke into the flesh of her thigh. Rubbing his nose into the crevice where her thigh and torso met, the teasing had her throbbing.

Panting, Buffy closed her thighs in an attempt to encourage him. She should've known it would be futile. Grabbing at her legs, Santiago pinned them to the bed. Spread open wide in front of him, she could feel his breath against her. He was incredibly strong despite his lean frame.

"Ask nicely." Santiago kissed her center gently.

"No," Buffy sneered, pulling a leg back to set her foot on his shoulder. She pushed him back gently.

Santiago took her foot and knocked it from his shoulder.

Kissing over her belly and hips, he dragged a wet tongue over her skin. "You're the most stubborn person I've ever met."

Buffy sat up on her elbows. "Likewise."

Santiago nipped at the skin of her belly. Buffy glared at him. He was almost there, where she wanted him most. She groaned.

He pulled away.

"No," Buffy whimpered.

"Ask nicely," Santiago countered.

"Can you just fuck me already?" Buffy huffed, exasperated and cloudy with arousal.

"With what?" Santiago licked her skin, a hair from where her pulse ebbed.

"Everything," Buffy breathed heavily as his fingers teased her wet skin. She couldn't take it anymore. "Please, Santi." Buffy squeezed her eyes shut.

He dove in as soon as she said the words, his fingers and tongue sliding easily into the places that made her squirm. A few pinches and kisses and she was floating through space, holding his head tightly against her.

Releasing him once she came back to earth, Santiago left open-mouthed wet kisses up her body until he reached her face. Rubbing his nose across hers, he nudged her mouth up to meet his. Buffy wrapped her arms and legs around him, sighing into his mouth with euphoria.

"Why are your pants still on?" Buffy frowned dramatically and reached between them to pull apart his belt.

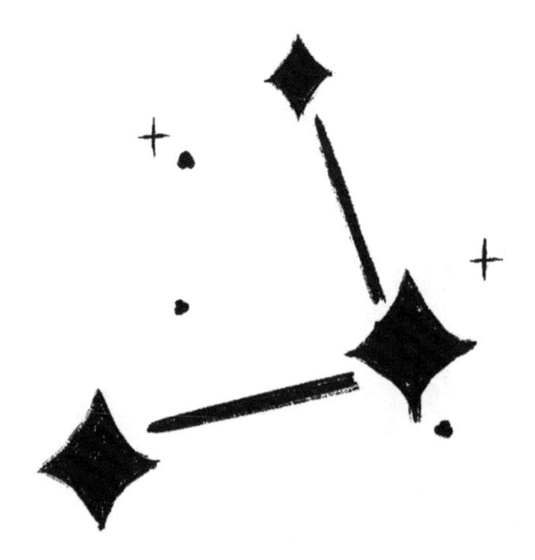

CHAPTER 8

Sunlight teased the darkness behind his eyes, rousing Santiago from his sleep. He stretched lazily, Buffy's leg falling from his lap. She grunted in her sleep, brow furrowing across her relaxed face. Eyes closed, Buffy reached out for him, sighing happily when he shuffled closer. Her lips tilted up just slightly at the corners, arm wrapping around his torso and squeezing tight. She rubbed her cheek against his bare chest and let a drowsy hum fall from her lips.

Santiago smiled and picked up the hand resting on his chest. Kissing her knuckles, he placed her hand over his heart, covering it with his. This, he wanted forever. If Buffy could let down her walls and open her heart to him, they could have *this*. Moments of utter peace where both of them could turn off the constant stream of thoughts and just *be*.

Running his fingers through her loose hair, he tucked her face into his chest. Buffy was still asleep and craving his touch. Santiago fell back asleep to the feeling of her breath against his neck.

He woke to that same hot air ghosting across his sternum, followed closely by a fire-hot tongue and lips that felt like pillows. Squinting, he blinked.

Buffy dragged her nose over his thigh, eyes on his in question.

"Good morning to you too." Santiago chuckled, gathering her long, red hair into his fist.

With his confirmation, Buffy took him in her wet mouth. A groan escaped him as he felt himself bump against the back of her throat. Still somewhat soft, she was able to press her lips firmly against the skin of his torso. Her tongue circled the base of his shaft and Santiago twitched in her throat. He tugged at her hair, pulling back until she released him somewhat. She laughed when he popped out of her mouth, a shudder rocking across her body.

Buffy relaxed completely between his legs, letting him guide the rhythm of her mouth at the speed he desired. Fisting her hair, he moved her head leisurely, setting a slow pace to prolong this moment with her. Santiago watched her expression closely. She almost seemed to smile around him. He was going to get used to this quickly. Buffy was going to have to use all her might to push him away after waking him up like this.

She hummed around him and the vibration trembled across his body. He shivered, pulling her out from under the sheets before it was too late.

"Come here." Santiago waved his hands toward his face.

Buffy shook her head.

"Trust me."

Buffy glared at him. With a grunt of frustration, Santiago hooked his arms under her thighs and pulled her hips over his mouth. Palming her flesh in his hands, Santiago devoured her like water in a desert. He licked and sucked at her in earnest, begging her to place her full weight on his face.

Santiago opened his eyes, looking up at her above him. She was already staring at him, her lip caught between her teeth. Buffy had a hand on her breast, the other gripping the headboard behind him. She looked like a goddess above him.

Santiago reached down to stroke himself. Buffy glanced behind her and pushed his hand off, replacing it with hers. Finally, she let her full weight rest on his face and chest. Santiago gathered her ample backside in his hands and held her against his face so tightly he couldn't breathe.

Before long, she was falling apart above him, her muscular body squeezing him in a myriad of places. Santiago felt as though he was ascending to Heaven. The heat of her body encompassed his entire face and chest. Her nails scratched across his scalp and shoulders. He hoped the marks would stay for a few days, a reminder of the way she let him take control. A reminder of her letting go.

Buffy shimmied down his chest, kissing over his entire body before sinking onto him. Tucking her feet flat on the bed under his torso, Buffy leaned forward and took hold of the headboard. Using the bed for leverage, Buffy moved above him. Santiago's brain emptied of every thought while he watched her bounce up and down in front of him. All he could hope was that this wall wasn't shared with any neighbors, or they were going to start receiving complaints.

"Open your eyes." Santiago spoke through gritted teeth, trying to stay present until Buffy finished. He reached between them and brushed his thumb over her center.

Buffy's eyes snapped open, sucking in a sharp breath. She held his gaze, mouth dropping open wide as she plunged them both over the edge. Santiago wrapped his arms around her waist, moving with her until she released the headboard and sagged against him.

He glanced up at the headboard, thankful it hadn't split in Buffy's piercing grip.

A content sigh fell from her lips and she wiggled her thighs tighter around his hips to snuggle closer to him. Her lips were featherlight against his chest, kissing across the panther curling over his shoulder. He could feel her eyelashes fluttering against his sensitive skin.

Santiago wound his fingers through her bright red hair, closing his eyes to take in the softness she kept hidden. Buffy kept her emotions and feelings under lock and key and Santiago could never truly tell how she was feeling. Except after an orgasm.

For a few precious minutes, she opened up to him in slivers. Tiny rips in the fabric of her mask allowed her true feelings to shine through. It did nothing to comfort Santiago.

Instead, it only made him desire her more, need her more, chase her more. He wanted all of her.

"Meet me for lunch tomorrow?" Santiago took advantage of her post-orgasm bliss, hoping she would let her soft side answer. She was her sweetest when her mind was cleared with euphoria.

Silence ebbed for too long.

"Why do you always ruin it?" Buffy huffed and threw the covers from their sweaty bodies.

He grunted when she rolled off him, shivering as the cold air met his body. Grabbing her hips, he pulled her back into the bed. Santiago watched her hesitate, letting him hold on to her for a moment before wrenching herself from his embrace.

Santiago reached for her as she stood, her wrist dancing barely out of his grip. Reaching forward, he used their momentum to pull her off balance and onto the bed with him. Buffy wrinkled her nose in annoyance and bit him on the shoulder.

"I want to talk about work." Santiago flicked her nose gently, pulling her teeth from his flesh. "We're a pro bono firm, so I wanted to pick your brain a little about Clara's case."

"Fine," Buffy relented, flipping onto her back beside him. Santiago tried not to show his disappointment at the physical space she put between them. "Can we have sex after?"

"Absolutely," Santiago laughed, pulling himself from her bed. "I'll pick you up at one." He dressed easily, not a hair out of place and looked as though he had donned fresh clothes rather than picked them up from the floor. He held back a laugh when he saw himself in the mirror. On the outside, he was put together and looked the same as always. On the inside, his heart was racing and grasping at anything that would keep Buffy beside him. He only hoped she perceived him with the chill he was attempting to emit, otherwise she would be scared off for good.

Leaving a quick kiss on her lips, Santiago let himself out with a promise to see her tomorrow.

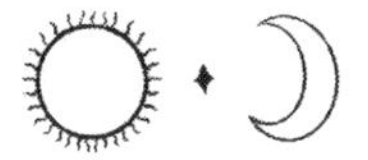

Buffy giggled, pulling her mussed sheets up to her chin. Last night had gone well. Santiago was starting to learn just how she liked things. He was turning out to be a great booty call. Calling him that made her feel like she was in college again. But what else could she call him?

Friends felt too intimate for the arm's length she was keeping him at. Letting him stay over was simply out of ease of access to his dick, *not* because she enjoyed his company. Buffy was certain that he could sew his mouth shut and never speak to her again, and she would still feel the same.

"Coffee or wine?" Camila shouted through their apartment, clanging through the front door to announce her arrival. "My parking space was open so I hope I'm not interrupting anything!"

Buffy rolled her eyes as Camila stomped through the house, announcing her arrival to all corners of their apartment.

"Is that sushi in the fridge?" Camila screeched, the sound of her feet shuffling across the floor frighteningly quick. Appearing suddenly in the doorway, Camila threw her hands on her hips and glared at Buffy. "Did you get Sushi House without me?"

"The rolls in the fridge are for you." Buffy sang the last word, shaking her head as though Camila should've known that.

"No, they aren't, you liar," Camila said. "Three of them are ahi and I hate ahi. Who are they for?" Camila punctuated her question with an intense glare.

"Well, obviously I need something for breakfast," Buffy argued, pointing at herself. "I'm a growing woman."

"Fess up. It smells like sex in here and I know you're naked under there."

"Santiago," Buffy answered.

"Hot lawyer with the tattoos?"

"Yes." Buffy threw the blanket over her face in anticipation of Camila's squeal. With a screech, Camila threw herself onto the bed, ripping the blanket from her grasp.

"Tell me everything."

"There isn't anything to tell. It's just sex." Buffy feigned nonchalance and hoped the smile she felt on the inside was not reflected on the outside.

"And sushi?" Camila quirked her head to the side.

"I paid for our half."

Camila scoffed. "You could let him buy you dinner if he's making a mess of your sheets every night."

"Hey!" Buffy kicked at her from under the blankets. "He's been here, like, twice!"

Camila dropped her chin and looked at Buffy from the side. "Be for real."

Huffing, Buffy kicked her once more. "I can't help it. He's just...so *good*." Buffy closed her eyes as memories flooded her senses, the ghost of Santiago gliding against her skin.

"Marry him." Camila spoke with earnest.

"He isn't *that* good. Get out of here." Buffy pulled the covers over her head and burrowed into the sheets until she heard her roommate clinking around in the kitchen. Slinking out of bed, she could smell Santiago like he was still sleeping beside her. Fingertips ghosted over her skin and she swore she could feel his lips on her neck. She tasted pan dulce on her tongue like he was still here.

Buffy smiled, enjoying the memory for a moment. Movement caught her eye and she turned her gaze to the mirror above the sink. A warm smile split her pink lips and her eyes were glossy and soft.

Who the fuck is that?

Buffy didn't recognize the person in the mirror. Her smile dropped instantly and she glared at her reflection. She could *not* be stupidly smiling about a man.

A *MAN*!

Glaring at herself in the mirror, Buffy chewed her lip. A penny-sized red bruise decorated her left breast.

She needed a shower.

Immediately.

Throwing back the curtain, she turned the knob as cold as it would go without losing pressure.. Buffy stepped under the frigid stream. Shock spread through her body and numbness danced over her skin.

Santiago had accompanied her last few showers and she hadn't wanted to subject him to the icy torture she normally endured. Now that she was alone, she let the entire shower happen beneath the freezing water. The constant chill kept her mind occupied and away from that dark spiral of guilt.

It made her miss Santiago. Whenever she was with him, she didn't have to fight to keep the thoughts at bay. Somehow, they vanished in his presence. There were few other people in her life that had ever done that. One of them was Frankie, her nephew, a spitting image of her sister with the calm demeanor of his father, and Calehan, her eldest brother. Before them, her mother had been her lighthouse in the storm.

After her mother's passing when she was a teenager, those dark spirals were next to impossible to avoid. Muskwa did his best, Calehan tried his hardest, and Juniper baked bread and brewed teas and made salves. But the darkness could not be healed from the outside; only Buffy could pull herself from the depths.

She still hadn't quite figured out how to get all the way out yet.

Tears fell beneath the ice water, scalding the skin of her cheeks. The darkness of her mother's death was something she had never fully emerged from. Truthfully, she didn't know if escape was possible. Maybe this was always who she was meant to be, married to the dark with a heart leaking forever from the hole ripped into it.

All Buffy had been doing the past decade was surviving, making it to the next day, and then the next one until it was time to die. Even the anti-depressants in college hadn't changed the constant darkness. When she was totally honest with herself, the only reason she hadn't already died was because of her family. She couldn't do to them what their mother had done to her.

Guilt flamed.

Wasn't that what she was doing by ignoring their calls and texts?

Buffy let her head fall forward, banging against the cold tiles.

Where was the way out? Either she felt nothing at all, no emotions, no happiness, or she felt the all-encompassing sorrow of guilt and regret. There had to be a middle ground but, nearing thirty, Buffy figured she should've found it by now.

Perhaps the dark was where she belonged.

Chapter 9

"What do you think about redheads?" Armando took her empty coffee cup and filled it with fresh brewed coffee. As head chef of the center, he often took it upon himself to be the center's barista too. He stirred in milk and sugar, dusting the top with cinnamon and chili powder.

Buffy took the mug from him with a thank you. The cinnamon tickled her tongue while the chili sent a comforting burn down her throat. It woke her up in a way plain coffee never had before. She smiled.

"My brother is a redhead," Buffy said.

Armando's eyebrows shot to the sky. "You have a ginger sibling?"

Buffy nodded. "He has brown eyes, but my sister, Winona, has blue eyes." She shrugged. "My brother's fiancé says there is more genetic diversity within a group than between groups. I guess my parents having seven kids was a little showcase of the diversity in our genes."

"That's dope." Armando bumped her fist. "The redhead I was referring to is the new physical therapist at my gym. He's perfect for you – insanely tall, hugely muscular, and his hair is *long*."

Normally, Buffy would've been drooling already. There wasn't much more to ask for than a big, long-haired, barrel-chested man. However right now, she couldn't even conjure an image of a man that was not Santiago. No matter how hard she tried, the only thought bringing an increase to her heart rate was a lean tattooed lawyer.

For fuck's sake.

How had she become so obsessed with him so quickly?

Maybe she needed a palette cleanser. Buffy wondered if Camila had plans tonight. Her roommate almost never turned down a happy hour.

Armando waved a hand in front of her face. "Earth to Buffy."

"Sorry." Buffy shook her head. "This grant is making my brain move like molasses." She scrubbed her eye with a fist. Luckily, her black eyeliner was smudge-proof. "I'm not really looking for anything serious right now."

Armando smiled. "I don't think he is either."

Buffy bit her lip. That did sound fun. She could at least meet the guy, see if he was worth further STD testing.

"Alright, you can give him my number." Buffy kissed Armando's cheek and turned to leave. Keeping Santiago at arm's length was turning out to be harder than she thought. Going out with someone else might be a good thing. There was no reason she couldn't casually see other people. A free dinner here, a new scary movie there, what was the harm?

Santiago was keeping her insatiable hunger in check, and she felt confident she could say no before things went too far. They didn't have any rules against kissing other people.

Sunlight filled her eyes and forced her to squint as the shuttle unloaded a group of community members. Waving hello to them, Buffy smiled wider when she saw Clara and her son walk in. Stretching onto her tiptoes, she peered behind them, searching for their lawyer.

Santiago wasn't with them.

Disappointment flared in her gut. Buffy sipped her coffee, the bitter taste mixing with the sadness at his absence. Clara had come with the shuttle group after all. She shouldn't have gotten her hopes up.

Now that Clara was in temporary housing, she had been stopping by the center more frequently—without Santiago in tow. Buffy should've been glad that Clara was gaining independence and utilizing the center. Instead, she selfishly wanted Clara to rely on Santiago and bring him around more often.

He's just a guy! Buffy screamed at herself.

"Buenos días!" Buffy waved to them. She smiled at the relief in Clara's eyes when she recognized Buffy's familiar face. "This is Armando." Gesturing toward Armando, he introduced himself to them in Spanish. Buffy smiled to fake comprehension.

She felt more and more like an idiot the longer she lived in California without speaking Spanish. The center demographics last year had fifty-three percent of their members listing Spanish as their first language. Honestly, it should have been part of annual employee training. The center should offer language classes for clients too. Buffy made a mental note.

"Can you put together a box of dry goods for them to take home?" Buffy asked Armando, nodding to the small family. "I'm getting her set up with employment aid today. She's going to be hungry."

Armando nodded and asked Clara to stop by before she went home. Clara moved to follow Buffy but halted when her son didn't follow them. Wide brown eyes roved over the countertop, following the fluid movements of Armando and his knives. He was swiftly chopping vegetables and sorting them into designated containers. The little boy's eyes were glued to his every move.

"I can take him to the kids room." Armando waved Buffy away and handed Poncho a stool. The little boy climbed up, his excitement clear.

"Todo bien?" Buffy used her minimal Spanish.

"Si, todo bien." Clara smiled, her gaze soft on her son. One of relief, hope, and joy.

Buffy felt her shoulders relax. Clara was going through one of the scariest experiences of her life. Immigrating was frightening, being homeless was isolating, and Clara didn't speak English yet. She deserved every ounce of relief that Buffy could provide.

Leading her through the building, Buffy attempted to explain the different rooms and services the center offered with her very limited Spanish. She found herself frustrated each time she didn't know a word or phrase and Clara couldn't understand. She needed to start lessons sooner than later. Maybe a call to her Spain-anchored brother was in order.

"Clara, this is the employment center. We hold classes, resume workshops, job fairs and the like. Veronica is my incredibly capable assistant." Buffy pulled out a chair at the computer bank where Veronica was waiting.

Veronica introduced herself to Clara in Spanish. Clara's eyes brightened and she shook Veronica's hand with vigor.

"Veronica is going to help you start the paperwork for a work permit and maybe set up a job board profile?" Buffy glanced at her assistant for confirmation.

Veronica nodded.

"Perfect. I'll be back when you're finished. Call me if you need anything." Buffy patted Clara's arm and thanked Veronica for her help.

Veronica was technically an executive grants assistant. Helping center members apply for jobs was not part of her job description. However, Veronica was a team player to her core, always willing to jump in wherever help was needed. Buffy distinctly remembered the time she gave Veronica a half day and then found her after closing, mopping the kitchen. At that point, Veronica had only been on the team for a few weeks. Her assistant's large heart hung on her sleeve.

Buffy paused at the doorway, listening to Veronica and Clara converse in Spanish. Buffy was proud of her assistant. Only on her second year at the center and her first since graduating college, Veronica had adjusted to every twist and turn with a smile on her face. Veronica easily conversed with everyone and always reminded Buffy of the positive.

Armando caught her in the hallway, Poncho happily following behind. "When did you start giving tours?"

"Clara is a friend of a friend," Buffy explained with a shrug.

"Would that friend happen to be the cute guy that was here last week?" Armando raised a brow.

Buffy rolled her eyes. "Actually, it was your rival, Myra."

"Are you serious? You eat from her truck and take her clients?" Armando stomped his foot, eyebrows pulled together and nearly touching in the center.

Buffy shrugged and turned, heading toward the elevators.

"I told you that I can make you a breakfast burrito! For free!"

"I like supporting the community." Buffy smiled wickedly as she entered the elevator. "You two really should just have a battle of the food trucks and be done with it. Otherwise, people are going to start getting some ideas about you two."

Armando scoffed, screwing his face up on one side. "That is not what is happening."

"Bye, Armando!" Buffy shouted through the closing doors.

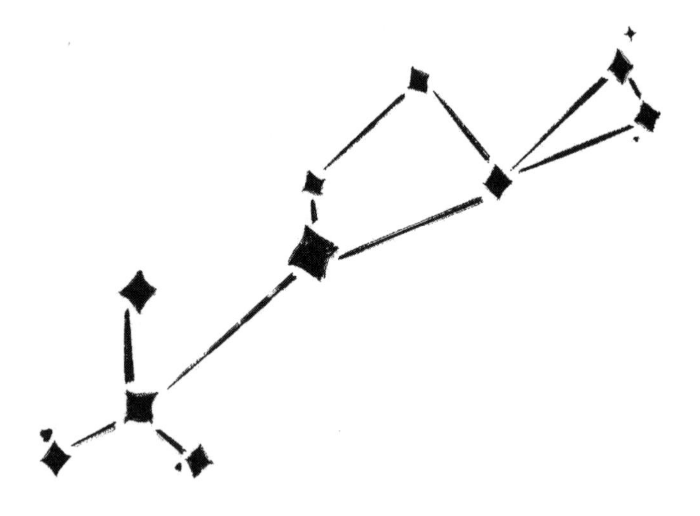

Chapter 10

Buffy pushed the button for the first floor, before Santiago leaned forward and took them to the garage instead. Work lunches, in her experience, didn't require vehicular travel. He was up to something.

Anxiety flared in her belly. Agreeing to this had been a mistake. Santiago was getting the wrong idea about her.

"Are you kidnapping me?" She scowled.

"Do you want me to kidnap you?" Santiago invaded her space, staring into her eyes with a heady look. He licked his lips and Buffy squeezed her thighs together. Damn, he had some kind of power over her.

"I could be into that." Buffy dragged her eyes over his lean frame, imagining all of the ways his muscles would flex as he manhandled her. She bit her bottom lip.

"Noted." Santiago took her hand, pulling her through the garage. Buffy wiggled her fingers free.

"I'm at work," she whispered. The reminder doused her in cold water, and she shook her head to clear her thoughts. They had to keep their distance in public. Not only for their professional lives, but because Santiago was getting way too comfortable. She had to draw the line somewhere.

Santiago offered a quick apology, opening the passenger door for her.

"Where are you taking me?" Buffy questioned.

"To lunch." Santiago acknowledged her with a warm smile. "Get in the car."

"I'm getting in because I'm hungry." Buffy pointed at him accusingly. "*Not* because you told me to. Bossy."

"Yes ma'am." Santiago flashed all of his teeth then, a completely full smile that stole the beats from her heart. Buffy smiled back, surprised at his reaction to her abrasive behavior. He seemed to like it when she was mean to him. Buffy liked that more than she wanted to admit. Forcing her gaze away from the jeans stretched across his thighs, she glanced out the window.

Opening her phone, Buffy shared her location with Camila. Always better to be safe than sorry.

"Mexican or Indian?" Santiago asked, turning down a large hill that left her stomach at the top.

"Indian like me or Indian like the continent?" Buffy said.

"I meant Indigenous." Santiago chuckled at her method of distinction.

"There's a new restaurant near the wharf my sister was telling me about," Buffy said softly. Thoughts of her siblings flashed across her mind. They deserved better than her. No matter how hard she tried, responding to the family group chat or calling them felt like pulling teeth in slow motion. Just the anxiety of typing a response or scheduling a call was enough to derail her entire day. She needed to get better at being a big sister. It was harder than it seemed.

Juniper was a fantastic older sister and mother. Maybe they didn't really need Buffy at all. Wasn't Juniper enough?

"I know the place." Santiago turned north. His hand made its way to her thigh, the warmth seeping through the thin fabric and into her skin. Buffy gulped. Acid burned in her belly at the tender gesture.

"No thigh touching." Buffy pushed his hand away.

"Why not?" Santiago glanced at her with a smile.

"It's too intimate." Buffy crossed her legs and turned toward the window.

"It's foreplay." Santiago smirked.

Buffy scoffed. "Everything is foreplay to you."

Santiago simply shrugged and put his hand on the gearshift between them.

The guilt only doubled in her belly as she stared at the hand she pushed away.

They had to park six blocks from the restaurant, the lunch rush in full swing by the time they arrived. The growing crowd took advantage of the break in the thick San Francisco clouds, sunlight flooding the street and bathing the diners in a warm, golden light. Buffy gazed at the side of Santiago's face, admiring the way his chubby cheeks reflected light from the top of them. They were like two stars, putting out their own source of light.

"Come on." Santiago gripped her waist while they navigated the crowded streets, putting himself between her and the horde of strangers and cars.

She fought the initial urge to push him off, but the fear of losing him in the crowd gripped her soundly. Buffy slid her hand into the pocket of his denim jacket, keeping a hold of him just in case. A warm hand enveloped hers inside his pocket, Santiago lacing their fingers together and giving her hand a squeeze. Buffy rolled her lips in to fight her smile.

"Santi, ¿cómo estás?" The host of the restaurant greeted them, engaging Santiago in quick chatter while he guided them straight through the restaurant.

Ignoring Buffy's look of puzzlement, Santiago laid a comforting hand on her back and urged her forward. She felt out of place, a conversation going on right beside her though she had no idea what they were saying.

Buffy listened to Santiago speak in another language. His voice seemed to drop a few notes deeper, as if the romance of the Spanish language demanded a romantic voice as well. The words sang as they danced out of his mouth and wrapped themselves around Buffy. A shiver went down her spine each time his tongue rolled over a new word.

The host smiled knowingly at her and winked.

What was Santiago telling him? Buffy glared at the side of his face. She listened intently but aside from a few nouns and verbs like trabajar, she didn't comprehend a thing.

Santiago was able to have all kinds of secret conversations right in front of her and she was none the wiser. For all she knew, he could be telling people they were married.

Buffy groaned. That was exactly the kind of thing Santiago would do.

The raven-haired host seated them at a table in the corner, a floor to ceiling window beside them offering an unobstructed view of Alcatraz. Buffy gazed through the glass. Alcatraz Island had been many things, but to her it was a memory of strength. AIM's occupation of the 1970's was almost as well known as the prison. The thought made her smile.

Turning back to the table, she caught Santiago watching her with a grin on his lips. Buffy opened her menu between them to block his eyeline.

"Have you been here before?" Buffy narrowed her eyes at Santiago from behind her open menu. Santiago sipped his water, no menu in front of him.

Santiago nodded at her. "The chef is a family friend."

"Do you know everyone in this city or something?" Buffy spoke behind the menu, only her eyes visible to Santiago.

"Something like that." Santiago pulled the menu from her hands. "Trust me to order for you?"

"Absolutely not." Buffy snatched the paper back from him. Without opening it, she gazed out the window. "I want the salmon dip."

"That's my favorite dish here." Santiago smirked. Waving to their waiter, Santiago ordered for them both. Salmon dip up first. Bison meatballs with veggies and cornbread for him, smoked rabbit with slaw and a frybread bun for her. Buffy's mouth watered.

"Did Clara come into the center today?" Santiago said.

Buffy perked up. Finally, a work-related topic. "She did, should be done with employment by the time we get back."

"Does the center finance their permit applications?" Santiago asked.

"We do." Buffy evaluated him with a grim look. The center attempted to finance as many things as it could for members and it was Buffy's grant work that made that possible. If she failed, it impacted their clients directly. She cracked her neck, the kink between her shoulder and spine throbbing at the mention of work.

"From grant money?" Santiago watched her muscles roll.

"Usually." Buffy thanked the waiter as he placed the steaming salmon dip in front of them. She could smell the jalapeños nestled into the bed of thin sliced nopales and cream cheese. Their dipping 'chips' were bite-size pieces of crispy frybread.

"Are you the only one working on grants?" Santiago handed her a chip overflowing with jalapeños and salmon.

"I take an intern every summer but otherwise it's just me." Buffy took the frybread slice from his hand and devoured it. The salmon turned to smoke in her mouth and she held back an audible moan.

"That sounds like a lot of work." Santiago said.

"I'm well suited to the challenge." Buffy replied. She narrowed her eyes at him. Did he think she wasn't capable?

"I know." Santiago smirked at her. His gaze darkened and drew over her neck and cleavage. She felt his eyes like a hand, warm on her flesh. Buffy sat up straighter, adjusting her shoulders and posture. Santiago licked his lips. Buffy crossed her legs.

The return of the waiter broke their silent communication. Simultaneously, they thanked him as he set their dishes in front of them. Santiago skewered two meatballs and dropped them onto her plate. In turn, she sliced her sandwich and handed him the smaller piece.

"No, you keep it." Santiago tried to push her hand back.

Buffy squinted. "Then I don't want your meatballs."

"You wanted them yesterday." Santiago snickered.

"And you wanted me." Buffy glared. "Eat the sandwich."

"You don't always have to reciprocate," Santiago let his foot lie gently against hers beneath the table. "I would've shared with you anyway."

"Not allowed." Buffy wagged a finger at him. Rubbing his foot against the outside of her ankle, Buffy let her legs lean into his. "You know what? Actually, that's going to be a rule. No paying for me, no gifting me things. We split everything evenly."

"Orgasms included?" Santiago raised a brow at her. "Because you're in a steep debt already if that's the case."

Buffy bit into her sandwich and stared out the window, ignoring him.

"How about you let me do what I want?" Santiago tapped the inside of her foot, waiting until she faced him. "And you do what you want? Pay me half, don't. It doesn't matter to me."

Buffy stared at him. She was uncomfortable with this entire arrangement. It was easier when the guy was as disinterested as she was. Santiago was nothing like other men. His actions matched his words and Buffy believed him when he said he wanted to pay for her, take her to dinner, and hold her hand.

That was the whole problem.

She didn't want the same from him. A time would come when Santiago would tire of their arrangement and of giving more than she returned. At some point, he was going to realize she wasn't worth his effort.

But for now, she was going to enjoy it.

Buffy snatched the bill before Santiago could move, thumbing her card into the fold. She held the bill tightly in her grasp.

Santiago watched her coolly, relaxed and leaned back in the chair. He made no move to wrestle the check from her grip. "What are you doing Saturday?"

Buffy sighed. She knew exactly where he was going.

"Let me take you to dinner."

"No." She shook her head. "Are you doing this to irritate me?"

"Come on," Santiago leaned his forearms on the table, bringing his head closer to hers. "I've tasted every inch of you. Go to dinner with me."

"No." Buffy handed the bill to the waiter with a smile that dropped as soon as she turned back to Santiago. "I told you this is just sex."

"I'm fine with that." Santiago looked at her plainly, no anger in his eyes. "But I want to fuck you after I buy you dinner. Think of it as foreplay."

Buffy tapped her chin, miming deep thought. "No."

Santiago smiled.

No matter how much she rejected him, Santiago took it in stride. It was almost as if he had no emotions, or as though Buffy had no effect on those emotions outside the bedroom. He never seemed to tire of her or become irritated by her sour mood. Maybe he was well suited to their sex-only arrangement, after all.

Holding the car door open for her, Santiago caught her around the waist. Holding Buffy tight, he brought her in for a quick kiss. Releasing her, he jogged around the car, climbing in beside her.

"Look," Buffy sighed, "I don't have time or energy for a relationship right now. I have a career and I live halfway across the world from my family. I don't have space for any more responsibility in my life."

Santiago nodded, gentle as he picked up her hand and held it in his lap. Buffy gripped his fingers back. She didn't have the courage to pull away again. It seemed like all she did was reject him.

"I get it," Santiago said. "I'm not asking you for a relationship either." He kissed her palm. "Don't you think we both could use a few extra hours of foreplay?" Santiago's lips brushed over the sensitive skin of her wrist and Buffy shivered.

Buffy grunted and pulled her hand away. "I'll think about it."

The shrill ring of her phone broke the silence around them. Buffy wrestled with the layers of her clothing until she located her phone.

Incoming Call: Juniper

Buffy silenced her phone and shoved it to the bottom of her bag. She shook her head, a rush of anxious thoughts clouding her mind.

"Parents calling?" Santiago glanced at her as he maneuvered them out of the parking space.

Buffy shook her head. "Oldest sister."

"How many do you have?

"Sisters?" Buffy asked.

Santiago nodded.

"One older sister, two younger sisters."

"What about brothers?"

Buffy nodded. "One older, two younger."

"You're the perpetual middle child," Santiago chided.

"Exactly." Buffy nodded. "You give firstborn energy." Buffy gazed at him accusingly.

Santiago roared with laughter. "You would be correct."

The car pulled left and Buffy saw the center come into view. They only had a few minutes before she had to return to work. Strangely, she felt anxiety crawl up her spine at the thought of saying goodbye to Santiago. His presence brought a strange calmness over her that allowed her to push all thoughts to the back of her mind. She had almost completely forgotten about the budget for food and housing.

Almost.

"Are you an only child?" Buffy wasn't sure why she asked. She didn't care, not really. But she was curious. Who had shaped Santiago into this ever-patient man? Surely, he came from a big family.

"I used to be."

"Used to?!" Buffy shook her head in confusion. "What does that mean?"

"I was twenty-four when my little sister was born."

Buffy dropped her jaw in shock. "Twenty-four?!" A million questions filled Buffy's mind, but she couldn't make any words form in her mouth.

Santiago pulled up in front of the center and flicked on his hazard lights. The car rumbled under them.

"I'll tell you the whole story. Are you free Saturday?" Santiago turned to face her in his seat. His fingertips brushed against her thigh. Buffy leaned into his touch, encouraging his palm onto her skin.

"I'm free." Buffy wanted to go, in truth. The idea of him feeding her and fucking her was all too alluring. So what if she had to let him romance her a little.

"Great." He kissed her cheek and sprung from the car. Walking to her side, he opened her door, a hand reaching in to help her out. "I'll pick you up at ten a.m. on Saturday."

"Ten a.m.?!" Buffy screeched, wide eyes raking over him as he ushered her out of the street. "Why in the hell—"

"You get what you want, and I get what I want." Santiago leveled his gaze at her. Buffy could tell he wasn't going to budge this time.

"Fine," Buffy said with a huff.

"Try not to dream about me tonight," Santiago called, watching her as she opened the heavy door.

Buffy slid through and turned. Santiago was still there, waiting until she was completely in the building before climbing back into his car. With a wave, he was gone.

CHAPTER 11

Anxiety plagued Buffy the entire night. She barely got a wink of sleep, even after consuming two cups of chamomile tea. Santiago had plans that he neglected to share with her. It set her heart racing and her stomach on fire, and she longed to see him. She wanted to know what his plans were, where they were going, what they would be doing. Buffy wasn't used to being outside of the loop. She was used to being the ringleader.

This feeling of unwaning energy was unusual for her. Buffy normally passed out as soon as she closed her eyes, sleeping for as long as possible. Instead, she spent the night tossing and turning. She agonized over every possible option and realized she knew very little of Santiago.

The smell of his skin, the look on his face when he came, his favorite sushi roll, all of that she knew. But aside from his dedication to his grandma, Buffy had no idea what he cared about. His hobbies, his passions, his goals, she didn't know any of it. Guilt burned her gut. Keeping him at a distance had come back to bite her in the ass. If she had ever asked about his interests, she might have a guess as to where he was taking her. It made her feel selfish, like she was just using him.

Vibration buzzed beneath the pillow under her head, and she pulled her phone out, squinting at the bright light.

Santiago: See you in an hour.

Buffy groaned. Butterflies of excitement erupted throughout her stomach as worries began to filter through her head. She shouldn't have agreed to this. His heart was going to break and she was going to be the one holding the hammer. She debated calling him to cancel but figured he wouldn't let her back out anyway. Resigned to her fate, Buffy took a peek in the mirror.

Her red hair was knotted and sticking up in multiple directions. Dry, cracking drool covered her chin and neck. Buffy tried to recall her dreams from the night before. When she finally passed out, she woke up again and again. It had to be a nightmare. She tried to recall a dream but nothing came to mind. When she reached back into her memories of the night before, it was just darkness. Like so many of her memories.

Buffy showered the night off, replacing the scent of sweat with a much more pleasant fruity smell. She pulled her hair into a thin braid on each side of her neck. Buffy shook her head. She looked like a mascot for a 1950s diner. All she needed was French fries and a burger.

The doorbell rang and pulled her from thoughts of the fast-food character. Releasing her hair and quickly shaking it loose, Buffy opened the door to Santiago holding two cups of coffee and a bag that smelled like fresh dough and oil. He raked his eyes down her body, pausing at the open gap of her robe. She hadn't had the chance to dress yet, being that she didn't know where they were going. She wore a black cotton bra and matching panties beneath the untied robe.

"You going like this?" Santiago followed her inside, placing the coffee and paper bag on the counter. "'Cause if so, I'm going to fuck you in the bathroom." He reached for her, palming the cheeks of her ass. "And right here on this counter before we leave."

Buffy scrunched her nose and swatted haphazardly at his exploring hand. She opened the paper bag and sipped her coffee. Fingering a sugar-coated fried donut, the sickly-sweet smell flooded her nose and her stomach twisted with nausea. It was too early to eat. It was too early to be awake on a Saturday. She needed more coffee.

Santiago was behind her now, slipping her robe off her shoulder to kiss the exposed skin. Her breath caught in her chest. Suddenly her stomach was burning with desire and she felt heat rising to her skin.

Buffy danced out of his grip and tied the robe shut over her undergarments. "What are we doing? I do *not* hike, Santiago. If you are taking me hiking, I swear—"

"I'm not taking you hiking," Santiago laughed, pulling her in for a kiss. Sugar scratched against her lips, his tongue tasting of the sweet donut against her coffee-flavored mouth. "Jeans and a T -shirt, closed-toed shoes." Santiago kept an arm around her waist and pulled a malasada from the bag.

He held it between them. Buffy glared at him.

Santiago smiled.

Dragging out a heavy breath, Buffy bit into the malasada, sugar falling past her lips. White crystals spilled across her golden chest like stars.

Santiago licked his lips at the sight and Buffy clenched her thighs tighter. She needed relief. Buffy ate the remainder of the donut. It did nothing to quell the sudden hunger in her belly.

Santiago kissed down her neck and across her chest. Slipping his tongue out, he licked at the sugar on her skin. "Get dressed." With a heavy smack to her ass, Santiago directed her toward her bedroom.

Buffy finished her coffee while she dressed, chugging it as though it would somehow dull the butterflies swimming in her belly. Damn Santiago. Why did his presence have to be so enticing? Her breath stalled in her chest and she commanded her heart to take a chill pill.

"You want another?" Santiago asked, rolling the bag of donuts up to bring with them.

"I'm good." Buffy threw her hair over her shoulder and led him from the apartment. "Have you seen Clara this week? I haven't seen her at the center lately."

"I forgot to tell you she got a job," Santiago said.

Buffy whipped around, glaring at him accusingly. Santiago simply smiled at her. "It's nothing much, nights cleaning for a budget movie theater," Santiago explained, following Buffy into the elevator. "But it's something."

"I'm happy for her."

"Me too."

"Does that mean you'll be hanging around my office less?" Buffy quirked a brow. Her breath held in her chest.

No, she thought. *Say no.*

Desperately, she hoped he would find more reasons to show up at her work. He had quickly become a welcome reprieve in her day, and she looked forward to seeing him. She would never admit it out loud, but she wanted him to continue stopping by and seeing her.

"Not even a little bit." Santiago gripped her chin and brought her mouth to his.

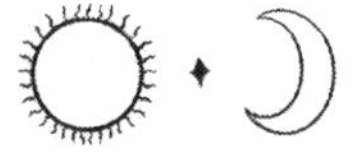

They drove across the bridge and pulled into a wide parking lot at the base of the mountain. Buffy squinted, searching for signage to tell her where she was.

Instead, a quick succession of bursts boomed through the air, and she recognized the sound instantly.

"You brought me to a shooting range?" Buffy raised her eyebrows at him.

"I promise you'll have fun." Putting the car in park, Santiago wiggled the bag of donuts. "Sure you don't want another?"

"I'm sure." Buffy continued staring out the window in front of her. Her gaze was accusing, narrow where it evaluated the building and people milling about outside.

Santiago took the last donut from the bag and went to bite it. He hesitated, noticing a huge chunk of golden dough was missing. Buffy watched him from the corner of her eye, nervous of how he would react. She had felt silly for just a moment, laughing at the thought of eating his donuts without his knowledge. To her, it was a funny joke but very well could be the test of Santiago's sense of humor and kindness towards women. Buffy knew that most men didn't treat women with kindness unless she was family. And sometimes, not even then.

"You're such a little shit." Santiago laughed, tickling Buffy along her ribcage and upper thigh. She didn't fight the laugh that rose in her chest, nor did she try to hold it as it came tumbling out. Soon, the two of them were laughing so hard Buffy was gasping for breath.

"I did change my mind." Snatching the last bite of crispy golden malasada from his hand, she stuffed it in her mouth and made for an escape.

Santiago caught her around the waist when she bolted in front of the car, his infectious laughter warm against her back. She relaxed in his grip, allowing her hips to settle into the cradle of his. His gasp of breath tickled her neck and she smirked in satisfaction.

"You're naughty." Santiago dropped a kiss to the crook of her neck.

Buffy followed him inside, trailing after him in silence while he paid and collected their items. The lobby was loud, most patrons already wearing ear protection, their voices carried through the room. Buffy plugged her ears, dampening the overwhelming noises. Between the gunshots, rambunctious laughter, and talkative patrons, the shop was playing heavy metal music that only further assaulted her eardrums. Santiago turned to her then, pushing her hands away and sliding a heavy headset on.

The noise dampened and Buffy felt herself breathe normally again. Santiago tightened the headset to his satisfaction, then flipped a switch on the bottom of her left ear covering. White noise crackled in her ears like a radio and the voices nearest her were amplified. Santiago spoke, drawing her attention.

"Does that feel okay?" His voice was clear through the headphones.

Buffy nodded, gazing at him. Santiago smiled and returned to his conversation with the employee. With the other distracting noises dampened, Buffy tuned in to their conversation.

Santiago conversed easily with the staff, switching between Spanish and English as though they were one language. Buffy listened to him in awe, elated that she could understand a majority of the conversation thanks to the extra English context. She watched his lips move around the words and realized suddenly why he was so amazing with his tongue.

Memories flooded her mind and Buffy hoped her blush was contained to under her clothes. Santiago shook hands with the worker and turned to Buffy.

Wedging protective eyeglass onto her face, he led her outside to a partially sectioned-off stall from the rest of the patrons. "Ever shot a pistol?"

Buffy shook her head. Pulling her in front of him, he freed one of her ears from the thick cushioned headphones. Santiago demonstrated how to safely use the pistol, watching as she loaded it in front of him. Palming the weapon in his hand, he showed her the proper way to hold and cock the gun.

"Squeeze." Santiago spoke over her shoulder. His body enveloped her in warmth and she leaned closer to him. "Don't pull. The kickback isn't too bad." Kissing her neck, he stepped away to give her space to shoot.

Buffy squeezed, one eye pulling shut in anticipation.

Nothing happened. Glancing over her shoulder in confusion, Santiago stepped up behind her, wrapping his hand around hers. Squeezing their fingers together, they pulled the trigger. They hit the target above the left shoulder.

"Are you sure you're good enough at this to teach me?" Buffy said.

"I wasn't aiming!" Santiago defended himself. He stepped back, giving her the space to aim and fire again.

Buffy adjusted her grip and squeezed the trigger. A squeal left her mouth as the bullet fired, the gun recoiling in her grasp. The pistol had a significant kickback and she struggled to maintain her grip on the weapon.

She glanced over her shoulder, hoping Santiago hadn't noticed her fumbling. Santiago smiled, giving her an encouraging thumbs up, excitement clear on his face. Lining up her shot again, Buffy fired. Her grip was like iron this time, and the gun barely moved in her hands. A smile rose on her face as she began to get comfortable handling the gun. She took aim and fired again. Her shots were landing all over the torso. Buffy aimed for a cluster in the center but she was off no matter how hard she tried. She had far better aim with a rifle.

Every burst from the weapon sent tingles down her spine, an inexplicable rush of adrenaline flooding her veins as the bullet left the chamber. The slide moved back finally, the gun empty.

"Try this one." Santiago handed her a shining silver revolver. It looked like something from those old western movies her dad loved. "This one has more kickback. You're going to love it."

Buffy watched eagerly while he loaded the rounds one by one. She tucked the handle into the web of her thumb and pointer finger like he showed her, lining up her shot once again. Squeezing the trigger, she felt the power of the spark ripple through her skin, her muscles tensing tightly to control the fierce movement.

Santiago watched her with a smile stuck to his face. Buffy smiled back. The smile she wore was genuine, a natural reaction to the adrenaline release. But the way he looked at her only deepened her smile even more. The tension had all but evaporated from her shoulders and Buffy couldn't remember her current work project even if she tried.

She was having *fun*.

Emptying the chamber again, she placed the revolver on the table in front of them. Finding Santiago already watching her, she poked him in the stomach, throwing her arms around his neck and pulling him into a kiss.

They laughed into each other's mouth, Buffy unable to wipe the wide smile from her face. She bounced in his arms, squeezing him around the shoulders.

"Thank you." Buffy kissed him again. "This is kinda fun, I guess."

"Don't mention it." Santiago kissed her again, sweetly, lips closed, matching smiles on each of their faces. "This one next." He pointed to a black handgun barely bigger than her palm.

Buffy went through three paper targets before she tired of the gun range. Her body felt light for the first time in a long time and she was grateful to Santiago for knowing just how to get her out of her own head. Somehow, he was able to read her like a book and knew just what she needed. This was something she just couldn't be mad about.

Watching Santiago clear the weapons and return them to the front started a fire in her belly. He handled everything effortlessly but with assured, careful movements. She wondered how often he came here to let off steam.

"You do this a lot?" Buffy cocked a brow, glancing down at his hands.

"Back in Colorado, yes." Santiago settled their bill and led her outside. "Out here, not so much." Lacing their fingers together, they strolled the parking lot underneath a peculiarly warm sun. Spring was on the way, flower buds of all colors growing in every patch of dirt in sight.

With a deep breath, Buffy gazed at Santiago. He was framed by sunlight, black hair shining almost blue in the sun. She smiled when he caught her staring at him and pressed a kiss to his cheek to cover her own blush at being caught.

Nearing the car, Buffy realized she wasn't ready to say goodbye to him yet. Maybe he was on to something when he suggested a few hours of foreplay.

"Can we get tacos?" Buffy asked. Santiago paused beside the passenger door. He gazed at her with a knowing smile and Buffy had to remind herself not to crack a mood-destroying joke.

"I know just the place." Santiago ushered her into the car. Back on the road, Santiago settled his hand on her bare thigh. Buffy smiled for the entire ride.

Nearly.

She should've recognized the neighborhood sooner than she did. It wasn't until he turned the corner of Abuela's street that Buffy finally realized where they were. A purple painted mailbox stood tall out front, the name *Morales* painted beside a golden constellation of stars.

They were at Santiago's house. Abuela Paulina's house.

Buffy saw Pear as soon as they pulled up to the small row home.

This could not get any worse.

Pear was seated on a porch swing beside Abuela Paulina, talking to a blonde woman. Dressed in a white T-shirt and oversized, low-slung pants, Pear looked straight out of a magazine. The gold-foil capped beer in his hand only added to the picture-perfect California family they formed together on the porch. Buffy cursed herself. It was easy to tell that Pear was not her biggest fan. His face might as well have a neon sign explaining his every thought. Buffy figured that was because he was the only one Santiago talked to about their arrangement. Pear wanted something better for his cousin.

Buffy couldn't blame him. Pear was right. Santiago deserved better than her.

"Santi!" Pear shouted his name so shortly that Buffy would've assumed he was angry if she didn't know better. He seemed like the type to love hard and loud.

Buffy climbed the stairs behind Santiago. She was irritated he hadn't told her where they were going, but she was equally as excited to try Abuela's homemade tacos. If the pupusas Santiago brought her were a sign, these tacos were going to be the most incredible thing she'd ever tasted. Her mouth watered at the thought.

Santiago hugged his cousin and pulled Buffy onto the porch behind him. Pear kissed Buffy's cheek and motioned to the woman behind him. "This is my cousin, Myra."

"Myra!" Buffy gasped.

"Buffy!" Myra jumped up from her seat and wrapped her arms around Buffy.

"You know each other?" Santiago motioned between the two women while his thumb grazed the skin above Buffy's jeans. "Wait, is Myra the one who keeps making you breakfast burritos?"

Buffy rolled her eyes. "I pay her for them."

Santiago muttered under his breath and rolled his eyes at Buffy. "Well, now I know why you won't let me cook for you. How am I supposed to beat a literal chef?"

"That's not why." Buffy muttered.

"Are you joining us for dinner?" Abuela Paulina asked, wide brown eyes gazing up at Buffy. Her stomach turned at the thought of eating a family dinner with Santiago. It turned more when she imagined rejecting Abuela Paulina's invitation.

"Of course," Buffy answered reflexively. "Can I help you?"

"Nonsense." Abuela Paulina waved the request off and headed inside her quaint home. "Santiago is my assistant." Myra and Pear followed her inside, leaving Santiago and Buffy on the porch alone.

"It's true." Santiago squeezed the flesh of Buffy's hip and kissed her cheek. Guiding her inside in front of him, he washed his hands and tucked his hair into a backwards baseball cap.

Fuck. The word bounced around in her head, echoing in her ears and drawing her attention to the scruff of his face and the curls poking out from under the cap.

How did one accessory change his entire appearance and make Santiago twelve times hotter? She was going to bring that hat into the bedroom with them as soon as possible.

Buffy itched to kiss him, the instinct to be beside him while he cooked drawing her in like a flame. She had spent all day with him, yet she didn't feel satisfied. Her feet gravitated towards him without her approval. Luckily, the rest of the house placed themselves in the kitchen as well, and Buffy didn't seem out of place. She kept the island between them as a physical barrier.

"Will you chop these for me?" Santiago rounded the island to stand beside her.

So much for keeping a barrier between them.

Hands above the belt, Buffy reminded herself.

Santiago reached over her shoulder and placed four tomatoes on the cutting board in front of her. Butterflies overwhelmed her stomach and she leaned into his touch, her hand ghosting along his forearm so that he couldn't pull away. Electricity hummed in her skin as he leaned into her grasp. Santiago dropped a quick kiss to her temple. "Please?"

Unable to conjure her voice, Buffy nodded and took a knife from the block. She quartered the first tomato, glancing up at Santiago for approval before continuing.

He nodded at her with a smile so warm it reflected on her mouth too. Avoiding Myra's pointed gaze, she went back to slicing.

Selfishly, she wondered if Myra would stop making her burritos once she broke Santiago's heart.

"Pues, tienes novia Santiago? You're not getting any younger." Myra looked between Buffy and her cousin. "You're dating, right?"

"We work together," Buffy answered.

Myra raised her eyebrows and glanced between Buffy and Santiago. "You're not getting any younger, primo."

"I'm barely in my thirties," Santiago argued.

"Exactly," Myra continued.

"Santi has plenty of time!" Pear defended his cousin.

"Basta, Myra. You're twenty-eight," Abuela Paulina said.

"Whatever happened to Marisol?" Myra pressed. "She was hilarious."

Buffy tried not to fixate on the name Marisol. Santiago was only someone she was fucking. Nothing more.

"Can we talk about literally anything else?" Santiago grimaced, glancing up at Buffy. "Pear is the oldest. Why aren't we worried about him?"

"Pear is a whore." Myra dismissed him with a wave.

"Ouch." Pear clutched his chest and fell to the ground as though he had been shot. "I'll have you know I went on a second date not too long ago." Pear spoke from his position on the floor.

"Did you invite them for a third?" Myra quirked an eyebrow.

"I'm thinking about it."

"So no," Santiago elaborated for Pear.

"Ay basta ya, we have a guest." Abuela Paulina dismissed the discussion and assigned Santiago to tortillas. Pear tuned the radio to a local Mexican station and took a begrudging Myra in his arms. They spun around the kitchen and living room like two Hollywood movie stars. Buffy wished she could dance like that. They moved in sync and their bodies swayed with the song naturally. It was beautiful and something Buffy could never do. She had two left feet, unfortunately.

Santiago placed a small ball of dough in Buffy's palm, wrapping his hands around hers to flatten it out. Together, their fingers and palms worked the ball into a thin flat disk. His breath tickled her ear when he took the rolling pin in hand, rolling over the flattened dough once in each direction before throwing it on the hot thin griddle. Without words, Buffy copied his movements on her own piece of dough.

They worked quickly together, filling the griddle with sizzling tortillas in no time. Heat rose in the kitchen, the smell of warm flour permeating the area. Once the pan was full, Santiago swept Abuela Paulina into his arms. He led her around the kitchen, singing along to the mariachi song playing on the radio. Buffy couldn't help but watch him dance with his grandmother. The smile on Abuela Paulina's face radiated through the kitchen and lit the room like a sun.

Carefully, Buffy tucked herself into a corner between the counter and wall, content to watch the others dance. Being a wallflower was one of her specialties. She should've known that Santiago wouldn't allow her to spectate.

Abuela Paulina escaped his grip and returned to peeling and slicing nopales. Santiago, now empty-handed, set his sights on Buffy. Frantically, she shook her head back and forth.

No.

Buffy was a horrible dancer and the way they twisted and turned and swung their hips intimidated her more than the first time she danced with him.

Santiago refused to take no for an answer.

Taking her hand in a strong grasp, he pulled her into his chest.

"You're lucky I wore flats today," Buffy grumbled into his ear.

Santiago shrugged. "I like how tall you are." Spinning her under his arm, he wrapped her up against his chest and whispered in her ear. "I like being the only man you let between those long legs."

Buffy shushed him with a hiss and stole a frantic glance at Abuela Paulina to ensure she hadn't heard his scandalous comment. She was staring directly at them with a smile on her lips. Her lips moved softly as she watched Buffy dance with her grandson, but Buffy didn't know what she was mouthing. She was probably singing along to the song, imagining the two of them as a couple. Embarrassment flared in Buffy's gut. She probably looked like the title character of some dumb romantic comedy.

Twisting their bodies around the kitchen, Santiago hummed the music against her neck. He stole her attention away from the rest of the room and eventually, she relaxed in his arms. Santiago tucked them even closer together, rubbing at the exposed skin between her shirt and jeans. Buffy couldn't keep the smile off her face. Mirroring Santiago himself, their beaming grins were enough to drown out everyone else.

Wrapping Buffy under his arm once more, Santiago caught her around the waist and pressed a kiss to her lips. Buffy almost pushed him away in surprise, but she couldn't bear to separate her body from his. She let him press a long kiss to her closed lips before turning her head and offering her cheek. Santiago was unbothered, pressing a kiss to her cheek, her jaw, then her ear before finally releasing her.

This kind of public display of affection wasn't convincing anyone that they were merely coworkers.

They ate outside on the porch beneath a nearly full moon. Abuela Paulina finished eating promptly and then set her easel up beside the table and began to paint. With so much moonlight, they ate and she painted without any artificial lights and it felt more intimate than anything Buffy had done in a while. Looking at Abuela paint and listening to stories of the cousins growing up together, Buffy felt like she was with family.

Guilt set in when she remembered she already had a family. A family that ate outside beneath the moon often. Muskwa loved to eat outside before the freeze, and she was more accustomed to eating in the light of a fire than fluorescents.

Juniper's reminder to buy a ticket home tickled at the back of her brain and rolled in her gut. Acid burned her throat and black clouds moved into her mind. She sighed slowly, the air escaping through her nose in a long stream.

Santiago wrapped his arm around her waist and tucked her into his side. He kissed her forehead, whispering a story about Myra and Pear wrestling as kids. His breath tickled her ear while his fingers rubbed over the cool skin of her arm. Just like that, the darkness was gone. Buffy was focused on him and the toxic waste turning in her belly disappeared.

Myra boomed Santiago's name and startled them apart. Bidding goodbye, she offered them both hugs and kisses to their cheeks.

"I love this look on you, by the way," Myra said, bumping their hips together.

Buffy looked at her expectantly. Myra laughed and started down the steps. Buffy followed her. Myra paused beside her car and pulled Buffy into a tight hug.

"You look happy," Myra whispered.

Buffy waved at the retreating car. She could feel Santiago's gaze on her back like a fire poker. Heaving a sigh, Buffy kicked at the rocks beside the road and ambled through the house to the backyard. Now it was her turn to tell everyone goodbye. Myra's departure was the perfect excuse. Anxiety bloomed in her chest.

"My grandson is quite taken with you." Abuela Paulina spoke into the night air. She sat on her porch swing just outside the door, hidden by the trellis of white moonflowers.

Buffy let out a scream of shock and covered her mouth with her hands. With reddened cheeks, she kept her eyes on the stars.

"Coffee?" Abuela Paulina offered her a steaming mug.

Reluctantly, Buffy took it between her palms and sat beside Abuela on the swinging couch.

Abuela Paulina laughed and patted Buffy on the thigh. "He hasn't said a thing to me, don't worry." She reclined further into the cushions of the porch swing, clicking her tongue in her cheek. "The two of you are like little magnets, pushing and pulling and constantly hyper aware of the other one." Abuela Paulina giggled softly. "It's cute."

"It's nothing, Abuela." Buffy attempted to brush it off. "He's a nice man—that's all."

"You're a nice girl."

"No." Buffy sighed. "I'm not."

The two sat in the quiet, listening to the coo of an owl nearby. Chills ran across her skin, as if the owl was reminding her that she was a bad omen too.

"Stars always think their neighbor is brighter than them. They live their whole lives in fear that the other star will grow bigger, shine brighter, and eventually suck them into their light until the first star ceases to exist. But it is simply a fear, that's all." Abuela Paulina spoke softly, her eyes on the night sky. "You have a heart of gold, Buffy. We've all seen it."

"I do good work. That's it." Buffy said. "I'm not good in my personal life. I hurt everyone who gets close to me."

"Sometimes we perceive another's hurt as greater than it was," Abuela hissed through her teeth like her statement was a secret just for them.

Buffy shook her head. "I'm too far gone, Abuela. All my teeth are sharp and I don't know how to dull them again." Buffy looked inside, watching Santiago and Pear throw bubbles and whip each other with wet dish rags. She ran her fingers through her hair, tugging on the uneven ends as a physical reminder of the darkness inside. "If anyone is a star, it's him."

"Even stars have teeth, mija. Santiago has his vices, like anyone, like me, like you. Perfection doesn't exist in humans. Give yourself a chance." Abuela Paulina stroked over Buffy's cheek, her hand soft and smelling of almond soap. Buffy wondered if that was the lingering pan dulce smell that was often stuck to Santiago.

"I'm not worried about you hurting my grandson, but I can see that you're hurting yourself already. Sometimes we get addicted to the pain and we forget that life isn't supposed to hurt like this." Abuela Paulina sat in silence with Buffy for a moment, pain written into every curve and wrinkle of her face. "Our sharp teeth are for protection from others, not from ourselves."

Pear burst out of the screen door and onto the porch, interrupting their conversation. He stooped beside the swing, wrapping Abuela in a tight hug. "I'll see you this weekend, Abuela." Kissing her cheek, Pear hugged Buffy and disappeared into the dark.

"I better get going." Buffy stood to follow him out.

It was now or never.

"Ay, basta. I'm old, not stupid. Stay here tonight, Buffy," Abuela Paulina grumbled and wandered back inside. Santago raised his brows at Buffy as his grandmother passed him.

"She told you," Santiago snickered and knocked Buffy with his hip.

"Shut up!" Buffy whisper-shouted, attempting to conceal her shock at Abuela Paulina's bluntness. "I'm only staying because she asked. Not for you."

"Yes ma'am." Santiago faked a salute. Buffy rolled her eyes and followed Abuela inside. Santiago gripped her hand and led her upstairs. The hallway was narrow and long, only three doors. Santiago stopped at the only door on the left.

"Welcome to paradise." With a flourish, Santiago ushered Buffy into his bedroom.

The room was simple, tucked into the corner of the house. It had windows on two walls. His bed was beneath the smaller window, a fluffy chair placed beside the larger window that faced the courtyard. Books surrounded the chair, on the walls, on the seat, on the floor, in the windowsill.

Other than the perilously stacked piles of books, his room was clean.

"Did you decorate or Abuela?" Buffy nodded to the extra throw pillows on his bed.

"Abuela." Santiago smiled sheepishly, throwing the excess pillows into the book chair. "This was my dad's room as a kid." He opened the closet door and pulled the chain to turn on the light. Stepping aside, he pulled Buffy over to look at the closet. The door frame had black notches starting at about knee height and extending to the top of the frame.

The names Alberto and Santiago alternated going up the wall, the years following. Alberto's name ended towards the top beside the numbers 1982. Santiago's ended at the year 2012, only an inch above Alberto.

"Your dad?"

Santiago nodded.

"No wonder your grandmother refused to leave." Buffy ran her fingers lightly over the dimpled wood. "I couldn't leave something like this behind either."

"You gonna be a mom one day, Buffy?" Santiago sat at the edge of his bed and began undressing for sleep.

"God, I hope not." Buffy grimaced.

Santiago laughed loudly, the sound echoing through the silent house. He seemed surprised by her honesty. "My parents having little Paulina sealed the no-kids deal for me. I love my baby sister to death but kids are a lot of work. Luckily she got my grandmother's name and not me. I'm not much of a Paul."

Buffy curled her lip in disgust and repeated the offending word, "Paul." She mimed a fake retch. "Kids are just *so* gross. And loud," Buffy elaborated. "And stinky."

"Sticky too," Santiago continued.

"They're better as nieces and nephews," Buffy said.

"Or baby sisters," Santiago laughed.

"Yours is allegedly cute," Buffy huffed and threw the covers back. "Mine was a walking ball of chaos."

"Is she still?"

Buffy shrugged. "I think so. Winona has leveled out a lot. But Joy, the youngest, she is a spitball of 'I don't give a fuck.' I would admire it if she hadn't stolen half my clothes as a kid and gotten them covered in horse shit."

Santiago laughed. "It's been a while since you saw her?"

Buffy nodded. "She graduated from high school right before I took this job. That was the last time I saw her."

"Three years is a long time."

"Almost four, I think." Buffy's voice came out in a whisper. "Joy was always closer to Juniper than me. Juni was like a mom to her, and I was the middle child, always starting fights."

"That does sound like you." Santiago snickered.

"Hey!" Buffy smacked his bicep, hiding her smile behind an eye roll.

"Who was mom for you?" Santiago whispered.

"My mom. I was old enough to remember her, to miss her." Buffy sighed. "But it's fine. She's gone and I'm still here. Joy is here, Juniper is here, Winona is here. That's all that matters." Buffy's brows pulled together in the center of her forehead, her eyes tight and narrow. She blinked furiously.

"Joy sounds like fun," Santiago said, lightening the conversation.

"You would say that. The two of you could torture me." Buffy shook her head and threw her hair over her shoulder to gaze at him. "You do anything to that curly mess when you sleep?"

"If that is your way of nicely asking to borrow a hair tie," Santiago said as he leaned close to her, their noses millimeters apart, "then yes." Pecking her nose once with warm, wet lips, Santiago took off into the adjoining bathroom. "Follow me."

Santiago offered her two options, one fluffy black scrunchie and one extremely stretched out elastic. Grimacing, Buffy took the scrunchie and attempted to tie up her shortened hair. Gathering it at the back of her head, all of the shorter top pieces fell from the tie. When she moved the tie higher, all of the shorter hair at the bottom of her head fell and covered her neck. With a grunt of frustration, Buffy gave up and left her hair haphazardly tied up.

Santiago snickered, offering her a green toothbrush already topped with minty paste. While she brushed her teeth, Santiago removed the scrunchie from her hair and combed through it with his fingers. Carefully, he started at the top of her head and separated her hair into three strands. Gently, he braided down the curve of her head, adding sections of hair as he went. Tying off the braid into a bun at the nape of her neck, Santiago wrapped the black fabric twice around the tiny tuft of red hair.

Buffy struggled to control her breathing. His fingers grazed against the back of her neck and lit her on fire. Her blood raised to the edges of her skin to meet him and her heart began to thump loud enough she could hear it. Hopefully Santiago couldn't.

"I like this look on you." Santiago spoke softly, wrapping his arms around her waist and leaving a lingering kiss on her cheek.

Before Buffy realized it, she was dressed in Santiago's T-shirt and rinsing her mouth with an old mug painted to look like a gorilla. They stood shoulder to shoulder in front of the bathroom mirror, comfortable silence stretching between them.

"I'm kind of surprised that it didn't disintegrate in your mouth." Santiago nodded toward the toothbrush she left beside his. Likely a children's toothbrush from his own childhood, the item was green with drawings of turtles in colorful masks. It was probably close to twenty years old.

"Keep this up and I'll use yours next time," Buffy threatened.

"You wouldn't."

"Try me." Buffy was struggling to keep her eyes open. The family festivities and never-ending supply of delicious food was tugging her towards the dream world. She flopped into Santiago's bed on her back, waiting for him to finish preparing for bed.

"I hope you have a vibrator in this room!" She called out to him, eyes closed in the copious sheets and pillows on his bed. Santiago had promised that tonight would be just like any night they spent together, meaning he was going to fuck her so good she passed out afterwards.

She didn't need the extra help tonight.

Buffy was asleep before he turned off the light.

CHAPTER 12

Buffy woke up alone, the space next to her still warm with body heat. Ice seized her heart. Staying here had been a mistake. She knew better than this.

Where was Santiago? When did he leave? *Why* did he leave? Had she done something wrong? She couldn't remember anything after they brushed their teeth.

Buffy played memories of the night before in her mind like a movie. Sure, she was her usual bitchy self, but Santiago had never seemed put off by that before. Speaking of her mother had been a mistake. Regret flooded her veins at the memory of their conversation.

She shouldn't have told him anything. People always ran when they realized how fucked up she was.

Shame burned across her skin. Buffy chewed at her lip, the sharp pain and taste of iron almost a comfort against the guilt. She shouldn't have stayed the night. She shouldn't have gone on this date at all. Now Santiago had made her feel things for him and *left*. Anger bubbled over her anxiety and acid burned her throat.

Sitting upright, she pulled the covers up to her chin and contemplated her options. She could get dressed and escape out the window. They were only on the third floor. She peered down at the street below. No awnings to cushion her fall but the sidewalk didn't look all that far away. Buffy figured she was tall enough to make the drop without breaking anything.

"What are you doing up?" Santiago opened the bedroom door, a glass of water in his hand.

Buffy let out a breath of relief at his appearance, the hammering of her heart finally beginning to slow. The sadness quickly vacated her chest, only the flames of anger left behind. Anger that should've been directed at herself.

"I need to pee." Buffy scrambled out of the bed, shutting the bathroom door harshly behind her.

What the fuck was that?

Splashing cold water on her face, Buffy attempted to calm her sprinting heart. She gripped the edge of the countertop. Embarrassment filled her throat. Her reaction to his absence had been so visceral, so intense, so immediate. It scared her. She shouldn't have had any reaction to waking up alone other than peace. He was changing everything about her. Buffy wasn't herself.

She wasn't supposed to feel anything for Santiago. They were sex buddies, nothing more. Drying her face, she took a deep breath. Space. That was what they needed: space. She had gotten too comfortable having him around, craving the heat of his embrace as much as his dick. This had to stop.

Taking a deep breath to steel her nerves, she opened the door. Santiago was lounging in bed, reading the newspaper. What was he, seventy-five? It pissed her off to see him relaxed while she was panicking.

"I've gotta go." Buffy kept her back to Santiago while she pulled her clothes from the floor. Dressing quickly, she headed back into the bathroom, exiting with a toothbrush between her lips. "I have a meeting at the center."

"It's Sunday."

"And?" Buffy didn't withhold the bite in her voice. "There's always events on weekends."

"I'll drop you off." Santiago followed her into the bathroom, watching her through the mirror.

"No! I can get to work on my own," Buffy huffed and pushed past him out of the bathroom.

"Hey." Santiago stopped her with a firm grip on her shoulder. "Nothing has changed. We can take one night off from bumping uglies without falling in love, okay?" He rubbed his thumb under the sleeve of her shirt, gently skirting along her skin. It calmed her instantly and Buffy fought to find the remnants of her anger.

"You knocked out before I even got to bed. Slept like a log all night." Santiago smiled, pushing a hair back into her braid. She leaned into his touch.

Reluctantly, she met his gaze.

"I don't think fuck associates hang out without the fucking part." Buffy spoke in a whisper, as though the words had less meaning at a lower volume.

"Associates?" Santiago raised an eyebrow, a smile pulling the corners of his lips.

Buffy shook her head in exasperation. "Seemed a better choice than booty call."

Santiago smiled and stroked the high ridge of her cheek. "You know, associates usually buy each other dinner, at least in my expert experience."

His attempt to lighten her mood only partially worked.

Buffy pulled his hands from her face and moved to stare out the window. A cat was prowling along the fence line, her white body blending in with the clouds hanging low in the sky. She wished she could trade places with the stray. Hunting rats was probably such a release, like the shooting range had been yesterday.

Thoughts warred in her mind but only one stuck out. *Santiago.*

"I don't know how to do the 'associates' part. The 'buddy' part of fuck buddies has always eluded me." Buffy kept her back to him. "They don't usually stick around this long."

Santiago let out a gruff laugh behind her.

"I like playing with fire." Santiago's breath teased her ear.

Buffy turned toward his voice. His gaze bore into her with lust and interest blazing in his deep brown eyes.

"What if I burn you?" Buffy whispered.

"Then I'll burn." Santiago shrugged.

"You're insane." Buffy stared at him.

"I know that you want to protect me." Santiago stood and crossed the room until they were chest to chest. "But I'm a big boy. I can make my own decisions. And right now, I would like to continue fucking you and sometimes convincing you to eat with me." He smiled broadly.

Buffy scoffed.

"Help me with breakfast." Santiago nodded towards the door and handed her a pair of sweats. He took her hand and led her downstairs.

Abuela Paulina was already in the kitchen, smashed plantains on their second fry in the spitting oil.

"Buenos días, mijos." Abuela Paulina greeted each of them with a kiss on the cheek. "Coffee is on the table."

"Abuela, sabes que puedo hacer el café." Santiago replied. "I'm supposed to be the one taking care of you."

Buffy figured he was typically awake earlier and brewed the coffee. She had distracted him this morning.

"If that's the case, then I only made coffee for Buffy." Abuela Paulina placed a cup of hot black coffee in front of Buffy. "Hands off." Abuela pointed at Santiago, wiggling the oily tongs and glaring.

"Thank you, Abuela." Buffy smiled deviously and picked up her coffee, taking a slow sip. It was more bitter than she was used to but there was an underlying taste of chocolate that coated her tongue and made her moan. "It's delicious."

"We only drink Cuban coffee in this house." Abuela Paulina removed the smashed plantains from the oil and pressed them between two towels. "Anything else is just water."

Buffy laughed and made a mental note to add Cuban coffee to the center shopping list. Abuela Paulina would absolutely not approve of their single-serve coffee machine, nor the bulk light roast Armando usually kept in stock.

Abuela Paulina set fresh plates on the table in front of them. Santiago handed Buffy a plate and placed another out for Abuela. A plate of golden rolled tortillas was on the table in front of them.

"What's this?" Buffy whispered to Santiago, pointing at the fried tortillas.

"Flautas. Beans and cheese rolled up in a tortilla and fried." Santiago took one and cracked it in half, showing her the brown refried beans and crumbled white cheese.

Dipping it in salsa, he ate one half himself and offered the other to Buffy. His fingers brushed her lips when she took the food from his outstretched hand. Santiago smiled while she chewed. "How is it?"

Buffy nodded, swallowing coffee quickly before she could speak. "It's spicy." Her throat felt dry and scratchy when she spoke. She coughed and drank from Santiago's glass of water.

Santiago cracked up laughing, leaning all the way back in his chair with his hand over his heart.

"Baby, that's the *mild* salsa." Santiago tucked a piece of her red hair behind her ear, looking at her like she was Bambi struggling to stand. She tried to ignore the way her skin tingled at the pet name.

"I can handle the heat," Buffy argued. She scrunched her nose up in disgust. "I'm not a bitch."

"Prove it, then," Santiago challenged, crossing his arms over his chest. He leveled her with a challenging gaze.

Abuela Paulina laughed in the kitchen behind them. She plated the plantains and joined them at the table.

"Give me the spiciest one." Buffy shook her head at him with impatience.

Santiago returned to the table with a tub of dark-red salsa. Once he opened it, the smell of chiles permeated the air and tickled her nose into a fit of sneezing. Coughing reared in her chest again and she felt like she was suffocating.

"See! You're coughing just from the smell." Santiago tried to take the salsa away but Buffy stopped him and took the salsa from his grip.

She dipped one of the fried tortillas into the thick merlot-colored salsa and ate it. Buffy chewed quickly, regret setting in before her mouth was fully closed. Burning took over her entire mouth immediately. Chewing quickly, she swallowed and drank water. The water didn't help, and she hacked out a string of coughs that slowly turned her face the same color as the salsa.

Buffy felt Abuela and Santiago watching her. She had to regain her composure. Shrugging, she leaned back in her chair and leveled Santiago with a glare. Tears filled her eyes as redness creeped up her neck. It felt like her head was going to explode from holding back the vicious coughing.

Abuela Paulina broke their silence with laughter, looking back and forth between the two of them with a knowing gaze. She ate a hot salsa-drenched flauta with ease and Buffy watched her in shock.

"Buffy, will you come to the family dinner this Friday?" Abuela Paulina placed her hand over Buffy's on the table.

"Sure," Buffy answered in reflex. *No, absolutely not*, should've been her answer, but she was quite literally incapable of saying no to an Elder.

"It's Abuela's birthday," Santiago elaborated. "Just the same people from last night." Santiago looked at his grandma with a smirk. "Maybe one of her new friends from the center."

Abuela Paulina blushed and suddenly Buffy's panic wasn't the center of attention. She could work with this.

"Do I know this friend?" Buffy asked, casting a sidelong glance at Santiago. It was as though they shared an inside joke and together, they lovingly teased his grandmother. She felt strangely at ease and like a member of their small family. Her heart felt full.

"No, of course not." Abuela Paulina waved her hand in the air as though waving away the thought. Buffy suspected she was actually trying to fan the blush in her cheeks.

"Norman, I think you said, right, Abuela?" Santiago continued, relaxing into his seat and draping an arm across Buffy's shoulders.

"You and Mr. Norman?" Buffy didn't conceal her shock. "He's a tough nut to crack." Buffy nodded and tapped her chin quizzically. "I think we have to invite him."

"Me too," Santiago agreed enthusiastically.

"You two are going to be the death of me," Abuela Paulina groaned and finished her coffee in one gulp.

Buffy and Santiago shared a laugh. Abuela Paulina was blushing like a teenager and her smile was the brightest thing in the room. She deserved to have a birthday surrounded with love.

"Can I get you a gift?" Buffy asked. Going to Santiago's grandmother's birthday party was not an *associates* activity but she wasn't going to show up empty-handed now that she had committed to the birthday girl.

"Oh no." Abuela Paulina shook her head. "Just bring yourself. Maybe some tequila." She winked.

Buffy laughed with her then as she had no doubt Abuela Paulina was still capable of doing tequila shots in her eighties.

"I'll be there." Buffy kissed Abuela's cheek.

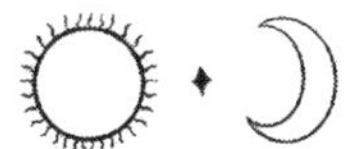

Camila and Miguel were on the couch when Buffy got home. Camila was speaking in hushed tones, her hands wildly animating her words. Miguel was staring at the wall behind his sister's head, clearly tuned out to her rambling. Neither of them had even noticed her entry. Tension filled the air and Buffy groaned. At least she had slept well last night and had the energy to mediate.

"You smell good," Camila called out as soon as Buffy stepped into the living room. "Did you pick up breakfast?"

"No," Buffy answered, smoothing over the waves in her hair from the braid last night.

"Where did you just come from?" Camila twitched her eyebrows and took in Buffy's rumpled clothes and makeup-free face.

"Good morning, Miguel." Ignoring her best friend's baited question, Buffy poured herself a glass of lemon water and joined the siblings. Miguel melted further back into the couch. Buffy took the half-eaten pink concha from Camila's plate and finished it in three bites. "You guys okay?"

"Miguel is being evicted," Camila explained, chewing the skin of her thumb. Miguel glued his gaze to the ground, cheeks and neck a deep red.

"What happened?" Buffy asked, looking between the siblings. This was terrible timing and Buffy was certain Miguel's confidence was rocked. He needed their support now more than ever.

"He got into a little scuffle—" Camila squished her pointed finger and thumb together in front of her eye.

"It was a fist fight." Miguel sighed, glaring at his older sister.

"It was less of a fight and more of a misunderstanding," Camila said, speaking to Buffy.

"Cami! I broke his nose." Miguel scrubbed his dry hands over his face. He sighed loudly and Buffy swore she could hear his heart thumping in his chest. "I deserve to be kicked out," Miguel muttered behind his hands. He stormed off then, slamming Camila's bedroom door behind him.

Buffy remained silent until Camila was ready to talk.

"Can he sleep on our couch? Just for a few days until he can find someplace," Camila whispered.

"Yes," Buffy responded immediately. "Of course. I can always stay at Santiago's for a night or two." She hoped at least.

"Oh you can, can you?" Camlia winked suggestively. "Got yourself a nice little sugar daddy finally?"

"Ew," Buffy gagged. "He is not a sugar daddy."

"He owns a house in the city. That's pretty sugary." Camila said.

"It's his grandmother's house," Buffy specified.

"You know that means it's basically his," Camila argued.

"He wants to move back to Colorado eventually, anyway." Buffy waved her hand through the air. Even if the lines blurred a little, it wasn't permanent. "Regardless, Miguel can stay here as long as he needs. We can figure it out." With six siblings, Buffy was used to sharing her space. It wasn't her favorite thing in the world, but she could deal for a while. "He's family."

Camila grasped Buffy's hand in hers, pulling it into her lap. She squeezed it tightly.

"I'm so lucky to have met you," Camila said.

"Me too." Buffy squeezed her hand once and withdrew.

"Is he doing well at work?" Camila lowered her voice.

"He's doing fine as far as I can tell." Buffy shrugged. "He's quiet but he's on time and he finishes his tasks so, can't complain."

"My brother is a good boy." Camila spoke more to herself than Buffy.

"I know," Buffy said.

"He just got mixed up. We were kids." Camila mumbled.

"I know." Buffy took Camila's hand again. Comforting people was not her specialty, but she hoped the physical touch would be enough..

"Going to jail ruined his life." Tears cut through Camila's gentle voice.

"No." Buffy squeezed her hand tight and shook her head. "It derailed him a little bit but his life is not over. He has a job, a sister who loves him, and a couch to sleep on. That's more than a lot of people in his position typically have." Buffy watched Camila digest her words. "You're doing great and Miguel will be able to do anything with you by his side." She tried to ignore the burn of guilt that came with her words. Camila was a fantastic sister. Buffy, however, was not. Buffy was a better friend to Camila than she was a sister to her siblings. All she did was disappoint them. It was better to let Juniper be the sister and for Buffy to keep her distance.

"Ew, I sound like an angel or something," Camila groaned.

"Or something." Buffy laughed. Camila, like many Chicanas, had a complicated relationship with her God. "Did you order groceries yet?" Buffy could attempt to take some stress off.

Camila shook her head.

"Should we do fettuccine or linguine this week?"

"Miguel loves bow-tie," Camila muttered, glancing at her closed bedroom door.

"I will suffer through bow-tie pasta for one week." Buffy opened the grocery delivery app on her phone. "After that, I want my noodles back."

Camila laughed and assured her Miguel wouldn't mind. Buffy added four boxes of bow-tie pasta to their order. They'd probably need more parmesan and tomato sauce too. She added them both.

"You could invite Santiago over for dinner." Camila glanced at Buffy from the corner of her gaze.

Buffy glared at her roommate.

"I never should've told you about him." Sighing, she pulled herself from the couch and filled their electric kettle. She needed something to distract her from this conversation. Tea should do it.

"As if you could keep a secret from me." Camila cackled from across the room.

"I could keep a secret," Buffy muttered, mostly to herself. She thought she was keeping a pretty tight lid on her emerging emotions for Santiago. If Camila had seen her panic at his absence this morning, she'd know just how right she was.

"Come on." Camila came into the kitchen and took a seat across the counter from Buffy. "If I am going to try working things out with Elena, then why can't you try with Santiago?"

"Those aren't even close to the same situations." Buffy shook her head. "You've been with Elena off and on for almost a decade. I've only known Santiago for a few months."

Camila shrugged. "It just seems different with him. You seem different."

"Well I'm not." Buffy crossed her arms. "I am the same cold-hearted bitch I have always been. No man or woman is going to change that."

"I'm just saying you don't have to self-destruct this time." Camila put her hands up as though she was calming Buffy like a horse.

Buffy poured them each a cup of mint tea and shut her bedroom door behind her.

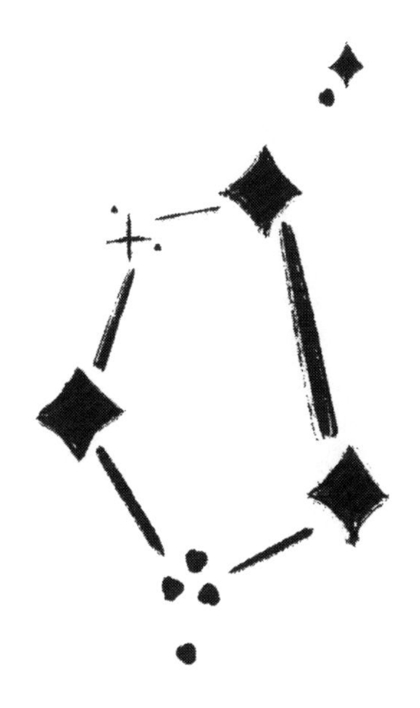

Chapter 13

On Monday morning, Buffy found Abuela Paulina in the kitchen with Armando, elbows deep in masa.

"You putting Elders to work now, Mando?" Buffy clicked her tongue against the roof of her mouth in disapproval.

"I was coerced." Armando put his hands up, arguing his innocence.

"He had the dough so dry we would've been having tostadas instead of tacos." Abuela Paulina shook her head at Armando, clicking her tongue in the side of her cheek.

"Well, as long as you promise to join everyone as soon as you're finished here. I wanted to introduce you to some ladies that live near your house." Buffy stole a small piece of steamed masa and popped it into her mouth. The corn melted on her tongue and Buffy felt at home.

"Oh really?!" Abuela Paulina turned bright eyes to Buffy.

"I can take it from here, Abuela." Armando relieved her of the masa, helping clear it from between her fingers before she washed up.

Abuela Paulina followed Buffy out of the kitchen and to the community room. The sweet buttery smell of pan dulce flowed off her skin and mixed with the smell of masa. It reminded Buffy of Santiago. She missed him.

"Good afternoon, Aunties." Buffy approached a table of three women, stooping to kiss each of their cheeks one by one. "I wanted to introduce you to Paulina. She just started coming to the center. I thought you might show her the ropes, maybe introduce her to some others."

"Sit with us for a while." Auntie Mae, a short woman with an even shorter face, surrounded by short white hair, nodded to Buffy.

Buffy hesitated. The urge to resist died on her tongue when Mae looked pointedly at Buffy over the top of her glasses.

Pulling out the empty seat beside Abuela Paulina, Buffy sat, rolling her shoulders back in an effort to relax. She prayed Abuela Paulina would keep the details of Buffy's time with her grandson to herself.

"You look stressed," an Auntie commented.

Buffy felt her blood pressure spike.

"She always is," another chimed in.

Trying to keep her cool, Buffy swallowed the bile in her throat. She glanced beside her at Abuela Paulina, who offered a comforting smile and pat to her thigh.

"Are you seeing someone yet?" a third Auntie piped up.

Buffy held her palms face up, a blank look on her face. Panic stole her voice and Buffy prayed no one would fill the silence with rumors. Thankfully, Abuela Paulina kept the information about her relationship with Santiago to herself.

"Well, that's okay." Auntie Mae was one of Buffy's favorite clients. Born in Louisiana and brought to San Francisco as a child via adoption, Auntie Mae was an incredible mix of Black, Cherokee, and Chicano culture. A longtime Spanish speaker, Auntie Mae often served as a "bridge". Santiago was considered a "bridge" too, or as some might call him, a blendian. That was a new word for Buffy, having grown up on tiny Bunchberry, but the term was widely used in the urban community, as far as she knew. Blendians were Natives who belonged to more than one culture and were able to communicate effectively across them. People like Auntie Mae and Santiago bridged the gap between communities and created unity within their people.

This also meant that Auntie Mae had more power than anyone in the center, and Buffy was smart enough to know that she wouldn't take no for an answer.

"I'm dating." Buffy shrugged her shoulders, begging Creator to keep the blush from her neck and cheeks. On second thought, her chest too. The V-neck had been the wrong choice this morning.

"Anyone special?" Auntie Mae asked.

"I'm not sure yet." Buffy avoided the heat of Abuela Paulina's gaze. "It's all new. Just seeing what's out there." She hoped her breathing was calm because her heart certainly wasn't.

"When is Calehan getting married?" Another Auntie called Buffy's attention away. Her elder brother had only visited the center once, but every woman in the building had fallen in love with him. It was like they'd never seen a six-and-a-half-foot tall Cree man with good manners before.

Happily, Buffy launched into minor details about Calehan and Xiomara's life in Europe. Once the Aunties were satisfied that at least one of the Yellowbirds had found a partner in life, Buffy was free to make her escape.

As soon as they were absorbed in a new topic of conversation, Buffy made her silent departure. Slinking away from the table, she beelined toward the elevators with barely a glance to the people she passed by.

The Aunties' interest in her love life brought a rotten taste to her mouth. The truth was she wasn't dating anyone. She was fucking someone, but that was it. Nothing more.

Then why did it feel like something more?

Lines had blurred to the point of erasure between them. She had gotten far too comfortable with him too quickly. They had fallen into a romantic relationship despite her hardest efforts. Bile rose in her throat.

If she and Santiago really were just fucking, then she should be seeing other people. At minimum, she could be flirting with strangers. Instead, she had allowed Santiago to take her on a date and blur those lines even more.

How had she let herself get tied down without even realizing it? She didn't have to sleep with other people, but she could at least be going on dates.

Stupid, Buffy thought. *That is exactly what you need.*

Grabbing her phone, she opened up the app store and redownloaded her favorite dating app. Time to play the field.

Swiping through the photos on her phone screen, Buffy couldn't seem to find someone worthy of her effort. Rubbing her hands over her face, she leaned her head back in her desk chair, a heavy sigh falling from her mouth. Every thought in her mind was plagued by him, the smell of eucalyptus filling her nose, his face conjuring behind her eyelids. She swore she could hear his voice too.

This was not good. She needed to get over Santiago and she needed to do it quickly. She set the filters to both genders, forty-years maximum, closed her eyes and started swiping. After a few minutes, she opened her eyes and slid to the messages. Three matches. Two men, one woman. Perfect.

By the end of the day, Buffy had thrown out both men and arranged to meet the woman for dinner and drinks a few blocks from the center. Nerves tickled in her gut, but they weren't butterflies. Instead, they felt like hot drops of lava, burning her from the inside out.

Guilt, she thought.

Shaking her head, Buffy attempted to dislodge the thought from her mind. She shouldn't feel guilty. They had an arrangement, and she and Santiago were not exclusive. Going on this date didn't mean she was going to sleep with this woman, and therefore she had nothing to feel guilty about. She wasn't breaking any of their rules.

Failing to go on this date because of misplaced guilt would only give Santiago the relationship and feelings he wanted. She *had* to go on this date. It was her duty to both of them.

The rationalizing failed and Buffy threw up her lunch in the bathroom. Brushing her teeth and pulling her hair back into a braid, she mustered up the courage to meet someone new and left.

Buffy found her date easily at the back corner of the bar. The woman had curly brown hair styled similar to a mullet; the bangs at the front blended into the longer parts at the back, creating a fluffy halo of curls. Buffy liked it. Santiago had similar curls.

Dammit, Buffy admonished herself.

"Buffy?" The woman asked as she approached, brown eyes warm behind folded lids.

"Rona?" Buffy hugged her. Rona was as tall as Buffy in her platform boots and smelled like mint. It made her think of Santiago, who often smelled like the woods and eucalyptus and fresh wild mint—the flavor of her toothpaste that he always used.

"Do you live nearby?" Rona asked.

"No, I work at a non-profit just up the road." Buffy let their knees touch beneath the bar. Rona pressed their legs closer together. "What about you?"

"I'm a preschool teacher." Rona winked one clear, blue eye.

Buffy felt her eyes widen. She had a hard time picturing the leather-clad woman reading on the floor to a bunch of small kids.

Rona laughed. "I leave the platforms at home when I'm teaching, but the rest stays."

Buffy evaluated her outfit, chains and black stones sparkling in the low light. She absolutely would've had a crush on Rona as a kid.

"You would be my favorite teacher, for sure." Buffy clinked their beers together and let their thighs mold together. Rona made her laugh and the conversation felt easy. If she focused really hard, she could almost forget about Santiago.

Almost.

Full of garlic knots and buffalo chicken wings, Rona took Buffy by the hand and guided her out onto the foggy San Francisco street. Buffy let Rona press their lips together. Rona's lips were dry, rough and bruising where they bulldozed her mouth open. Her tongue was cold against Buffy's, swishing through her mouth like a harebrained snake. Rona tasted like beer. She hated it.

Santiago filled her mind. The way he kissed her, his hands gentle on her hips, he absorbed her wholly—conscious of every minute movement she made. Rona was a bull in a china shop and Buffy was the shattering china. Everything felt wrong.

Buffy pulled away, gently taking Rona's hands from her hips. They felt small against her skin and she missed the way Santiago encompassed her despite being her same size.

"Thanks for dinner," Buffy kept her voice high, feigning an interest in an effort to keep herself safe.

"I'll take you home." Rona licked her lips, looking Buffy up and down.

Buffy felt guilty. She had been flirty up until they actually kissed. It was frustrating. She wanted to be into this, she wanted to like Rona, but Santiago was the only thing on her mind. All she could think about was that she would rather be with him, that she would be scared for him to see her on this date, that she didn't want to hurt his feelings.

Regret settled into her bones.

"I've got to be up early." Buffy smiled, batting her lashes slowly to soften the rejection. "A girl has to work."

Dancing out of her arms, Buffy bumped into the people waiting at the Peruvian food truck beside the curb. Turning around to apologize, she met a familiar pair of dark brown eyes. Pear.

Fuck.

"Hi, Buffy." Pear's smile was wicked, sharp, a smirking smile as though he knew her intimate secrets.

Santiago had loose lips evidently.

"There you are!" Buffy said, praying that Pear would play along.

Her date wrapped an arm around her waist, "I'm Rona." Rona's protectiveness was appreciated, but unnecessary in this situation. Pear was annoying but she had about four inches and fifty pounds on him, so to be honest, he wasn't a threat.

"This is John. He's my brother. He came to pick me up." Buffy looped her arm through his.

"I was waiting for you," said Pear, standing straighter. He was dressed in a three-piece suit, two boxes of food in his hands. "You ready?" He offered her one of the takeaway boxes. Rona nodded and looked between them. She took a step back.

"Text me when you get home!" Rona waved, biting her lip.

"Bye!" Buffy waved at her over Pear's shoulder, letting him hurry her up the sidewalk and away from Rona.

They turned a corner together with their arms still linked. Safely behind the cover of a building, Buffy pulled her arm away. Pear stopped at a red door and typed a code into the keypad.

"I'm gonna catch a cab." Buffy offered him the tub of food.

"Yeah, right." Pear opened the door and stood to the side, waving her in. "Santi would kill me if I let you call a cab."

"He's not my keeper," Buffy huffed, anger flashing across her face.

"That's obvious." Pear waited expectantly, holding the door open. Buffy wanted to see Santiago, but not like this. Knowing he was so close made it hard to resist. Relenting, Buffy followed Pear. He led her up the stairs and into a large room, windows lining the entirety of one wall. "Santi! Tu novia está aquí!"

Santiago wore a sage green button-down, the top three buttons undone. Black ink peeked through the opening, teasing the frustration in her belly to the forefront. He held a stack of files and a tape recorder. Buffy felt her heart thump. He looked *good* at work.

Though Rona had been beautiful, Buffy's thoughts had stayed permanently on Santiago and now he was in front of her, even sexier than she remembered.

"What are you doing here?" Santiago's smile was wide, energy visibly filling his body at the sight of her. Leaning in to kiss her, Buffy turned, offering him her cheek. It felt wrong to touch his lips with hers after kissing someone else. She felt guilty, as though she needed a shower before kissing Santiago.

Santiago, however, didn't miss a beat, wrapping an arm around her waist and nosing a kiss to her hairline just above the ear. He squeezed her tightly to his chest, keeping an iron arm around her waist to anchor her beside him.

"I was with a friend at the bar around the corner," Buffy lied. Her tongue tasted like salt.

Santiago pulled her with him into his office. The walls were painted a creamy taupe, with modern and historical Mexican art hanging on the walls. His Pueblo side was evident here too, the black and white striped shapes dancing on the walls. "I didn't know your office was nearby," Buffy said, hesitating in the doorway.

"Lucky coincidence." Santiago winked, pulling her back into his arms. He hummed against her neck and pressed a kiss to the exposed skin of her shoulder. She hoped that he couldn't smell Rona's flowery perfume still clinging to her clothes.

"Things are never a coincidence," Buffy spit, angered by his lack of irritation at her obvious lie. She knew Santiago was smarter than he let on and being caught in her lie while he knowingly played along was worse than him yelling at her.

Why couldn't he just get mad at her?

Santiago gazed at her. He took in her outfit and tired eyes.

"You can tell me if you were on a date." Santiago held her hand between both of his, pressing a kiss to the thin skin of her wrist. "You don't have to hide from me."

"It wasn't a date," Buffy scoffed.

"Your lipstick begs to differ," Santiago teased with a smile, flexing his fingers against her waist.

"It was just drinks." It had been drinks at a bar...that also had appetizers.

"I can smell the garlic on you." Santiago crossed his arms, leaning back on his desk. He watched her easily, but Buffy couldn't read his expression. He looked calm and that only freaked her out more. "Be honest with me."

"Fine, yeah. I went on a date. I'm allowed. We're just fucking, remember?" Buffy threw her hair over her shoulder.

"You'll go on dates with someone you aren't having sex with." Santiago raised one lone brow. "But you won't let me buy you dinner?"

"I like your cock more than I like dinner," Buffy retorted.

"I'm happy to give you both."

"Are you trying to ruin this right now?" Buffy crossed her arms, digging her fingernails into the soft flesh at the back of her arms. Anxiety began to boil in her gut. She was a bomb ready to explode. "If sex isn't enough for you, then this should end here."

Fear was burning her gut into a rage, liquid hot rage that bubbled up her throat, filled her head and blinded her. Buffy saw red.

Santiago blinked at her, stood, and closed the door behind her. He turned to face her.

"I don't care who you drink with," Santiago said. His face was directly in front of hers, her lack of high heels allowing him to gaze directly into her eyes. "But I deserve honesty, Buffy."

"You're crazy," she scoffed, stepping to the side to put distance between their beating hearts. "Santiago, this has to end."

"Buffy." Santiago sighed, thumbs against his temples.

"Clearly, you're developing strong feelings, and I am not."

"You don't feel anything for me?" Santiago stared her straight in the eye. His unwavering gaze made her feel sick with guilt. She was hurting him. It was written plainly across his face. "The first thing you do in the morning is reach for me. You really think you don't have *any* feelings for me?"

Notably, he didn't deny having feelings for her. Buffy's heart squeezed in her chest and she wanted to throw her arms around his neck and kiss the frustration from his face.

"You're warm." Buffy shrugged, glaring back at him. "That's it." Buffy watched fire stir in his eyes.

"I'm not asking you to change anything." Santiago turned to face her. "We can stay fuck buddies or whatever—" He waved his hand when she made at face at his word choice. "I want to be able to take you to dinner and romance you and tease you and then take you home and fuck you until we can't stand." He took another step closer to her. "What is so wrong with that?"

"No romance." Buffy focused her eyes on his chin, desperate to look anywhere but his eyes. "That was one of the rules."

"Your rule." Santiago's voice was deeper than she had ever heard it. "Not mine."

"I eat sushi with you!" Buffy didn't know what more he wanted from her. "I go to lunch with you. I let you bring lunch to my office." Her voice was rising now and she hoped the walls were well insulated. "All of that is against the rules and I have selfishly been allowing it because for some inexplicable reason I can't say no to you." Buffy sighed and ran a hand through her hair.

"Then let me take you to dinner." Santiago reached for her hand. His face softened.

"No." Buffy jerked her hand out of his grip. "I can't give you more than a good fuck. If that isn't enough for you, then we should end it right here."

Santiago blinked at her in shock. "What is happening right now?" He shook his head.

Buffy scoffed as the anger continued to boil in her belly. The fear of losing him was screaming in her brain but she silenced it with rage. Santiago was ruining their arrangement, not her.

"Why are you angry with me?" Santiago asked, frustration lacing his voice.

"Because you're trying to change me!" Buffy shocked herself at the admission. Santiago made her feel things she never had before and the desire to change her rotten core was overwhelmingly scary. This was supposed to be a sex-only relationship. "I told you this was sex and nothing more." Buffy waved her hands in front of them.

"I'm not asking you to change, Buffy." Santiago stepped closer to her. "I'm asking you to let me be myself. I want to take you to dinner. I want to drive you home. I want to pick you up for coffee and shooting before I take you home and fuck you. That is all that I want, Buffy. What do you want?"

"I don't know," Buffy whispered, the anger completely depleted. Fear was controlling her now and it had stripped her naked in front of him.

"That's okay." Santiago stepped closer again, resting one palm on her upper arm. "You don't have to know right now. But for us to keep doing this, I need you to tell me the truth. I deserve at least that."

They stared at each other in silence. Buffy knew better than to make a promise she couldn't keep. She looked at the floor, his gaze too intense to watch. The fight trickled out of his blood and onto the floor in front of them as if she had cut him open and bled him dry. He stepped back.

"Come on." Santiago grabbed his briefcase and suitcoat. "I'll take you home."

A stone dropped into her stomach, fear and guilt creating a spirit-sucking monster inside of her. Another relationship ruined by her and her alone. Self-sabotage was her middle name, after all. Camila was going to be pissed that she self-destructed again.

Santiago watched her calmly from beside the door, waiting for her to join him.

Annoyance flared in her veins at his calm demeanor. She refused his dates, kissed other people, told him she wanted to end it, and yet he barely showed any anger. He was impossible.

"I'll take a cab." Buffy wrenched the door open.

Santiago's hand slammed it shut before she could open the door wide enough to step through, "No. You will not."

"You don't get to tell me what to do." Buffy's words spit like fire.

"Buffy." Santiago looked her in the eye. "You can't hide from me. I've already seen all of you."

"You don't know me," Buffy argued.

"And who's fault is that?" Santiago's mask slipped then, just for a second. Long enough for Buffy to see the flash of hurt in his eyes, the tension in his jaw and the thinning of his lips.

Then, it was gone.

All of the fight evaporated from her body in an instant.

"Come on." Santiago opened the door and guided her through with a gentle hand on her back.

Their drive was silent. Buffy kept her eyes locked out the passenger window, pretending she was in a taxi. For all the words Santiago had to say to her, he offered little emotion or anger. It left Buffy confused. If he liked her so much, why was he okay with her going out with other people? Why hadn't he tried to make them exclusive yet? It was a game. It had to be. Nothing else made sense.

"You're thinking too loud." Santiago chuckled when she met his gaze. The car was no longer moving, the darkness of the garage brighter than the night outside. He unbuckled his seatbelt, then hers.

"I'm drunk," Buffy lied. "Can't you tell?"

"Anyone ever told you that you're a bad liar?" Santiago kissed her cheek and slid from the car.

"Oh shit, I forgot." Buffy stopped in front of the open passenger door. "Miguel is sleeping on our couch. I can't bring you in there."

"Who's Miguel?" Santiago questioned.

"Camila's younger brother."

"How young?" Santiago raised a brow.

"Like twenty-something."

Santiago shrugged. "He's old enough."

"Gross." Buffy grimaced. "Thanks for the ride."

"Stay at my place tonight." Santiago spoke flatly and she knew he wasn't asking it as a question. Her heart leapt and she climbed back inside the car before he could change his mind.

A while later, he was parking in the tiny driveway of Abuela's walkup. All of the lights were off inside the house and Buffy figured Abuela had been asleep for a few hours by this point. She probably wouldn't even know that Buffy spent the night.

Buffy went straight up the stairs to Santiago's bedroom. By the time Santiago reached her with two glasses of water, she was stripped bare and filling his bathroom with steam.

She could feel him as soon as he stepped into the hot room. He radiated warmth and made her desperate to wrap herself in him. Resistance waning, she found herself the next best thing: a boiling hot shower. Buffy feigned anger at his presence, tried to convince herself that she wanted to be alone, that she wanted him to leave. If she kept the front up for herself, eventually it would stick. But the truth was that she was counting each second that he waited to join her in the shower. She swallowed. Maybe he didn't plan to join her after all. Maybe she had succeeded in pushing him away. Her throat tightened.

A bite of cool air teased the back of her arm before Santiago was there, molding his warm body against hers, protecting her from the chill. One arm snaked across the wet flesh of her belly, wrapping around her torso and holding her tightly to his front. Using his other hand, he trailed his fingertips across her warm flesh, droplets of water sticking to each other and following his path. Reaching her neck, his thumb rubbed gently over the edge of her jaw before he turned her face to his and claimed her mouth.

Santiago was harsh, holding her tightly to him, lips equally firm against her own. Buffy gripped his forearm for purchase, going light-headed under his sensual embrace. His fingertips dug into her hips, dimpling and turning white where they met her skin.

She wondered if the punishing grip would leave bruises behind. She hoped they would. Santiago had been rough before, they had explored somewhat, but he had never been so clear with what he wanted before tonight.

He wanted *her*.

Buffy pulled herself from the bed, slinking lazily to the bathroom to clean up. Pausing in the doorway, she watched Santiago dress. Gray slacks covered his tattooed legs, his sage green button-up glowing against the desert-brown skin of his neck.

"I've gotta run back to the office for a bit," Santiago explained.

She felt sick. He didn't normally leave right after sex, and she found her thoughts spiraling. He was asking her to leave. She was sure of it.

Catching her eye, Santiago met her in the doorjamb. Pushing her hair from her neck, he held her face between his palms. He waited until she met his eye, smiling softly as he brought her in for a kiss.

Against her own will, Buffy gripped his waist and held him tight to her front. He was slipping through her fingers and the fear was all-consuming. People could only be pushed away for so long until they finally tired of the fight. She could see Santiago's fight waning and the thought of him leaving gripped her heart.

"I don't want you to go," she whispered against his lips, eyes squeezed shut. The words were out of her mouth so quickly she didn't process them until they were already out of her mouth. Shit.

Silence stretched between them and bile rose in her throat. He clearly did not want to stay. Buffy tried to pull away.

Santiago held her firmly against him, one hand still holding her face to his.

"I don't want to go either." Sighing, he rested his forehead against hers. "Ride with me to pick up my files? We'll get some ice cream and come back?"

No, Buffy. Say NO.

"Okay."

Traitor.

Santiago held her hand until they reached the car, opening her door and ushering her inside. They rode in silence, the radio playing softly while Santiago's fingers tapped the beat on her bare thigh. Buffy traced the veins in his arm as his fingers moved, mesmerized by the ink of his tattoos seeming to come alive. She felt at peace in the car beside him. It felt like everything was going to be okay.

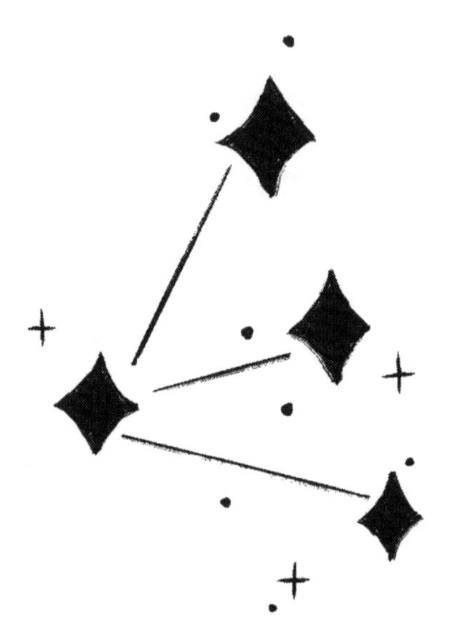

Chapter 14

"Stay here." Santiago unbuckled and straightened his shirt. "I'll be right back." Kissing Buffy on the back of her hand, he left her with the keys and heat blasting.

"Figured you weren't coming back," Pear chuckled when Santiago entered their shared office space.

"What are you still doing here?" Santiago ignored Pear's teasing comment.

"Shit, I need to pick up all that work my fool cousin left behind." Pear gestured to the stacks of files strewn across his desk.

Santiago rolled his eyes. "I'm taking it with me."

"Oh yeah?" Pear raised his eyebrows. "Bringing work home to your little shooting star?"

That was Pear's way of calling Buffy flaky.

"Don't call her that." Santiago gathered the documents he needed and tucked them under his arm. "You should go home."

"I will." Pear crossed his arms against his chest and leaned back to stare at his cousin. "You sure you know what you're doing?"

Santiago's stare could cut glass. Pear was stronger than glass. He had the scars to prove it.

"She was making out with that other girl, Santi." Pear sighed. "I don't want to see you get hurt again."

"I know what I'm doing." Santiago let the door slam behind him.

He shook his head in an effort to dislodge the look of anger Pear had pulled from him. Before opening the door to the street, Santiago huffed out all the air in his chest, cheeks blown wide. Pear was right, Santiago was on his way to getting hurt. Buffy had been concrete in her no feelings rule and he feared she wouldn't break her own rules—even for him. It was impossible to tell Buffy's true feelings. At times she looked at him with stars in her eyes. Other times, her gaze was made of daggers. He had no idea if she was falling for him or tolerating him because he was a good fuck.

When Buffy saw him emerge onto the street, she waved gently. Santiago felt her eyes watch his every move as he walked around the car. He waited until Buffy unlocked the door, then slid inside. Buffy caught his hand after he tossed his files into the backseat, settling it onto her bare thigh.

The forward display of interest stole his breath. This was new behavior from Buffy and he was scared if he showed how much it affected him, she would stop.

"You okay?"

"Hm?" Santiago met her gaze.

"Penny for your thoughts?"

"Just thinking about you." Gripping her fingers in his hand, he lifted their entwined hands to his mouth and pressed a kiss to the fragile skin on the inside of her wrist. Buffy kissed his palm before returning their joined fingers to her thigh. "Cherry or chocolate dipped cone?"

"Chocolate, obviously." Buffy looked at him from the corner of her eye. "What kind of psycho gets cherry? It tastes like cough medicine."

"No, it tastes delicious," Santiago argued.

They ate their dipped ice creams in the parking lot of the shop. Buffy stretched her long legs across the dash, her toes just barely missing his windshield. He wished she would let her toes touch the glass. To leave a reminder of her behind.

Chocolate gathered in the corner of her lips and dripped across her chin. Santiago reached out, wiping the chocolate mess from her face. Buffy watched him suck the chocolate from the pad of his thumb. Her eyes glazed over before she spoke.

"Are you sure that you're real?" Buffy asked.

"What do you mean?" Santiago was puzzled.

"You!" Buffy was exasperated, munching through the sugar cone at lightning speed. "You're the perfect man and I have you tied up in this situationship with *me*. In comparison to you I am basically evil incarnate."

"Stop." Santiago didn't hold back the laughter that bubbled at her dramatics. "I am not perfect and you are not evil. I'm a big boy, I can make my own decisions. I chose this. I chose you, Buffy."

"Ew, shut up." Buffy turned away from him and hopped out of the car to throw away her trash. Red neon light from the ice cream shop silhouetted the sway of her hips in front of the car. Santiago kept his eyes glued to her languid figure. By the time she returned to the seat beside him, the sheen in her eyes had passed, though Santiago was certain tears had been there.

Santiago started the car and pulled onto the busy city street. There was a gentle tug on his forearm and suddenly his palm was resting on the bare flesh of Buffy's thigh. Squeezing the muscle of her thigh twice, he smiled to himself and relaxed into the short drive. He felt like he had finally made a breakthrough with Buffy. Now, it finally felt like they were on the same page.

Pulling up to the house a few minutes later, Buffy was sleepy against his shoulder. He slid out of the car and came to the passenger side.

Santiago opened her door and leaned inside. Her brow furrowed at the intrusion but her eyes remained closed. "Come on. We're home, it's time to go inside." He whispered, raking his hands through her hair to wake her. Santiago knew he was taking full advantage of her agreeable state but she leaned into his hand and he knew she was enjoying it just as much as he was.

Buffy squinted her eyes open and let him pull her from the car. Closing the door behind her, Santiago wrapped an arm around her waist. Tucking her head into his shoulder, they climbed the steps to the sleeping house. Santiago unlocked the door and held it aside, guiding Buffy in front of him with a firm hand on her back. As soon as her shoes were off, she trudged up the stairs and threw herself onto the bed.

Santiago undressed her, tugging one of his T-shirts over her naked shoulders before tucking her under the covers. He stripped to his boxers then and joined her in the cocoon of blankets. He settled his files onto the nightstand beside him, flicking on the lamp.

"I've never slept beside someone I didn't just fuck," Buffy whispered.

"We just had sex a few hours ago," Santiago laughed into the dark.

"You know what I mean," Buffy whispered. Her eyes were closed, her face pointed towards him. With his arm resting heavily over her thigh, she fell into a deep sleep.

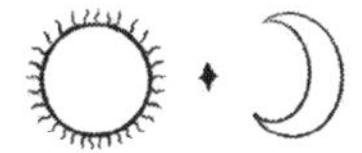

Santiago made breakfast burritos in the kitchen, washing the dishes as soon as they finished eating. It felt painfully domestic.

"I have a late meeting tomorrow night." Santiago topped off her cup of coffee. "I'll pick you up after?"

Buffy watched him move effortlessly around the kitchen. Abuela Paulina sat outside on the porch, gentle music playing from her phone. Suddenly, Buffy felt like she was back home on Bunchberry.

The line she had drawn between them had become completely erased. There were no boundaries between them anymore and Buffy felt oddly like she had gone to bed single and woken up married. Panic settled into her chest.

"I've got dinner with Camila and a few of our friends tomorrow," Buffy lied.

"Want to come over after?" Santiago asked. "I'll pick you up."

"No, I think I should stay home with Camila and Miguel."

Santiago turned his head to the side. "Buffy, let me do what I want."

"What you want is just going to get you hurt," Buffy argued. "I'm not good enough for you."

"Why not, Buffy?" Santiago hid the shock on his face. His voice was even, frighteningly controlled. "I know what I want. Why can't I have you?"

"I'm not right for you." Buffy kept her eyes on the floor. Shame flooded her veins and worked the water from her throat. She swallowed. "You're so good, Santiago. You help people, you take care of your grandma, you have like...no mental illnesses, which is just insane to me. You deserve someone like you." Buffy hardened her gaze before meeting his eyes. She glared at him. "Not someone like me."

"Buffy what are you talking about?" Santiago came to her then, palms engulfing her cheeks to tilt her head back until her eyes met his. "You are everything-"

"Don't." Buffy pushed his hands from her face and turned, walking around the counter to put more space between them. The pull to collapse into his arms, listen to him whisper and calm her was too strong to resist alone. "You don't know me, Santiago. You have no idea what I'm like when it's bad, and even when it's good—I am still bad." Buffy scrubbed at her face with the heels of her hands, roughly dragging over the skin until it was red and swollen.

"What do you mean you're bad?" Santiago rounded the counter, hands outstretched for her. Buffy practically ran from him, the dining table a new barrier between them. "Buffy." He said her name like a plea and she wanted to give in. It killed her to see pain on his face, hurt caused by her. She always did this, hurt the people she loved.

A sharp trill split the tense air between them, light flashing from Santiago's pocket. Hesitating, he asked her to wait a moment and answered the call. Buffy took advantage of his distraction and placed more physical distance between them.

"I've got to get home." Buffy gathered her things, shoving them into her purse. She couldn't hear Abuela Paulina's murmured bendiciones anymore and the thought that she was listening to their argument was vomit-inducing.

Shouldering her purse, she moved to put on her shoes. A flash of hurt moved across Santiago's face and Buffy felt herself waver. But just as quickly, her wall came right back up. He watched her tie her shoes while he spoke evenly to the person on the other end of the phone. Ending his call, he nodded toward the backyard.

"She'll want to say goodbye."

Santiago grabbed his keys from the mantle and headed outside to Abuela Paulina's spot on the back porch. Buffy trailed behind him, hoping that she wouldn't notice their harrowed expressions.

"Don't forget about Abuela's birthday dinner this Friday, yeah?" Santiago thumbed her chin and stepped onto the back porch.

Buffy nodded.

"Abuela!" Santiago shouted and Buffy's heart squeezed in her chest. His voice was strangled with fear.

Face down in the grass, Abuela Paulina wasn't moving. Her mug was shattered on the ground beside the porch swing. The bench of the swing was stuck in the bushes at the back as though Abuela had taken a hard fall.

"I'll call 911." Buffy gripped her phone until her knuckles turned white, holding it to her ear so hard it hurt. Backing away from Santiago, she watched him fawn over his grandmother. He rolled her easily to her back and moved to stabilize her neck. Abuela Paulina was squinting into the sun and calling Santiago by his father's name.

Buffy was impressed by the way Santiago stayed calm and moved efficiently. He spoke to her easily with questions that wouldn't confuse or scare her. This man was goodness at his core.

Buffy didn't deserve him.

Once the paramedics arrived, Buffy led them to the backyard and slipped away during the commotion. She was a distraction to Santiago and he deserved to put all of his attention on his grandmother.

Buffy walked home, the cool air biting at her cheeks. She held back the tears for three blocks before the dam broke. Tears cascaded down her cheeks. Buffy missed him as soon as she walked away. He was dealing with an injured grandmother and Buffy was wondering if he was missing her like she was missing him. What kind of sick person was she?

Buffy needed to clear her head.

As soon as she got home, Buffy beelined to Camila's dark bedroom. Slinking away with her sleeping roommate's laptop in hand, Buffy booked a last-minute flight to Malaga, Spain, leaving at nine tonight. She packed furiously, forcing Camila awake to help her choose outfits.

"Where's Miguel?"

"He picked up an extra shift today for the youth singers practice," Camila explained.

Buffy nodded. She was glad Miguel wasn't here to witness her breakdown.

"Is this about Santiago?" Camila groaned, rubbing at her sleepy eyes.

"Yes. He's fucking with my head," Buffy sighed, scrubbing her hands roughly over her face. "I need some space."

"Did you tell him you're going?"

"He's not my boyfriend, Cami."

"He sleeps here more than I do. At least call him on the way to the airport."

"No." Buffy was more stubborn than a bull. She would ram her head again and again, ignoring the pain until she no longer felt anything.

"Buffy," Camila sighed. "What happened?"

"Nothing." Buffy threw the remaining items in her duffel. "I can't stand him constantly wanting something more from me. I don't have anything left to give him and I need him to just get over me."

"I don't think he wants to get over you." Camila said. Buffy met her gaze, flames evident in the thinness of her glare. "Pear said—"

"Oh my God, are you guys talking about me behind my back?"

"No." Camila remained calm. "Pear said that Santiago really likes you, that's all."

"Why are the two of you talking about our relationship anyway?" Buffy crossed her arms, holding her fury back for as long as she could. "Why are you talking to Pear when you're dating Elena?"

"You're one to talk, Buffy." Camila met her gaze. There were many reasons the two of them were best friends, but their ability to stand up to one another was one of the greatest reasons they fit so perfectly in each other's lives. "Call him, okay? He cares about you."

Camila helped Buffy pack, tossing far too many bikinis into her bag than was necessary for the seven-day trip. Buffy's phone was vibrating nearly nonstop, Xiomara texting her with excitement and plans for her visit. Nerves settled into her at the thought of seeing her brother. He could always see straight through her as if she were glass. She doubted her ability to keep Santiago a secret.

It was only seven days. She could do a week without thinking of or talking about Santiago. If she could do that, then everything would be fine. If she couldn't make the week without him, she just might have to jump off a cliff.

By the time the sun set, Buffy was packed and ready to head to the airport. Santiago hadn't called her all day, though she had checked her phone constantly for any communication from him.

Her heart dropped each time her phone was devoid of his name, and each time she chastised herself and contemplated blocking his number for the duration of her trip. Buffy was too weak to do that and instead silenced his contact.

Buffy handed her duffel to the cab driver and climbed inside.

"Be safe, okay?" Camila leaned in the window to kiss her on the cheek.

"Always am," Buffy replied.

"Let me know when you land and send lots of photos, okay?"

"Yes, Mom." Buffy shooed Camila away and tapped on the metal of the car.

The taxi took off, rolling over the hills of the bay. Buffy's hands were dripping with sweat. Her phone was in an iron grip that threatened to crack the glass screen. She stared at the phone in her hand. Their frequent texts, calls, and meme sharing led to a complete and total memorization of his phone number to the point she dreamed the number from time to time. She had only saved his contact after she almost called him *Maybe: Santiago*, like her phone did with unnamed numbers. She hadn't wanted to hurt his feelings.

She should've known then.

With a deep breath, she summoned the courage to tap his name. Her heart thumped wildly in her chest, throbbing in time with the ringing on the line.

The phone rang.

And rang.

Then rang some more.

His voicemail picked up.

Buffy hesitated over his number, deciding just how desperate she was. Before she could lose the nerve, she called again.

Voicemail.

Buffy squeezed the phone in her hand until her skin turned white, then red again, before going numb. The numbness was enough of a distraction to stop the tears from forming in the back of her throat.

Santiago had never ignored her call before. Even when he was busy, he would answer the phone or send a text. She tapped her phone. No text messages.

Had her actions this morning finally been the end? Abuela Paulina was his focus today, she knew that, but Santiago hadn't even sent a text. Things felt different.

Buffy wondered if she had succeeded in pushing Santiago away. Finally, she had what she had wanted all this time.

Her stomach turned and bubbled and threatened to explode and devour her like a black hole. She felt embarrassed. Embarrassed that she couldn't tell Santiago how she felt, embarrassed she felt anything at all. Gulping, she forced her dinner to stay in her stomach, the fear of losing him forever burning her alive.

This was a good thing. If Santiago ignored her while she was away, they could have a clean break. He would move on easily, forget all about her. Buffy could wallow and eventually forget about him. She ignored the weight in her stomach, breathing deep.

Goodbye Santi, she thought.

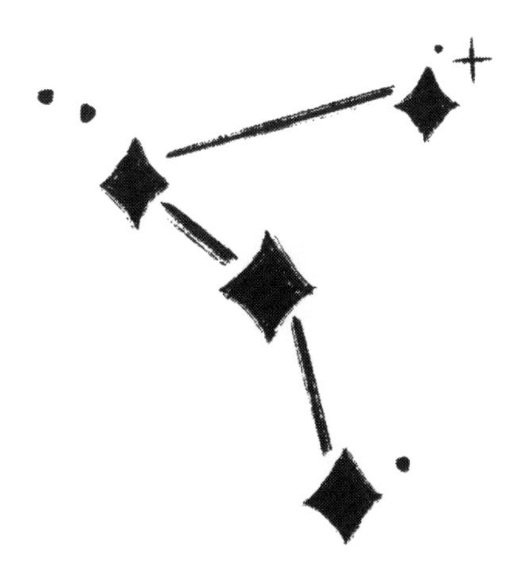

Chapter 15

Stepping out of the airport, all of the moisture in Buffy's skin was sucked out by the bone-dry air. No wonder Xiomara was willing to move here; it might as well be a desert like Chihuahua. Buffy checked her phone one more time, ignoring the texts Santiago had sent. He had called twice on her first flight, and by the time she landed for her layover, it was after midnight in San Francisco. Instead of texting him, she deleted the calls from her phone memory, telling herself it hadn't happened at all.

Day one of seven Santiago-free days had already begun, and she would be damned if she gave in before she got started.

A familiar white Jeep pulled up to the curb. Buffy rolled her eyes. She thought Calehan had been joking about bringing their mother's Jeep to Europe. Evidently, he was being serious. Buffy chewed her lip, the childhood car conjuring images of her mother so vivid she could smell her juniper scented perfume. Xiomara's petite figure launched out of the truck and pulled Buffy in, squeezing her tight.

"I'm so glad you decided to visit." Xiomara wore a radiant smile, her skin the same color as Santiago's from the warm Spanish sun.

Fuck, she was never going to get away from that man.

"Damn, your accent is crazy." Buffy leaned back to peer at the woman again, ensuring that it was truly the Xiomara she knew. Her eldest brother had fallen for the archaeologist a few years ago now, and she had been a full member of the family ever since.

"We speak Spanish now." Xiomara shrugged. "Your brother learned quickly and I even saved him from the lisp, Gracias a Dios". Xiomara smiled widely, as though she had protected Calehan from certain death. "Cal is at work but he's coming home early."

"Perks of being the boss?" Buffy asked, opening the backseat door to love on Xiomara's dog. She scratched Anubis under the chin and kissed his damp snout. The hairless dog's skin was soft against her fingertips. The whiskers by his mouth had turned white since Buffy last saw him.

"Damn straight." Xiomara smiled wide, pink in her cheeks.

"Can we go to the beach while I'm here?" Buffy climbed into the passenger seat beside Xiomara.

"Absolutely." Xiomara smiled and turned onto the sun-soaked highway.

Buffy showered while Xiomara made lunch. In keeping with the European lifestyle, she made a tasting board of jamón, four different cheeses, and two types of salami. Buffy's mouth watered at the smell. She slept on both of her flights and woke up with twenty-four hours' worth of appetite.

Anubis whined at the front door just before it opened, Calehan's long braids slinking through the short doorframe before the rest of him.

"Little sister." Calehan smiled wide, squeezing Buffy tight to his chest. Tears sprang to her eyes instantly, the familiar feel of her eldest brother releasing every emotion she had been holding back.

Clearing her throat, Buffy blinked the tears back and pulled from her brother. "You stink."

"We sprayed insulation today, shit reeks." Calehan laughed, dropping a sweet kiss to Xiomara's waiting lips. The two of them glowed when they touched, as though the love they shared had a physical aura.

Buffy hid a sneer, jealousy rearing an ugly head in her chest. She missed Santiago.

Damn it.

"I'm going to take a quick shower." Ruffling a hand through Buffy's hair as he passed, Calehan disappeared down the hall.

"Let's eat on the balcony." Xiomara picked up the board of assorted meats and cheeses and followed Anubis toward the sun.

Hanging high overhead, the sun beat down on their balcony and Buffy instantly began to sweat. Thankfully, Xiomara opened a large umbrella beside her and Buffy took the seat right beneath it. Xiomara tucked their food onto the table in the shade with Buffy before stretching out in the sun.

"You look happy," Buffy commented.

"We are." Xiomara sighed airily. "How are you?"

"Never been better." Buffy tasted bitterness between her teeth.

"Camila said you've been seeing someone."

"You two met one time. Do you really have to talk so much?" Buffy sighed.

"We're related!"

Buffy rolled her eyes. "Barely."

"Okay, colonizer." Xiomara teased, pushing Buffy's leg with her toes.

Calehan joined them in linen shorts and a button-down.

"You look like a little surfer boy." Buffy snickered.

"I am a beach boy." Calehan took the seat next to his sister, throwing an arm around her shoulders and tugging her close.

"Ew, get off me."

"No, I've missed you." Calehan held her tighter. "Give me a kiss."

"I will stab you with this cheese knife," Buffy threatened.

"Just stay away from the family jewels," Xiomara interjected. "I need those."

Buffy and Calehan's combined laughter broke them apart. Buffy faked like she was puking while shoving Calehan off the couch.

"Well, should we head to the beach?" Xiomara shaded her eyes with a hand and looked between the siblings.

Buffy changed into a strappy swimsuit and covered up with one of Santiago's button-down shirts. This one was short sleeved and white, embroidered with Otomí florals and animals along the breast pockets. It was one of his favorites. She totally hadn't kept it hidden in her drawer and packed it intentionally. She would *never* do that.

Her phone screen lit up, a text from Santiago. On impulse, she threw her phone in the open suitcase and zipped it up, shoved it in the closet, and shut the door. Buffy wanted nothing more than to speak with him and for everything to be okay—but she knew it wasn't.

Buffy skipped Abuela Paulina's birthday and likely broke both of their hearts. If Abuela was even okay from her fall. Buffy wouldn't know considering she wasn't speaking with Santiago. She couldn't bear to hear the hurt she had inflicted. Santiago had been nothing but calm and gentle with her and she couldn't imagine him angry. She was terrified at the thought of him being angry with her. Stars fear the brighter don't they? No wonder she feared Santiago; he was a sun if she ever saw one. He was grand and full of life and love while Buffy was already burnt out—on her way to the nearest black hole.

Putting physical space between her desire to contact Santiago and the incinerating fear from ignoring him, Buffy followed her siblings out of their apartment. She followed behind them, watching Calehan pull Xiomara to the side so that he could walk in between her and the traffic. Calehan picked up Xiomara's hand and took the basket from her arm. He linked their fingers together with ease.

Santiago was the same way. He didn't let her carry anything and she couldn't remember the last time she crossed a street without his hand in hers.

You don't want a relationship, she told herself. Repeating it over and over was like throwing pasta at the wall. It wouldn't stick anymore, no matter how hard she threw it.

On a weekday during siesta, the beach was packed, but they found space alone at the far edge on a hill just above the water. Grass was growing within the sand and she pictured Bunchberry. Their mom's island had a shore that looked the same. She took a deep breath and followed her siblings through the sand.

Xiomara threw herself face down on their picnic blanket, eyes closed to the sun, a smile on her resting face.

"She's recharging."

"Solar-powered girlfriend. I need to get me one of those," Buffy joked.

Calehan and Buffy walked to the water, standing at the edge of the tide. The ocean was warm here. It felt wrong on her skin. Water should be cold enough to leave her skin numb. It wasn't supposed to feel good.

"Speaking of..." Calehan looked at her from the corner of his eye.

"Not you too." Buffy grimaced and kicked water on his legs. "When did you get so tan?" Her eldest brother had always been muscular and tan but he looked different. His skin was darker and his muscles were rounded in a different way than they had been from working on the ranch. He looked...happy.

"It's sunny here every day." Calehan laughed, examining his dark brown skin. He shone like a bronze statue in the sun. "Do you want to talk about it?"

"Talk about what?" Buffy ignored him.

"Buffy." Calehan glared at her. "I know that Mom's birthday is hard on you and dating on top of everything..."

"It's been a decade since Mom died. I think I'm over it by now," Buffy said. "And I'm not dating."

"Hell," Calehan scoffed. "I'm not." He sighed heavily and kicked at the water, splashing it up onto their thighs. "I know you feel the same way I do, but Mom loved you. She didn't want to leave you."

"But she did."

"She was sick, Buffy."

"So am I! And I'm still here." Buffy breathed heavily, her chest rising and falling with speed. "I haven't left *any* of you." She looked away from her brother. "I've thought about it but I would never do what she did."

"I know, Buf." Calehan pulled her sunglasses down over her tears. "You love more than you hurt."

Buffy shook her head. "Loving you guys is different. You're family." Unwilling to make eye contact, Buffy watched the tide wash over her ankles. "What happens if it gets bad again and he has to leave me?" Her whisper was so soft that Calehan barely heard her. Buffy hoped he hadn't heard her and she could forget about this entire conversation.

"He will stay by your side through it." Calehan gripped her by the shoulders. "Time heals everything." Calehan tucked his head to meet her gaze. "Plus, it sounds like this new guy is pretty patient."

"He is," Buffy pushed Calehan's arms from her shoulders. She wiped furiously at her eyes before covering them with her tinted glasses again. "I think I love him." Buffy almost threw up as soon as the words left her lips.

"That's great!"

"It's not," Buffy sniffled, desperate to keep the tears at bay. "How do you do this?" Gasping for air, the tears fell. Calehan threw an arm around her shoulders, a heavy weight grounding her to the spot. "I'm going to ruin it."

"No, you won't." Calehan squeezed her shoulder in his palm. "When you love someone, you make it work. Tell the truth, be there for them, and fall in love with them again and again. That's all you have to do."

"You make it sound easy," Buffy scoffed.

"It is," Calehan said. "The loving part is easy. Choosing each other is easy. It isn't supposed to be hard."

"I'm scared," Buffy whispered. "I'm not good enough for him."

"Buffy, how can you say that?" Calehan bopped her in the head with the heel of his hand.

"Don't hit me." Buffy retaliated with a smack to the center of his soft belly. Calehan doubled over in pain, the laughter robbing him of breath.

"You're a catch. Anyone would be lucky to be with you." Calehan stared at her in confusion.

"I'm just-—" Buffy broke off and looked at the sea. The ocean went on forever from here, not an island or boat in sight from this little hill they had to themselves. "I'm so angry. I'm always in meetings that make me angry or writing grants that piss me off or dealing with shitty board members. I hate the world." She huffed and threw her arms. "I'm depressed and anxious and I'm mean and dismissive. I left home and went to college and got this job for what? I'm still just an Indian woman pimped out for money. Nothing has changed in five hundred years, and I don't know why I bother even trying."

Calehan shook his head.

"That's how it feels!" Buffy rubbed her temples. "No matter what I do, it is never enough. How can I ever heal myself when the entire world has their boot on my neck?"

Calehan looked at her, waiting for the storm to quiet in her mind.

"I don't know how to not be angry." Buffy shrugged in defeat. "I want to be all of those things for him, for myself, but I don't know how. I'm so mean to him and he keeps coming back and I don't understand why! Even when I'm trying my best, I'm hurting him." Sobs overtook her then, all speech turning to gibberish. Calehan pulled her into a tight hug.

"I can't convince you that you're amazing and kind and worthy of all the love in the world." Calehan spoke into her hair. "But what I do know is that this person knows all of those things. You said he's seen you at work, seen you with the community and your friends. Don't you think he's seen enough of you to love it all?"

"I'm not good for him," Buffy complained.

Calehan was silent, a heavy anchor to the world. "Why do you think you know what is best for him?" Calehan rose a brow at her look of fury. "It sounds like he has been clear. He wants you. You make him happy. Would you rather torture him and yourself forever?"

Buffy wanted to scream in frustration. That was the one thing she couldn't bear to do; hurt Santiago. The thought of him being in pain caused physical turmoil in her stomach and she couldn't bear the acid reflux much longer. Calehan was right, she owed it to Santiago to at least *try*. He deserved to make his own choices just like she did. If he wanted to choose her, then she had to let him.

"I should go back."

"Yes," Calehan agreed, "But not for a few days at least. You came all this way, after all."

"Fine," Buffy sighed, wiping her face. "Only if Xiomara makes menudo."

"She bought tripe this morning, just for you." Calehan held his sister to his chest. "You deserve a love like this. I've never seen you so happy, even though you're scared. I'm proud of you."

"Shut up." Buffy shoved herself free from his arms, taking off in the sand, kicking it back at him to deter his chase. She threw herself down beside Xiomara, freshly woken from her cat nap. Anubis was under a towel beside her and he stuck his nose out to lick Buffy's sea-sprayed legs.

"Lista, mi vida?" Calehan pulled Xiomara from the blanket, shouldering the picnic basket while Buffy shook out their picnic blanket.

Xiomara wrapped her arm around Buffy's waist, leaning on her shoulder.

"I'm so happy you came, sister."

"Me too. I missed you." Buffy held her back, Anubis weaving in and out of their legs.

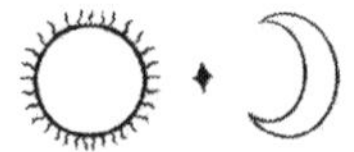

Tucked into the star quilt Rosebud had gifted them last Christmas, Buffy felt cold. When was the last time she slept alone? Now that she had decided to give Santiago a chance, she couldn't think of anything except him. Throwing the covers from her body, she dug her phone out of her suitcase from the back of the closet. Plugging it in beside her bed, she turned it on for the first time in more than twenty-hour hours.

Camila: Santiago came by. I thought you called him.
Buffy: I tried, he didn't answer.
Camila: He was worried about you.
Buffy: Did you get rid of him?
Camila: I told him you went to visit Calehan. Didn't say where.
Buffy: Was he mad?
Camila: No, he looked like shit though.
Buffy: I'll text him.

Taking a measured deep breath, Buffy steeled herself to finally read his messages. Instead, there was a voice memo waiting for her.

"Buffy." Her heart cracked open at the sound of his voice. Santiago sounded defeated, exhausted. "I'm sorry about missing your call. You didn't have to disappear on me. Could you just let me know you're okay and I'll leave you alone forever, okay? I'm just worried about you. I missed your call and then you just disappeared—" He cut himself off, clearing his throat before continuing. "Let me know you're okay, please."

Fuck.

Even when she was treating him poorly, he only worried about her. No regard for himself or how evil her actions had been to ghost him and run halfway across the world. Guilt plagued her, mind, body and soul. She had broken him. Once again, she ruined everything.

Checking her Wi-Fi connection, Buffy called him.

"Buffy." The relief in his voice brought tears to her eyes.

"I'm sorry," Buffy whispered.

"Are you okay?" Raw, his voice was deeper than she had ever heard it.

"I'm fine." She picked at a loose thread on the bottom of her shirt. "I came to visit my brother. You'd love his fiancé. She's Mexican too."

"I love her already." Santiago laughed then, a smile finally rising on Buffy's lips.

Buffy rushed to fill the silence between them. "I'm only staying for a week."

"Is it warm there?" Santiago asked.

"Super warm, you'd love it." Silence swelled between them. "I'm sorry I didn't tell you I was leaving. That was wrong of me." Buffy held her breath, terrified that she had ruined things between them forever, that she had succeeded in pushing him away. "And for missing Abuela's birthday. I feel horrible." Buffy held her breath, trying to control the guilt burning in her gut. "How is she?"

"She's okay." Santiago said.

"When I come back..." Buffy started, hesitating on what to say next. "Can we get that salmon dip again? I dream of it sometimes."

He laughed then, full-bellied and deep, a real laugh this time. Buffy smiled. She was making him laugh from halfway across the world.

"Definitely." Santiago sighed, and Buffy envisioned him rubbing the stress from his forehead. Stress that she had caused. Her eyes closed in shame. "Did you do anything fun yet?"

Buffy told him about everything, the dry air, the beach, her brother and his fiancée so in love it made her jealous.

"Tell me about your case," Buffy whispered, settling further into the bed.

Santiago's voice lulled her to a sleep heavier than she had in days.

CHAPTER 16

"Wake up."

A shrill voice cut through Buffy's thoughts at the same time a large weight pounced on her abdomen. Anubis licked all over her face before she was awake enough to duck under the blankets. Groaning, she used the quilt to wipe the spit from her face.

"If this is what having children is like then I don't want any," Buffy grumbled and let herself roll out of the covers and onto the floor.

Anubis followed her down, tapping his toes all around her in the hopes she was ready to play with him.

"Come on," Xiomara called the hairless dog out of the room. "We need to go run some errands and swing by my office."

"I'm fine with a book and your sunny patio out there," Buffy countered with a smile.

"Too bad." Xiomara smiled devilishly and disappeared.

Ugh.

Buffy felt like she had been hit by a truck. The forced correction to her sleep schedule might have been a mistake. Grabbing her phone, she took a quick selfie of her mussed hair and sprawled position on the floor and fired it off to Santiago.

Buffy: Remind me not to get a dog.

Santiago: Is that my shirt?

Buffy: No...

Buffy bit her lip to hide her mischievous smile. Showered and dressed, Buffy met Xiomara in the living room, where her arms were stuffed with tote bags. Xiomara struggled with the many straps of the tote bags before she wrestled her sunglasses free and onto her face. Hooking a leash to Anubis, she led them downstairs.

"You walk really fast for how tiny you are," Buffy grunted, struggling to keep up with Xiomara's rapid pace.

"Tiny body, giant attitude." Xiomara laughed and Buffy couldn't help but join her.

"Well, that's for sure." Buffy tapped her hip against Xiomara. "How'd my brother convince you to move over here for him anyway?"

Hoping her voice was casual enough, Buffy prodded for answers. Calehan had royally fucked up by keeping secrets from Xiomara, yet somehow it had all worked out in his favor. Buffy wanted to know how to make everything work out in her favor with Santiago.

"He didn't." Xiomara stopped at the first fruit vendor, conversing easily with him in Spanish. Buffy could only pick up words here and there. The accent here was vastly different from what she heard in California. She stood silently, watching as Xiomara picked out tomatoes, peppers, and limes. They moved on to the next vendor selling all kinds of bread and baked goods.

Buffy picked out a sugar-coated treat that was shaped like a heart made of thousands of shiny buttery layers. It cracked like ice beneath her teeth, the taste of cinnamon like coming home.

"I couldn't live without him," Xiomara said.

Buffy pointed her attention back to her sister, no longer lost in the sugary goodness of her pastry.

"Cal didn't convince me to come here. He begged, but he didn't propose marriage or threaten to leave the job and move back to Bunchberry." Xiomara led them to a small bench beneath a tree, sitting down to eat their matching pastries. "Well, he did offer to turn it down briefly, but he wasn't being serious."

Buffy laughed with her and threw a crunchy piece of pastry to Anubis.

"It hurt so much to be without him," Xiomara continued. "I was hurt, justifiably, pero dios mío I have never *ached* like that before. With Javier, he was taken from me and I had no choice but to move on. With your brother, all of that hurt and pain was my own doing. He was still alive, he still wanted me, he still loved me." Xiomara shrugged, looking Buffy in the eye. "I chose myself. He became part of me."

Buffy mulled over Xiomara's words in her head. Xiomara chose the happiest version of herself, which included Calehan.

"How did you know it was him? That he was a piece of you and not someone else?" Buffy said.

"You just know." Xiomara sighed. "I wish I had a better answer for you, but I don't. I can't see my life without Cal. He's there when I imagine our future and he's there when I remember the past. He is the first person I want to tell all of my good news to and the only person I trust with my bad news. Being without him is like breathing underwater, I'm alive but just barely. Being with him feels like the world will never end."

"You two are gross."

"You're such a bitch." Xiomara laughed and pushed Buffy in the shoulder.

Buffy fell exaggeratedly to the side, as though Xiomara's tiny frame had any effect on her heavier build. Anubis barked and jumped up to put his paws in Buffy's lap.

"Get her, Anubis! She's attacking me!" Buffy shrieked out between laughs, though Anubis only licked her.

"I have to swing by the lab to check on a few things for our new collection." Xiomara stood and gathered Anubis' leash. "By *I*, I meant *we*." Xiomara smiled wide, pleased with herself. Buffy sighed and resigned herself to walking further in the blistering sun.

"Collection of what?" Buffy stretched when she stood from the bench. The sunshine made her feel *alive*. For the first time, her head felt clear and her heart felt light, even without Santiago bringing her to orgasm. Hope filled her chest. Perhaps people could grow, even people like Buffy.

"Artifacts." Xiomara looked at Buffy as though she had three heads.

"Are they Native?" Buffy's mind was whirling.

"No." Xiomara chuckled. "I spent my first year here repatriating everything I could from this area. The rest of the country is harder to get on board with repatriation, but the university is pretty progressive. This collection we're working on now was seized by the cops a few months ago."

"The cops?" Buffy raised her brows. "Damn, you working for the pigs now?"

"Not at all." Xiomara laughed. "They were tracing drugs and ended up in this old man's apartment where they found six hundred and thirty-three ancient artifacts. Ceramics, bronze tools, rock fossils, even a piece of a fresco we think is Roman. It's insane. Almost impossible to catalog because we have no provenience."

"You're losing me."

"We don't know where the items were found, so we can't accurately date or assign them a culture or time period yet. We need more information that we might never get." Xiomara scanned a card in her wallet and opened a large glass door. "Anyway, the cops asked the university to authenticate and I took the lead."

They entered an office with Xiomara's name on the door. *Xiomara Chavez, Professor of Archaeology*. Buffy was grateful for the English translation underneath the larger words in Spanish. She could guess, but it would be an admittedly uneducated guess.

"You have an office and everything." Buffy whistled low. Xiomara was impressive when she came to Bunchberry three years ago. Her career trajectory had only benefited from the move to Spain.

"I'm some real shit out here." Xiomara threw her curls over her shoulder. "How are you, 'manita?"

Buffy fought the urge to cringe at the sweet nickname. The perception amongst all of these family members was too fucking great. Xiomara looked straight through her.

"Do you have x-ray vision or something?" Buffy huffed.

Xiomara laughed, ignoring the comment and continuing her fiddling over the artifacts in front of them.

"I'm fine," Buffy blurted.

Xiomara didn't answer, only the clink of the artifacts on her nails breaking the silence.

"I don't deserve him." Buffy whispered.

"Can I tell you what Javier told me?" Xiomara looked up at her.

Buffy nodded.

"I had depression before he died, who doesn't at some point?" The two shared a bitter laugh. "After he proposed, he was away for a few months and I had one of my darkest times ever."

Buffy held her breath. She couldn't imagine Xiomara depressed. She was a ray of sunshine, of light, of happiness who only smiled and never frowned. If people like Xiomara could have depression, how was there any hope for the eternally angry Buffy?

"Javier was so relaxed, so unbothered, no worries, no fears. I didn't get it, I didn't understand. Sometimes I would just get stuck thinking of reasons he should leave me, that my mood and negative thoughts and my sadness and my father's death—all of that was reason enough for him to move on," Xiomara explained.

"Why didn't he?" Buffy wondered. This was why she didn't get close to people—her darkness always dragged them down too. It wasn't fair. Her mother's choice had affected every member of their family and it terrified Buffy to know she was capable of the same thing.

"I asked him to, many times. Asked why he was with me, why he stayed with someone who couldn't control her own thoughts." Xiomara set the artifacts down, looking Buffy in the eye. "Do you know what he said to me?"

Buffy shook her head.

"He asked if the roles were reversed, if he was the one pulled into the dark, would I leave him?"

Buffy couldn't help the surprise and her mouth fell open.

"I think I did the same thing." Xiomara laughed. "But he was right. I wouldn't leave him for any of the things I thought he should leave me for. He loved me, not in spite of those things but because of them. He was happy to spend the rest of his life being my sunshine, the one who kept me out of the dark. As long as I tried my best too."

Buffy could hear the tears in her future sister's voice.

"And he did. Until the day he died." Xiomara sighed at the memory. "Then I took some meds, got some therapy, and so on, and I'm chilling now. Sometimes the darkness comes back but I'm strong enough to handle it. Plus, your brother radiates love just like the sun. It helps."

Buffy nodded. When she mulled it over, she could only come to the same conclusions. She would drop everything for Calehan if he was struggling the way she was. If Joy called her and asked to move in with her and Camila, she would do it in a heartbeat. If Santiago was pulled into the darkness, she would dive down with him to tear him away from it.

It was only right she let him do the same for her. If that was what he wanted.

Buffy looked out over the rooftop, buildings sparkling below her, the sea reaching toward them from the shore. She sipped her red sangria and cast a glance over to her brother. Calehan had Xiomara tucked between him and the railing, enveloping her completely with his significantly larger figure. Xiomara was laughing with her head thrown back, mouth open so wide that Buffy was shocked a bird didn't shit in it.

Buffy was jealous of them. She wanted to be wrapped in Santigo's arms, listening to him laugh in her ear. Spain hadn't given her the distance she'd been seeking. Instead, it had slapped her in the face with love and romance and pointed her toward the path she was most afraid to walk. So much for the seven days of no Santiago thoughts.

Snapping a quick photo of the lovebirds, she fired it off to Santiago.

Buffy: save me
Santiago: you look just like your brother
Buffy: take that back

"When is your flight again?" Calehan asked, fingers dripping with garlic wine sauce.

"It got canceled so they rebooked me on an earlier one." Buffy avoided Xiomara's gaze.

"They moved it sooner instead of later?" Calehan obliterated the fabric napkin he had, stealing Xiomara's to use instead.

"Well, they let me choose. But it's not like I can just take another week off work," Buffy said. She tossed her hair over her shoulder, feigning nonchalance.

"Sure, work calls." Xiomara eyed her knowingly.

Buffy ignored the quip and spooned another mouthful of seafood paella into her mouth.

"Can you tell me a little about this guy then?" Calehan asked. "I've been waiting so patiently but you haven't even said his name."

"Why do you need to know his name?" Buffy stared at him in confusion.

"Buffy!" Calehan exclaimed, covering his heart as though she had shot him.

Buffy rolled her eyes. "Fine."

Settling into the cushions behind her, she picked up her glass of sangria to hide her smile. "His name is Santiago. He's thirty-two, a lawyer, Pueblo and Mexican."

"Like brother, like sister." Xiomara snickered, nosing Calehan in the neck. "Is he tall?"

"About my height," Buffy said.

"What's he like?" Calehan pressed.

"He's nice."

"Never change, little sister." Calehan grinned at her like a proud father and Buffy wished the couch would absorb her.

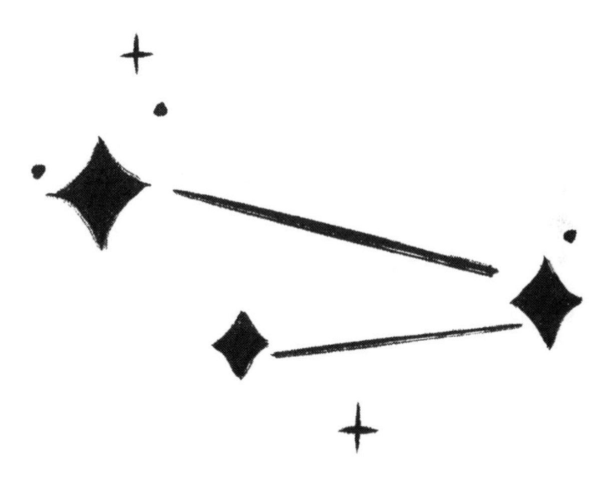

CHAPTER 17

Santiago blinked. His eyes were dry even though he had switched to glasses hours ago. Antiseptic burned his nose, the skin cracked and red from constant rubbing. Santiago couldn't resist the urge to rub it again, pain ebbing from the center of his face. Opening his text messages, Santiago pulled up his conversation with Buffy.

She was long asleep now, the time difference between them significant. Scrolling up until he found her most recent picture, he tapped on it and opened it larger. Buffy was seated beside her brother, identical smiles plastered on their faces. In mirror image of her brother, her left eye tooth was turned in ever so slightly. Santiago could close his eyes and envision her smile in the blackness of his mind. He couldn't wait to see it again. All he had to do was make it until he saw her smile again. He could do this.

Opening his patient app, Santiago scheduled a new appointment with his therapist. He hadn't had a session with her in a few months, but he figured sooner was better with what was coming. Abuela Paulina's kidneys had finally given out. Santiago knew that he had mere days left with her. Anxiety set up a home in his gut and stole his sleep and now here he was, at the hospital, praying selfishly for his terminally ill grandma to survive.

A deep voice ripped him from his thoughts.

"Are you alone?" Pear ambled into the waiting room, still dressed in pajamas. Golden shoulders stuck out of his white tank top, low-slung black sweatpants dragging along the dirty floor with his slides.

"Myra is getting coffee." Santiago nodded down the hall.

"No Buffy?" Pear sat down across from Santiago, his voice still raspy with sleep.

"She's out of town." Santiago kept his eyes on his knees.

"Missed Abuela's birthday and her death?" Pear whistled lowly. "That's gotta be some kind of karma, right?"

"Don't," Santiago huffed with exhaustion. He couldn't handle this right now. Abuela Paulina wasn't expected to make it through the night and he refused to call Buffy, effectively ruining her vacation. Santiago knew that she didn't visit her family frequently. Buffy deserved to have a happy time without all his baggage. He knew that she was likely already beating herself up for missing Abuela's birthday in the first place. Knowing she was dying would push her over the edge and he couldn't do that without being there to catch her. It would have to wait.

"What are you doing, primo?" Pear settled his elbows on his knees, leaning across the aisle toward Santiago. "You're head over heels for this woman and she's dating other people, disappearing without a word, and now she isn't here when you need her most?"

"I haven't told her about Abuela," Santiago muttered, too tired to argue with his fiery cousin. Pear was protective of him, like an older brother, even though they were the same age. He loved him for it but right now he couldn't take it. His heart was barely beating as it was.

"Okay, she still missed her birthday and flew to Europe without saying a word to you," Pear huffed with annoyance. "Buffy isn't good enough for you, Santi. You're worth more than being some chick's fuck toy."

"Can we not do this right now?" Santiago pressed his thumbs into his temples, searching for relief that eluded him.

"You could at least tell her that Abuela is sick," Pear said.

Santiago sighed and opened his phone, scrolling through messages until he found the photo. Buffy had her arms around her brother, a wide smile on her face. Anubis, who was obsessed with Buffy, was standing against them, begging for attention.

"Who is that she's with? I've never seen her smile like that." Pear squinted at the photo.

"Her older brother. She hasn't seen him in a few years." Santiago glared at his cousin.

"Oh." Pear crossed his arms. "Isn't Spain where they do all that clubbing stuff?"

Pear almost continued his thought but thankfully cut himself short with one look at his cousin's face.

Santiago sighed in relief. He knew that he wasn't looking his best, having been at the hospital for nearly forty-eight hours now. Myra had met him here that morning, only leaving to bring him food and a change of clothes. They had slept in Abuela Paulina's hospital room together the night before, sharing a footrest between their two hard plastic chairs. Myra reappeared now, two cups of steaming hot coffee in her hands.

Pear stood and kissed her cheek, squeezing her tightly to his side before sitting again.

"Did the doctor come by yet?" Myra asked, curling up in her chair like a little kid.

Santiago shook his head, drinking the bitter, over-steeped coffee and relishing in the toxic burn.

"It's Abuela, she's too stubborn to die." Pear bumped Santiago with his knee, trying in vain to bring a smile from the sullen man.

Santiago scrubbed his hands over his face, dropping his head into his hands with a heavy sigh. He stared at the ground, his cousins barely in his line of sight. Myra and Pear shared a glance, worry etched into their mirrored lips. Abuela's lips. The look on Myra's face said more than words; stubbornness wouldn't be enough this time. Abuela Paulina had lived a long life full of hardships. At some point, the body wanted to rest. He knew that she had fought hard for more than a decade. Abuela Paulina deserved to be at peace.

But Santiago didn't want to be without his grandmother. He was selfish and he desperately wanted her to survive. She was in every memory of his life up to now and he couldn't fathom saying goodbye for the final time. The world couldn't exist without her. Returning to normal life without her seemed impossible. Void of her presence, the house felt like it was turning against him, unhappy with Abuela's departure. He hated that house without her in it. The thought of going back alone made him want to vomit.

"Mr. Morales?" A nurse approached them, her fingers white against the clipboard in her hands. "Would you like to say goodbye?"

Together, the three cousins walked the short distance to Abuela Paulina's hospital room. Myra and Santiago walked straight in, taking seats on either side of Abuela Paulina. Pear hesitated at the door, his eyes glued to Abuela Paulina's blanket covered toes. They were still and Pear swallowed at her lifelessness. Santiago glanced at Myra, communicating with her silently. She stood and joined Pear at the door.

Santiago cherished this moment alone with his grandmother and sat beside her on the thin hospital bed.

"You look so much like your father," Abuela Paulina muttered, the whites of her eyes spotted yellow and brown.

"I think he looks like *you*," Santiago said, taking her hand in his.

"You two did not get those bushy eyebrows from me," Abuela Paulina chided, tapping him on the forearm with her pointer finger. She sucked in a breath, trying to regain what was lost with her speaking. Santiago bit his lip and looked away. His skin prickled to see his grandmother in pain with no way to stop it.

Clammy hands wrapped around his and he looked up at Abuela Paulina.

"Where is your Buffy?"

Santiago swallowed. "She's visiting her brother in Spain. I haven't told her about..." He trailed off, unable to finish the statement.

"That's okay, mijo, let her enjoy her trip." Abuela Paulina coughed, struggling to catch her breath. Santiago held onto her hand while she hacked, rubbing her back when she leaned forward. She reached for the cup of water beside her bed. Santiago held it to her mouth, helping her take a long sip. "Don't wait too long to tell her that you love her."

"Abuela," Santiago chided. She didn't need to be worrying about him right now.

"Life is short. I want my grandson to be happy." Abuela Paulina's hand shook as she reached up to caress Santiago's cheek. She wiped the tear from his eye. "Tell her how you feel, be there for her, and it will all work out. The two of you were made for each other."

"You think so?"

"I know." Abuela Paulina said.

Santiago smiled and leaned forward, tucking his head into her neck while they hugged. She smelled the same here as she always had, like coconut oil and pan dulce. If he closed his eyes, he could conjure the Abuela Paulina from his childhood, the one with no ailments, no heartbreak, and no goodbyes.

He felt a hand on his back and looked up to find Pear finally inside the room. Santiago leaned back, giving his cousin space to hug their grandma. With a hand on Abuela's knee, Myra climbed onto the bed at her feet and joined the boys.

"Somos niños otra vez," Myra said, bumping her forehead against Pear's.

"Son mis niños por siempre." Abuela Paulina looked at each of them with a smile that only grew wider.

Chapter 18

Camila was waiting in passenger pickup, her grandmother's wood-paneled station wagon roaring audibly beside the curb. Lips rolled in on themselves, Camila wore a tight expression. Buffy felt a rock drop into her belly.

"What happened?" Buffy asked.

"Santiago's grandmother passed away," Camila said.

Buffy blinked. "Abuela Paulina?"

Camila nodded.

"I just spoke with him though and he didn't say anything about his grandmother..." Buffy didn't understand. She had only been gone five days. Abuela Paulina was the picture of health less than one week ago.

"Santiago didn't want to tell you. He thought you weren't coming home for a few more days." Camila opened the driver's side door. "She passed last night."

Buffy struggled to comprehend Camila's words. Abuela Paulina had been old, but she had been full of life and energy and dying seemed so far off her radar that Buffy couldn't really believe she was gone. Nothing felt real anymore.

"Take me there," Buffy said, throwing her duffel in the back seat and sliding in beside Camila. "Quickly."

"Duh," Camila scoffed, pulling away from the curb.

Nearing two in the morning, the streets were fairly empty, though Camila had to navigate multiple construction detours. At one point, Camila took a downward hill so quickly Buffy had to close her eyes to save herself from throwing up.

Buffy pulled the extra set of keys from her pocket. Fingering the silver key, she gripped it tightly in her hand. Santiago had left them behind a few weeks ago and Buffy had carried them in her purse ever since. She meant to give them back to him, truly, she did. But it just never came up and Buffy never mentioned it. He never asked, so Buffy kept it her dirty little secret.

Clearly, keeping it had been the right choice. She wasn't confident knocking on the door and a phone call would wake a sleeping Santiago in the middle of the night. Hopefully he wouldn't be upset at her intrusion.

Letting herself into the walkup, she toed off her sneakers and left them beside her duffel bag in the hallway. Santiago's red Pueblo moccasins were beside the door, thrown haphazardly. She straightened their leather and placed them upright before heading upstairs.

Buffy found him in his room, facedown on top of his blankets, still dressed, socks on. She hesitated in the doorway. What if he didn't want her here?

Watching him sleep, Buffy examined his face. His eyes and nose were swollen and red, his mouth hanging open so he could breathe. Buffy felt guilty for being away. She wished he had told her what was going on. She would've booked the next flight home.

That was exactly why he hadn't told her. He was far too good to her.

Sighing, Buffy chewed her lip, still stuck in the doorway. Maybe she should sleep downstairs, see him in the morning. Buffy tried to imagine sleeping on the couch, beside

Abuela Paulina's now vacant armchair. Santiago grunted in his sleep, his eyes screwing up in a mask of pain.

The thought of sleeping away from Santiago made her heart ache. She needed to see, with her own eyes, exactly how he was doing. If she was the one in mourning, she would want him to lay beside her indefinitely. She would have to be pried from his embrace.

Buffy had to trust his words. She had to take a leap of faith and hope that the desire he expressed toward her was real and true. Santiago had shown her through words and actions just how much he wanted her. She hoped his feelings hadn't changed since she'd been away. With a deep breath, she stepped inside his room and shut the door behind her.

Crouching beside Santiago, she rubbed his arm gently. Softly, Buffy called his name, trying her best not to startle him. He likely wasn't expecting someone to be in his bedroom at two a.m.

"Buffy." A hazy smile pulled at his lips, his eyes closing again. Relief flooded her at his delight. He mumbled sleepily. "Star of my dreams." With a jolt, Santiago flipped over, wide eyes staring at her. "Are you real?"

"Hi," she said, offering a small wave. She bit her lip. "I heard and I wanted to check on you."

"Why are you here?" Santiago was stunned, still half-asleep.

Buffy's mouth went dry. Maybe he didn't want her here. Maybe he was already done with her. Maybe taking this risk had been a mistake after all.

"I didn't mean it like that." Santiago leaned forward and kissed her softly. Her lips were timid, but she kissed him back. "I thought you weren't coming home for a few more days?"

"I moved to an earlier flight." Buffy shrugged. Glancing away from his intense gaze, she contemplated saying more. "I wanted to see you." She hesitated. "I missed you."

It was as though Buffy had dropped liquid light into his eyes. The smile on his mouth was small, but his eyes shone brighter than the entire room. He pulled Buffy back onto the bed with him, rolling her under him in a tight embrace.

"Santi." Buffy rested a palm against his face, rubbing gently at his purple shaded eyes. "I'm sorry I wasn't here for everything. Can I stay with you for a little while? I want to make sure you're okay." Her other hand fisted in the comforter while she waited for his response.

"Please stay," Santiago whispered, his brows furrowed in worry.

"I will. I promise." Buffy tucked her nose into his hair. Wrapping her legs around his middle, she tucked his head into the dip of her neck, rubbing her fingers against his scalp. "I'm not going anywhere," she said against the top of his head, tightening her grip around him. "I am so sorry, Santiago."

Santiago responded in kind, pressing his lips against the skin of her collarbone, rubbing his nose across her neck. She could feel him fall asleep, his breathing finally turning slow and deep. Buffy fell asleep with butterflies in her belly, dreaming only of them—together.

They stayed molded to each other through the night, neither willing to let the other out of their grasp. Buffy was scared, but not of loving him anymore. She was scared to see Santiago in pain, in mourning. What if she wasn't enough for him?

Her mother's death had changed everything about Buffy. Before she died, Buffy's mean streak was easily managed by her mother's gentle guidance. Abuela Paulina had been one of Santiago's closest family members. What if her death changed him too?

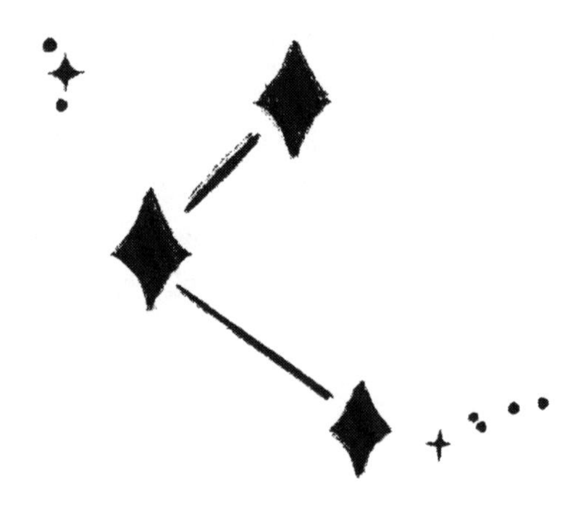

Chapter 19

Buffy woke up alone. Throwing the sheets from her body in panic, her gaze darted around the room in search of Santiago. She heard him chuckle behind her.

"Looking for someone?"

"You scared me," Buffy huffed, feigning annoyance despite the blush across her high cheeks. Her heart was hammering in her chest, as though she had tasted her worst fear on the tip of her tongue.

"I'm not going anywhere, Buffy," Santiago said.

"Neither am I." Buffy followed him into the bathroom.

"Are you sure?" Santiago turned to face her, peace in his eyes. "I am all in, Buffy. All of the feelings, all of the labels, all of you."

"Me too." Buffy met him chest to chest, wrapping her long fingers around his face. "I am all in for you, Santiago. All of you." Closing her eyes, she pressed her forehead to his and rubbed their noses together. "I'm sorry I made you wait so long."

Santiago laughed, pulling her in for a kiss. Taking advantage of his open mouth, Buffy licked against his tongue, savoring all the feelings she had withheld into this moment.

"I could get used to this." Santiago tucked a strand of red hair behind her ear.

"I want you to." Buffy blushed at the look on Santiago's face and turned him around to face the sink as he had been before she found him. She tucked her chin into the crook of his neck, inhaling the natural scent of his skin and hiding the smile stuck to her lips. She wrapped her arms around his middle.

"How long have you been awake?" Buffy watched Santiago in the mirror, his eyes closed while he rested in her arms.

"A while," Santiago whispered.

A horn blared outside, pulling Buffy's attention to the open bathroom window. Facing the busy San Franciscan street, the warm smell of masa floated through the open window and Buffy found herself imagining Abuela downstairs. She would've rolled them bean and egg flautas, using the corn tortillas from the night before. The smell was so vibrant and memorable that it conjured Abuela right there in the bathroom with them, her voice and scent of her perfume following.

Buffy squeezed her eyes shut. No wonder Santiago was awake.

"Do you cut your hair in mourning?" His gentle voice startled her and the scent of Abuela's perfume drifted away.

"Usually," Buffy answered him.

"You cut it a few weeks ago." Santiago turned around in her arms, sandwiching her face between his palms. Worry etched into his brow. It was true, Buffy cut her hair often. Sometimes once a month, sometimes only once a year. In the darkest of times, she cut her braids until there wasn't enough left anymore. Now, her hair remained at the center of her back, and twice a year, on her mother's birthday and her death day, Buffy cut the end of her braid and burned it. The dates were far enough apart that most people didn't even notice.

"I've been mourning for years," Buffy replied, opening her eyes to meet his gaze. "I cut my hair twice a year; the day of my mother's birth and the day of her death. It helps, a little bit." Buffy exposed herself to him and prayed he still saw her the same. She didn't want his pity.

Santiago blinked, wetness shining on his cheeks. He pulled her closer. Buffy rubbed under his eyes with her thumb, warming the cold skin beneath.

"We can cut yours, if you want," Buffy suggested. "Sometimes it makes me feel better. We'll burn it after, some tobacco, some sage. It will feel good."

Nodding, Santiago bent down wordlessly. When he stood, he held a black machine in his hands. Buffy lit the bundle of sage resting in the abalone shell on the counter, muttering a prayer as the flames singed the leaves. Carefully, Buffy buzzed Santiago's hair short to his skin. She rubbed over the short hair when she was finished, squeezing his neck softly before stepping away.

Santiago swept his hair into an empty corn husk and set it on the counter to be burned later. He smudged himself, then Buffy.

"Shower with me?" he asked, voice thin like a wisp.

"Always." Buffy took his hand and followed him into the water.

Squeezed into the tub together, they washed each other, and Buffy fought to keep from crying. Santiago hadn't made a move to initiate sex with her yet. It would've made her panic if not for the constant touch he kept on her. His tenderness held an intimacy she'd yet to experience, and the feelings were overwhelming.

His hands washed over her naked body, every wrinkle and crevice and roll. Somehow, this innocent touch felt more intimate than when he slid his fingers inside of her and it managed to keep her panic at bay. She knew in her rational mind that sex was the last thing on his mind, but she didn't know how else to connect without it. All she could do was take it one day at a time and hope that she could be enough for him. Even without sex.

Freshly showered together, Buffy started breakfast in the kitchen while Santiago read over funerary paperwork. She figured he wouldn't have much of an appetite and made him a two-egg omelet. Thin slicing a serrano, she mixed onions and cilantro into the eggs, cooking them slowly over the flame.

"Do you have to go to work?" Santiago asked, watching her cook.

"I'm going to work remotely for now," Buffy answered.

"Really?" Santiago didn't hide his surprise.

"Don't make it a thing." Buffy kept her back to him. She could hear him snickering behind her. "I had a few more days off anyway—they jumped at the chance."

"Thank you." Santiago caught her wrist when she placed his omelet in front of him. He waited in silence until she met his gaze. "For everything." As he kissed the inside of her wrist, Buffy stroked her fingertips across the shell of his ear before pulling away.

"Sap." She took the seat across from him, cutting a small piece of her toast off. Gingerly, she topped the small slice with a scoop of her scramble and set it on the empty plate beside them. Flipping the mug upright, she poured a small amount of coffee and cream and gave it a stir. One small piece of bacon next to the toast, and the meal was complete.

Buffy avoided looking up at Santiago. She knew he would be staring at her with a closed lip smile and eyes full of love.

He was annoying.

Santiago ate the rest of his breakfast with his eyes closed. Buffy watched his face while they ate, the purple circles under his eyes dark and deep set. He looked ten years older than he really was. The shrill screech of Santiago's phone cut through the room and popped his eyes wide open.

Buffy stood and retrieved his phone from the living room.

"It's your dad." Buffy handed his phone over. Santiago took it and pressed it to his ear, reaching out to lace his fingers with hers before she could pull away. Buffy fought to keep her face neutral at the action. It was as though he knew she needed his reassurance, and he was willing to give it over and over again. Or he needed her touch for comfort. Maybe it was both.

Buffy listened to their conversation with half an ear, instead focused on the impending doom of meeting his family. Thanks to her policy of pushing everyone away, she had never met a partner's parents or siblings before. Ice flooded her veins and her palms grew sweaty at the thought of making small talk with his parents. What would they think of her? How much had Santiago told them? If they knew half as much as Pear, they probably already hated her.

Abuela Paulina had met Buffy before. That made things different. Meeting a nearly six-foot-tall red headed Cree woman wasn't an easy swallow for anyone. Add Buffy's sharp personality, resting bitch face, and tendency towards sarcasm and *boom*. Perfect storm for parental hate. Oh, and she also couldn't speak Spanish to any of them.

Great job, Buffy.

"Yeah, don't worry about it, Dad. I'll give them a call." Santiago spoke tightly and ended the phone call.

Buffy stroked over his hand where it was nestled in hers. "Is everything okay?"

"The funeral director has some questions about her clothes and jewelry, I guess." Santiago sighed and rubbed his palms over his face. "They need me to come down in person. I told my dad I would take care of it."

"Don't worry about it." Buffy ached to ease the pain from his face. Unsure of exactly how to comfort him, she stroked over his fresh buzz cut. "I can go down there and pick up her jewelry, make sure she's well-dressed for her journey." Saying goodbye was hard enough, Santiago didn't need to do it twice.

Santiago looked up at her. "You sure?" His gaze was woefully hopeful.

Buffy's heart broke at the look of relief in his eyes. Her chest cracked open, a bolt of pain shooting across her body and tingling across every bit of her skin. Seeing him like this hurt more than her own grief. Settling into his lap, Buffy tucked his head under her chin and grasped him tight.

"Of course." Buffy felt his breath against her neck. "I'd like to say goodbye to her."

Santiago's grip dimpled into the thick muscle of her round thighs, and he kissed the exposed skin of her chest. He tucked his hand into the fleshy roll of skin above her hips.

Tilting back, Santiago kissed her cheek. "Thank you, Buffy Yellowbird." Peering at her, she watched his glossy eyes glaze over, her reflection sharp as a mirror in his wet eyes. "Buffy Morales has a nice ring to it."

Buffy raised a brow.

"Yellowbird-Morales?" Santiago raised a brow.

Buffy laughed to cover up the blush on her cheeks. It did have a nice ring to it, she had to admit.

"I'm going to marry you, Buffy Yellowbird-Morales." Santiago nosed her cheek until her lips met his.

"I'll think about it." Buffy kissed the surprise from his lips.

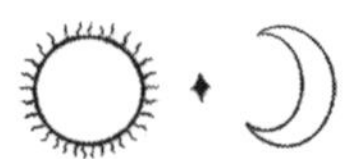

Pear took Abuela Paulina's favorite mug out of the cabinet and filled it with coffee. Taking it outside, he placed it on her favorite sunflower coaster and wished her a good morning. Whispering a prayer into a bundle of cedar, he lit the sprig and set it beside her coffee.

"Where's Buffy?" Pear asked, returning to the kitchen.

"She and Camila went down to pick up Abuela's effects." Santiago gestured to the bowl of bread on the table between them. "Buffy made bannock if you want some."

"Where's the frybread?" Pear took a piece of bannock and ripped it in half, inhaling the scent deeply.

"She likes bannock."

"What are you going to do with Abuela's room?" Pear said.

"Mom and Dad are coming here after the funeral so I figured they could handle it," Santiago said.

"That's good." Pear heaved a sigh and finally bit into his bannock. "I can't do it."

"I can't either." Santiago rubbed at his forehead as if he could hide the memory under his fingers.

"Is Buffy staying for a while?" Pear asked.

Santiago nodded. "She's working remotely and going with me to the funeral."

"Are you guys together now?"

Santiago nodded.

"That's what she said?" Pear raised one eyebrow.

"Yes, *John*. She told me that she wants to stay here and that she wants to be with me. Is that enough for you?" Santiago glared at him, exhaustion leaving his nerves raw.

Pear scoffed and bounced a piece of bannock off Santiago's forehead.

"I'm just making sure. Last thing I need is your heart broken right after all of this. I think I'll have to move." Pear laughed.

"I'm tired of you." Santiago rubbed at his forehead again. "I'm moving back to Colorado."

"With Buffy?" Pear raised a brow.

"Don't you have work to do?" Santiago muttered.

"I won my case yesterday, thanks for asking." Pear smiled at the guilty look on Santiago's face. "The interns are taking care of all of your paperwork while you're out. They've got us for at least a few weeks."

Santiago nodded. His eyes had glazed over while Pear updated him. At any moment, Abuela Paulina would come in the front door, fresh oranges and tamales in hand. She would join them in the kitchen and swat at Santiago for being an overbearing grandson. Then she would tap Pear upside the head and tell him to be nicer to Buffy and his cousin. And just like that, everything would be back to normal.

The door didn't open.

Chapter 20

Buffy sniffled and rubbed her nose. How long did it take for nose hairs to fall out from inhaling bleach? She should've worn a face mask. Funeral homes were supposed to smell like fake cookies and roses, not like the bleach scent of the emergency room.

A gurney wheeled by them, the white sheet almost flat against the bed. The mortician's assistant nodded at them with death in their ice blue eyes. Buffy glanced at Camila. They sat shoulder to shoulder on a white metal bench, the air suffocating them both.

"Mrs. Morales?" A man dressed in a suit and vest waved to them from the open double doors.

Buffy fought the urge to roll her eyes—Santiago had clearly embellished their relationship to the funeral home staff. It was exactly the kind of thing he would normally do to mess with her.

"Hi." Buffy shook the assistant's outstretched hand.

"Your grandmother is right this way." His blue eyes were bright in the dim yellow lights.

"Thank you," Buffy answered.

The mortician walked quickly, Buffy and Camila struggling to keep up with him. Buffy wondered how he had so much energy in a place actively decaying.

It smelled like mold down here, as though the death and decay had settled into the earth, grown within the building, and made this place its home. The chill tickled gooseflesh to both of their arms, Buffy grasping Camila's hand in hers when they entered the silver-walled room. A gust of cold air hit their faces and bodies as they stepped inside the giant fridge.

A body lay covered with a white sheet in the center of the room. There were a few other bodies out, pushed up against the walls on the far side of the room. Buffy blinked a few times, trying to comprehend the situation. It felt like she was looking through someone else's eyes, like it was a movie.

It wasn't.

Death was far different than this on Bunchberry. If an Elder died of natural causes like Abuela Paulina, they were handled and buried in tradition. The body wouldn't leave the family until it was to rest in the earth. Seeing so many unrested bodies stacked together like toy blocks turned her stomach. Human bodies shoved into a corner while they waited for their time in the autopsy spotlight. Buffy fought to keep her breakfast down.

The assistant unfolded the sheet down to Abuela Paulina's chest, her face and shoulders more purple than brown. Her veins were blue, no longer the warm-toned green of a sun kissed woman.

"This is a bag of the effects she came in with." The man handed an oversized plastic bag to Buffy. "This is the bag of effects that her family provided earlier." He placed that bag in Camila's arms. "I'll be right outside when you're finished. Don't worry about putting the jewelry on her—we have people to do that."

The door clicked shut behind him. Buffy and Camila stood in silence, eyes rooted to the closed door.

"*People to do that*?" Camila's eyes were wide with disgust.

Buffy was already evaluating each piece of jewelry with a level of scrutiny she hadn't employed since she was a science-nerd kid examining river rock. A small pair of gold cross studs were in the bag beside a gold cross necklace. Removing both items, she placed them gently on the stainless-steel table beside Abuela Paulina's head.

With shaking hands, Buffy pushed the first cross earring into Abuela Paulina's cold ear.

"Wait!" Camila whispered. "I brought offerings." Quickly, Camila lit a small sprig of sage and dropped it into a purple and white abalone shell settled at the bottom of Abuela Paulina's feet. She added a pinch of tobacco and a sprig of cedar and they returned to the task at hand.

Working together in silence, Buffy and Camila dressed Abuela Paulina in her favorite day dress. It was a lavender colored huipil, with multicolored flowers embroidered around the neck and shoulders. The flowers continued down to form a belt at the waist. Abuela Paulina was wearing it the first time Buffy met her and Santiago. Buffy wondered if Abuela Paulina had worn the same dress at her birthday dinner. Guilt rolled in her belly. She blinked the tears away.

Camila threaded a thin woven anklet around Abuela Paulina's death-swollen ankle. Buffy adjusted her long gray hair, combing it over her shoulders with her fingers so that it lay around her face like a halo. With her wedding ring in place and the gold warming her ashen skin, Abuela Paulina was ready for her journey into the afterlife.

Buffy and Camila held hands and gave individual prayers in silence, thanking Abuela Paulina for everything and wishing her a safe journey to the afterlife.

"I'll give you a moment alone." Camila disappeared from the room without a single sound.

"I'm sorry," Buffy whispered, her throat tightening to hold back tears. "I'm so sorry, Abuela. I shouldn't have left. I should have come to your birthday. I did it again. I'm so sorry." Buffy began to sob, dropping her head to Abuela's cold arm. "Everyone leaves me, Abuela. How am I supposed to do this? I don't know how to keep going when it hurts so much. Why did you have to go? Why couldn't you have stayed with me? How are we going to live without you? How is Santiago supposed to live without you? I'm not going to be enough for him. We both needed you."

Buffy cried until her tears turned cold against Abuela's icy skin, a reminder that the warmth of her spirit was long gone. Wiping her face and drying Abuela's arm, Buffy smoothed over her hair once more and opened the door.

"She's ready." Buffy nodded to the mortician and left before they could ask more questions.

Camila was waiting for her in the hall.

"I need to stop by the center really quick," Buffy said, following her down the long white hallway.

"You want to go to work?" Camila whined, pushing the door open behind Buffy.

"There's someone I have to see." Buffy slid into the car without another word.

"I'll check in on Miguel," Camila said, starting the engine. She parked in the garage underground and followed Buffy upstairs.

Buffy paused in the lobby. "Meet you back here in fifteen?"

"Vamos." Camila nodded in understanding and turned toward the kitchen.

Buffy took a deep breath to steel her nerves. Informing someone of a deceased loved one was the last thing she wanted to do today. But he deserved to know sooner than later.

She found him on the back porch, where the center hosted painting classes and yoga. Buffy nearly turned around and left. More than anything, she wanted someone else to deliver this news and take the responsibility off her shoulders. She forced herself to slide the door open and step outside.

Mr. Norman turned around at the sound, his face falling when he saw who it was.

"Hi, Mr. Norman." Buffy tried to smile.

"Buffy." He nodded once at her. "Haven't seen you around."

"I went to visit my brother in Europe." Buffy sat in the rocking chair beside him. "And then when I got home...I needed to take some time off."

Out with it already, Buffy.

"Paulina Morales passed," Buffy said, her eyes trained straight forward. She watched Mr. Norman out of the corner of her eye.

He barely moved, only his eyes moving across the mountains.

"I wondered where she was," he said.

"I'm sorry."

Mr. Norman waved her off with a thick hand.

"I hope I will still see you around the center," Buffy said.

Mr. Norman looked at Buffy. For the first time, he was smiling at her with his teeth.

Even stars have teeth, Mija.

"Can't get rid of me now." Mr. Norman patted her on the knee and settled back into his rocking chair.

Buffy took her cue to leave. Stopping by her office to gather a few things, Buffy found a pink envelope waiting on her desk. She didn't recognize the handwriting of her name. But as soon as she lifted the letter, she smelled masa. In shock, Buffy dropped the letter on her desk and hurried back downstairs.

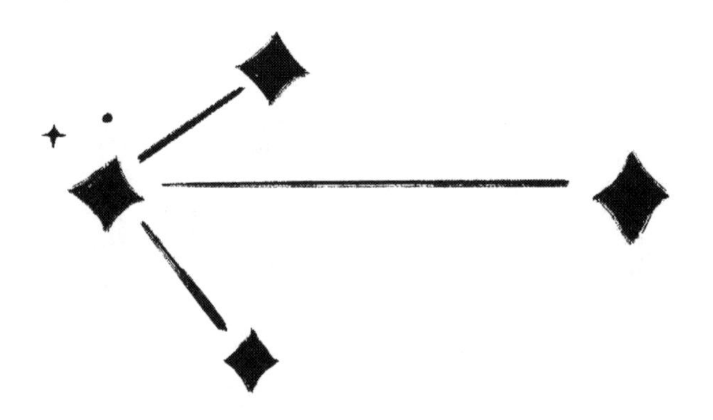

CHAPTER 21

Buffy squinted at the airline app on her phone.

"Why do our tickets say Vegas?" Buffy nudged Santiago with her foot. "We're not going to Colorado?"

"That's where Abuela wanted her ashes scattered," Santiago said. "There's a valley there. It's Abuela's favorite place in the whole world."

"Have you been?"

"Not since I was a kid."

"How much do I owe you?" Buffy asked without thinking.

Santiago glared at her with a playful smile.

Buffy sighed. "Thank you for buying my ticket."

"It's my pleasure, baby." Santiago lifted her leg and kissed the inside of her ankle. Sparks tickled up her like teasing fingers.

"What have you told your parents about me?" Buffy attempted to keep her voice even, but she expected Santiago could see through her like glass. Thanks to her no romance rule, Buffy hadn't met any of her partners' parents. The mere thought made her want to throw up.

"The basics." He leaned forward to grab the TV remote.

Buffy watched quietly as he turned it down a few notches.

"What do you want me to tell them?" Santiago asked.

"I don't know," Buffy whispered.

"We don't have to label this or anything yet." Santiago rubbed her calf. "They will probably call you my girlfriend—" Buffy groaned. "But it doesn't have to mean anything."

Buffy examined his face. She knew that Santiago would go weak in the knees if she called him her boyfriend. It meant something to him. It meant something to her too; she just didn't know how to explain how she felt.

But she owed it to him to try.

"It's not that I don't want to be your girlfriend." Buffy sat up, moving closer to Santiago. She folded her legs under her and scooted as close to him as she could. Santiago tucked the blanket tighter around them. "I just..." She sighed and tried to organize her jumbled thoughts.

Santiago rubbed his thumb against her thigh. She looked at him and blushed under his intense gaze. The way he stared at her felt like x-ray vision, as though he could see every thought like a neon sign above her head. Frankly, she wished he could and then she wouldn't have to say all her thoughts and feelings out loud.

"Don't look at me!" Buffy squealed and pushed his face toward the television screen. "I don't want to call you my boyfriend because you feel like more than that to me." The words came out of her in a rush.

Santiago tried to turn his head but she kept her hand against his face. He laughed and leaned into her grip.

"I said not to look at me!" Buffy squealed in embarrassment. She could hardly believe she'd said those words out loud.

"How am I supposed to focus on the TV when you say something like that?" Santiago smiled and Buffy giggled. His reaction to her admission made her heart feel light, as though it was going to break free from her chest and shoot through the ceiling and into the sky.

Buffy finally removed her hands from his face and let him tackle her into the couch.

"I'm going to call you my lover." Santiago rubbed their noses together.

"I beg you not to." Buffy scrunched her nose. Lover somehow felt worse than girlfriend.

"Soulmate?" Santiago kissed her jaw between laughs.

"How about ball and chain?" Buffy joked.

Santiago lifted his head from her neck and stared down at her. "You are the wind beneath my wings." He said it with complete sincerity, only his smirk afterward letting her know he was teasing.

Buffy laughed and pushed him off of her, scrambling off the couch and toward the stairs.

"I regret starting this conversation with you." Buffy hit the first step before Santiago caught up to her. Dropping to her hands and knees, she tried to make it up the stairs before he did.

Santiago was faster than her. He had her flipped on her back and pinned beneath him before she could even think to fight back. She sat down on the stair below her and let him climb over her.

"I'll be serious now." Santiago smiled and kissed her on the lips. "What do you think about partner?"

Buffy grumbled as she thought about it. It was better than boyfriend, certainly. But it still sounded weird to her ears.

Santiago kissed down her neck, distracting her from the over analysis going on in her head.

"Partner is fine." Buffy pulled his face back to hers. "For now."

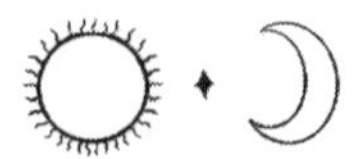

Locking the seat belt across her lap, Buffy opened the tiny airplane window. The air smelled cold and sterile. She pulled her surgical mask back over her nose and adjusted in the blue leather seat.

"I've never flown first class," Buffy muttered, stretching her long legs in front of her. It was a welcome feeling not being squished in an economy seat.

Santiago shrugged. "I had the miles, so why not?"

Buffy unwrapped a piece of gum and handed it to him wordlessly, following with a piece for herself. Her ears popped while she chewed.

"I promised my little sister that I would come home for Christmas this year." Buffy kept her eyes on the window. "Will you come with me?"

Santiago nodded, picking up her hand and holding it against his chin. "I would love to."

"I can't wait to see you on the ranch," Buffy snickered.

"Oh yeah?" Santiago looked at her with narrowed eyes. "What, you think I can't handle it?"

"Not at all," Buffy chortled. "You're my city boy."

"I'll be anything as long as I'm yours." Santiago gazed at her through half-lidded eyes.

"Gross." Buffy smiled freely behind the cover of her mask. "Are your parents picking us up from the airport?"

"Yep," Santiago checked the time on his phone. "The whole family is staying at my Uncle Rubio's house."

Buffy felt paralysis take over her body. They were staying in a house with the entire family? Satiago had certainly not mentioned this. She would've remembered and panicked for the entire flight.

Duh. No wonder he hadn't mentioned it to her.

"I thought we were staying in a hotel," Buffy mumbled.

"We can, if you'd prefer," Santiago responded, his gaze lingering over her face. "It's not a big deal either way."

Buffy's thoughts raced. What if they didn't like her? She barely spoke Spanish. Santiago assured her that most of his family spoke English, but her nerves persisted. She should've asked Camila for a crash course. Her vision began to tunnel in front of her while thoughts waged war in her mind.

"Hey." Santiago took her hand and pulled her attention back to the present. "They're going to love you, okay?" He tucked a stray red hair behind her ear. "And if you don't feel comfortable, we can go somewhere with a pool. Uncle Rubio refuses to get a pool. What kind of rich person lives in Vegas and doesn't put in a pool? It's ridiculous."

Santiago's rambling distracted her from the racing thoughts and gave her the space to refocus on him. This family would be mourning one of their matriarchs; they likely didn't care enough about Buffy being there to form an opinion. She could do this. Definitely.

"Please put your seatbacks upright and lock your tray tables as we begin our descent into Las Vegas." The flight attendant's voice crackled over the intercom. "Welcome to Sin City."

"Sin City, eh?" Buffy wiggled her eyebrows up and down and bit her bottom lip in suggestion. She dragged her gaze over him. They'd been busy with funeral preparations and hadn't made much time for rolling in the sheets. Vegas seemed romantic enough to set the spark for them.

"There's a brothel outside the city." Santiago smirked at her. Buffy squeezed his hand as the plane shook, gripping purchase on the dry runway. They left San Francisco under cover of heavy fog and now they were landing in Vegas under blaring sunlight; not a cloud in sight.

"Like...a historic brothel?" Buffy questioned.

"A currently open and operating brothel." Santiago laughed at the wide-eyed look of shock on Buffy's face.

"I know that I'm sexually adventurous but—"

"I'm not asking you to the brothel, Buffy." Santiago chuckled at her stricken expression. "Just sharing some fun Vegas facts."

He pulled their bags down from the overhead compartment. Pushing them both in front of him, Santiago led her off the plane and into the airport. He let her take her suitcase in exchange for wrapping their hands together. Buffy tried not to blush. Was everyone looking at them? They had to be, right?

Deep breaths, Buffy.

"I don't know why they don't just make sex work nationally legal," Buffy muttered, returning to the conversation which had originally distracted her from her nerves.

"I agree, babe." Santiago smiled at her furrowed brow, thoughts passing plainly across her face. They came to a stop with the other passengers from their flight. "We'll fix the world tomorrow, okay?" His thumb traced over the lines on her forehead, until the creases relaxed.

An alarm sounded, announcing the arrival of the tram. Santiago guided Buffy onboard in front of him, tucking her between the corner and his body. Tight spaces only heightened her anxiety and a crowd of people amped it up even more. The physical barrier Santiago made for her eased her nerves and made her feel safe.

He always made her feel safe.

Buffy slid her arm around his waist. Holding his face against her cheek, Buffy breathed deeply and let excitement move forward in her mind. They were in Vegas for a horrible reason, but she knew Santiago was still happy to see his family and to have Buffy beside him. They'd even made plans to spend a few days on the strip with his cousins. Santiago told her nearly every day how much he wanted her there. In all honesty, she needed to hear it every day. She believed it more and more with each time he said the words.

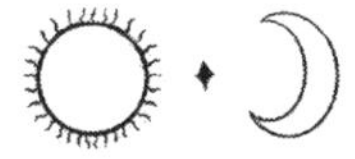

Holy shit, this air has nothing on Spain.

Buffy felt the skin of her hands tighten, as though the oil and water in her body was vacuumed out. She flexed her fingers, cracks slicing through the skin of her joints. The Las Vegas desert was trying to kill her. Rubbing her sweaty hands on her pants, she took Santiago's outstretched hand and followed him outside. Pressing his lips to the back of her hand, Santiago tucked her close to him.

"They're going to love you," Santiago whispered as they approached the passenger pickup.

A white SUV pulled up to them and the doors opened.

"Santiago."

Buffy recognized the voice immediately. Mirroring Abuela Paulina in face, voice, and stature, Santiago's father wrapped him in a tight hug. A few inches shorter than his son,

Santiago had to reach down to hug his father back. Buffy hung back, watching Santiago's mother join the family embrace.

Eventually, the woman broke away and wrapped her arms around Buffy. She could smell the sorrow in his mother's tears. They were clean, like ocean spray. Relieved.

Abuela Paulina had passed in her sleep at the hospital. Painless. Santiago's mother, Diana, kissed Buffy's cheek, sharing a breath before releasing her. Holding her at arm's length, Diana looked at her Buffy from head to toe.

"I'm so sorry," Buffy whispered, fingertips rubbing gently against her silk shirt.

"Don't be." Diana pulled back, holding Buffy's face in both hands. "You gave her friends again. She was happier than I've seen in a very long time. Mom knew she was ready."

"I'm happy to finally meet you Buffy. We've heard so much about you." Alberto smiled and wrapped Buffy in a warm hug.

"Oh no." Buffy grimaced.

"About half good and half bad things. Perfect balance." Alberto smiled.

"Oh goody," Buffy said.

"He's kidding." Santiago waved his father off and opened the back door, gesturing for Buffy to climb inside.

"Hi, Buffy!" A shrill voice squeaked in the small space and shattered her ear drums.

"Hi, Paulina." Buffy put on her biggest fake smile and hoped that the kid would quiet down once the excitement passed. She reminded herself that Little Paulina was just a kid and didn't understand how exhausted they were from traveling.

Be nice to the child, Buffy.

She squealed again when Santiago opened the door on her other side. Santiago climbed inside and embraced his litter sister, kissing her forehead and smoothing over her pigtails. Born unexpectedly six years prior, leaving Colorado and Little Paulina to care for Abuela Paulina had been especially hard for Santiago. He didn't talk about her much, other than how much he missed her and how smart she was. Buffy could see the relief in his eyes at Little Paulina's excitement to see him. Leaving behind young siblings always built a fear that one day they wouldn't remember you any more than a distant third cousin.

"Pau, say hi to Buffy." Santiago held his sister in his lap, her legs and torso facing Buffy.

"I did already!" Paulina said, tucking her face into her older brother's neck.

"Did you tell her you like her hair?" Santiago said.

"Shh!" Little Paulina attempted to cover Santiago's mouth with her tiny hand.

Buffy laughed and buckled into her seat. Santiago had easily captured his little sister's attention and Buffy was happy to sit there quietly. He buckled Little Paulina back into the car seat between them. Buffy slept on and off during the short ride. Once they arrived, it felt like only minutes had passed.

People slowly filtered into the house over the next few hours. With so many new faces and names she'd never heard before, Buffy felt lost. Thankfully, Little Paulina had taken to her red hair and cool-girl demeanor, giving Buffy the perfect excuse to stay rooted to her seat in a quiet corner of the living room, coloring with crayons.

After making his rounds and helping serve food, Santiago tucked himself into the corner with them. Using a scrap legal pad from his briefcase, Santiago had goaded Paulina into a game of tic tac toe. The little girl's intelligence was plain, and she quickly grew tired of tying with her brother.

"Have you ever played hangman before?"

Paulina turned wide eyes to Buffy and shook her head.

"You only have a few chances to win, so it's way harder than tic tac toe." Buffy exaggerated her statement with waggled eyebrows and a shared look with Santiago. Instantly, Paulina was enamored with her new game.

Santiago and Buffy set up hangman words and phrases again and again, Little Paulina solving them in less than five guesses. Clearly, she was related to Santiago and they shared the same sharp mind.

"You going to grow up to be a rocket scientist or something?" Buffy shook her head as Little Paulina completed another guess correctly.

"Nah, she's going to be a lawyer like her big brother." Santiago puffed his chest proudly.

"No thanks," Paulina responded without looking up from the game. "I'm going to be an astronaut."

"Hell yeah you are." Buffy high fived the little girl wearing Santiago's smile.

"What do you do for work?" Alberto, Santiago's father, had a heavy brow that cast his brown eyes in shadow.

"I'm a grant manager for the Urban Indian Center," Buffy explained.

"Do you like it?"

Buffy shrugged. "I like making a difference."

"Not a fan of the other stuff?"

"Not in the slightest." Buffy held his father's gaze, a look of understanding passing between them.

By the time midnight rolled around, Little Paulina was asleep upstairs and Buffy no longer had an excuse to abstain from socializing. Sticking to Santiago like glue, Buffy kept close to him while he walked through the home and introduced her to his family. Almost everyone spoke English, save for a few of the eldest members of the family. She was comforted by the ability to share understanding, but the desire to learn Spanish only rose. Camila spoke it with Miguel at home, multiple employees and clients at the center preferred to speak in Spanish, and they were constantly making more materials and courses in Spanish for Chicano community members. It was time she added a third language to her resume.

"Baila conmigo," Santiago whispered in her ear, pulling her out of the French doors and onto the back patio.

Buffy ground her heels down and let him tug her futilely. Santiago faced her with a knowing look.

"They are not going to judge you if you're not a perfect dancer." Santiago spoke lowly, so that only she could hear him.

"They'll judge you for being a terrible teacher, won't they?" Buffy raised one eyebrow.

Santiago considered for a moment.

"You're right." Santiago turned her around, pulling her back inside the house. Tugging her up the stairs, he kissed his mother on the cheek and told them goodnight.

Leading her into their bedroom, he closed and locked the door behind them. Santiago tossed their phones in the center of the bed. Without giving Buffy a moment to react, he swung her into his arms and began moving them around the room.

"Play the music from your phone." Buffy pulled from his arms, reaching for the phone in the center of the bed.

"No." Santiago tugged her back to him, their thighs sticking together from the heat. "I want to sing to you."

"Please don't."

"Yes." Santiago ignored her whining. "Should I learn guitar? Then I could sing to you all the time."

Buffy was laughing now, imagining Santiago following her around with a guitar singing melodies about her coffee and rounded ass. Dropping her hand, she squeezed her palm between them and over the crotch of his jeans.

"You're not being a good student. Where is your focus?" Santiago chided her, gripping her hand and putting it back on his shoulder.

"I think I'm plenty focused." Buffy reached for him again, sliding her hand effortlessly into the waist of his pants.

Santiago removed her hand and tucked it firmly into his grip. "Pay attention." With a startling smack to her ass, Buffy was even less focused on learning how to dance. The stinging of her butt cheek only made her stomach flame even more.

"Follow me, okay?" Santiago spun her around a few times, as though he was disorienting her in preparation. He stepped twice one way, tapped the floor with his toe, and stepped two times back the other way. Tap, again with his toe.

Buffy stumbled along and tripped over her own feet.

"Are you sure you know what you're doing?" Buffy complained.

"Yes, but you're not following me." Santiago laughed at the pout of frustration on her face. "I have an idea."

Unzipping his duffel bag, Santiago turned Buffy around and draped a cool piece of fabric over her shoulder.

"Really, Santi?" Buffy scoffed. He was not doing a good job of pulling her focus away from sex. Black fabric obscured her vision.

"Trust me, it will help you relax." Santiago tied the soft black fabric at the back of her head and turned her around to face him. Leaning down, he breathed along her cleavage before sucking a tiny purple bruise into the skin of her exposed breast. "You can have dick after."

Buffy huffed and opened her mouth to argue.

"Only if you're good." Santiago punctuated his words with a sharp bite to the skin of her neck.

"Oh my God." Buffy wove her hand through the air and smacked it against Santiago's chest. His skin was hot and bare. "When did you take your shirt off?!" she whined in desperation.

Santiago didn't answer, instead taking her back into his arms and pulling her along with a step, step, tap. Buffy dragged her hands up his arms and down his bare chest.

"Why are your nipples so hard?" Buffy snickered, pinching them between her fingertips.

"I should've gagged you instead," Santiago muttered, spinning her under his arm until her back melted into his chest.

Buffy opened her mouth to speak but her words were cut off with a squeal of surprise as Santiago pulled and twisted her around the room. He moved easily through different movements, their hips and feet hitting beats that only he could hear. She was out of breath and dizzy by the time he pulled the blindfold from her eyes.

Buffy fell forward into his chest, catching herself on his belt loops. "How am I supposed to remember any of that?"

Santiago shrugged. "Guess you'll just have to dance with me again."

"Ugh." Buffy hid her blush by turning her face into his chest. She felt overwhelmed with emotion. Tears teased the back of her throat. "Thank you for letting me come here. For letting me be with you."

Santiago wrapped his arms around her, a hand going to the back of her head to hold her close. "I know that you find it hard to believe, but I need you, Buffy. You're the only person getting me out of bed right now."

"Every single morning, you are awake before—"

Santiago cut her off with a sharp kiss. Pulsing into her lips she could feel his heartbeat begin to pick up, the breathing in his chest turning ragged. The air in the room switched from heavy with unspoken feelings to heavy with lust.

Buffy grinned and pushed her hands back into his pants.

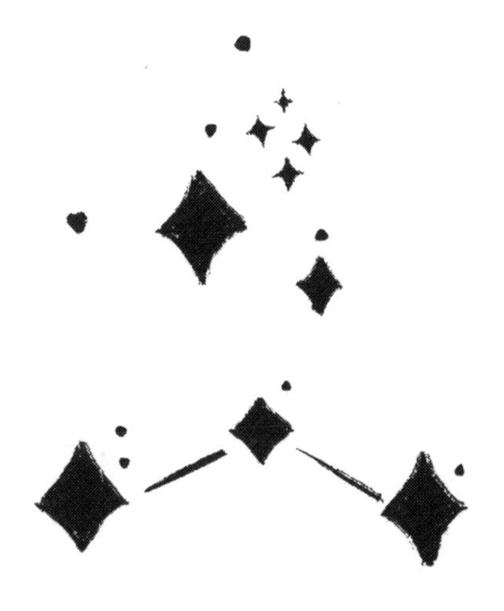

Chapter 22

A bell tolled outside the car, shaking the windows and eardrums of everyone in the vehicle.

"Are we at a church?" Buffy squinted out of the car window. They were in the middle of the desert, only cacti and mountains around for miles. A wooden one-room building stuck out against the blue sky, a white cross on the top reflecting the sun like a mirror. Buffy couldn't stand to look at it for more than a minute or two.

"Yep." Santiago straightened his coral bolero tie. "It's complicated."

"Isn't it always?" Buffy pulled the black lace veil over her shoulders and took Santiago's outstretched hand. She had spent enough time in churches to know that while some believed in Creator and others in God, everyone believed in each other.

The veil whipped with a sudden gust of wind, tickling the hairs on her nose and upper lip. A loaner from his mother, the black mantilla hung to her elbows, the lace curling forward over her collarbones. Santiago placed the black cowboy hat on his head and Buffy held back a giggle. She pressed her fingertips to her lips to quell her laughter.

It felt wrong, seeing her slick, suit-wearing, hot-shot lawyer city boy dressed in country clothing. To her, it seemed out of place, but Santiago looked more comfortable than she had ever seen him. He walked on the clouds of worn-in cowboy boots and seemed to stand taller, his shoulders taking up more space, confidence visible in his posture. His chin held high, pride on his face matching the rest of the family. They had lost their matriarch but it hadn't been a death of sorrow. Instead, her life brought their family pride, love, and solace, and they celebrated the fulfilling life she had.

Santiago trudged around the car to take her hand, tucking it into the crook of his elbow. Buffy squeezed her thighs together.

Stop it, Buffy thought. She could *not* get horny at a funeral.

They walked into the church together, sitting in the pew behind his parents. The building was small but packed to the brim with family members. Situated on the way to the top of the mountain, the small white church had an incredible mountain view out every window. High in elevation, snow topped the nearby mountains and brightened the already blinding sun. Everywhere she looked, Buffy had to squint in the bright light.

"Your grandma made the sun super bright today." Buffy squinted at Santiago, only one of her eyes open—just slightly.

Santiago didn't respond with words, but he squeezed her hand warmly. Gazing at Buffy, Santiago took in a long, shaking breath. He turned his gaze out the window. Buffy rubbed her thumb across the inside of his wrist.

Music played, calling attention to the front of the room. A large portrait of Abuela Paulina was encircled by orange, pink, and white flowers. Candles burned in the four directions around her. An eagle feather was tucked into the corner of her portrait, peeking out of the orange flowers.

A large band was behind the priest, arms full of all different types of instruments. Mass at a Mexican church was unlike any church service Buffy had ever attended before.

Not that she had attended very many.

His family joined in on multiple songs the band played, singing along to words Buffy couldn't understand. The priest spoke for long moments, flowing effortlessly between Spanish and English. While Buffy didn't believe in these things, she could feel the love and comfort the family gained over the service. It settled over her and warmed her from where Santiago's hand sat in her lap. Buffy didn't understand the lyrics of the songs, but she could feel them.

Santiago and Pear spoke in Spanish at the funeral. While Buffy could only understand a word or two, she followed along with the reactions of their family. She recalled the translation Santiago had spoken to her in bed that morning and watched as his family teared up with memories just as she had. He told the story of the first time he made tortillas with Abuela, how she had warned him not to touch the stove like she did. The way she had held him, rubbed his burnt fingers, and sang about a frog making the pain go away.

Church pews shook with laughter when Santiago recited the frog poem, Pear's clapping echoing through the entire room. Santiago thanked his grandmother with a final prayer and took his seat beside Buffy. Myra leaned forward and squeezed Santiago's shoulder, patting his cheek once before sitting upright.

Santiago pulled Buffy's hand to his lips. He pressed a kiss to each knuckle, using his thumb to wipe his tears before they could drip onto her skin. Reaching for him, she wiped the tears from his face and thumb before turning her attention back to the priest.

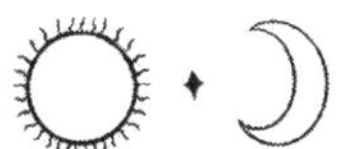

"No one thinks it's weird you brought a random redhead to your grandmother's funeral?" Buffy whispered when they finally headed back to the car. They had stood in the greeting line for what felt like forever, hugging family, accepting condolences and tears, then kissing the pain away on their cheeks. Myra spent the entire time whispering the family chisme into Buffy's ear.

"You're not a *random* redhead," Santiago argued. "Besides, I'm sure they're gossiping about it behind our backs." Holding the car door open for her, Santiago smacked her on the ass as she climbed inside.

They rode silently in the back of the car, Little Paulina strapped in a car seat between them. She fell asleep with the long, bumpy ride across the desert floor. Her head lolled onto Buffy's shoulder and she caught his mother's eye in the rearview mirror.

Smudged black from hours of crying, her eyebrows blurred from crossing herself, Diana's eyes were tired. Santiago leaned over then, wrapping his arm over Little Paulina and tucking his hand into Buffy's lap. He kissed his sister's sleeping cheek and squeezed the flesh of Buffy's thigh.

Diana smiled as fresh tears fell down her cheeks, her eyes never leaving the reflection of the three of them.

Buffy was swept up by the family as though she were one of Abuela Paulina's own grandchildren. In a panic, she had attempted to beeline for the car and escape the attention, but Santiago caught her around the waist and kept her tight to his side.

He looked at her then and she gripped him back. Shining with tears, his eyes were sunken into purple cheeks and exhaustion was written all over his face. He needed her. Kissing his cheek, Buffy took her place beside him.

Buffy helped Diana and Alberto unload the car: slow cookers, bags of chips, and tortillas overflowing the trunk. Arms loaded with tote bags full of miscellaneous take-out containers, she stumbled into the house behind Santiagos' parents. All of the smells assaulted Buffy's senses, the sneezes kicking in almost immediately. Little Paulina sat at the island laughing at her as Santiago dragged Buffy away from the kitchen and back outside.

The memorial was an all-out party. There was no other way to describe it. Hosted by Uncle Rubio and a distant cousin, the house was overflowing with music, food, and more tequila than Buffy had ever seen in her life.

Changed into vibrant white-and-gold mariachi suits, the band was playing a Gloria Estefan song that had a familiar melody. Buffy figured her mother had played it when she was alive. Her chest felt tight and Buffy tried to push the memories from her mind.

Easier said than done, however.

Santiago deposited her on a porch swing and returned with two plates piled high with food. He balanced two pieces of sugared bread between his lips.

A bowl of thick chocolate-colored soup was balanced on the bend of his elbow. Mole, she realized. Buffy took the bowl from him, holding the couch swing still for him. Rich spices from the soup filled her nose, tickling her skin and bringing a symphony of three sneezes in a row from her.

"I will take that one." Santiago took the steaming bowl with a smile and gave her a plate of beans and rice, pork, and carne asada. He topped it with the pickled veggies Buffy recently discovered she liked. "Are you going to dance with me?"

Buffy scrunched her nose up and peered at the dancing aunties and uncles from the corner of her eye.

Santiago squeezed the flesh of her hip in his warm palm. "Please, mi amor."

"That's cheating." Buffy pointed her fork at him. He knew the easiest way to bring her to her knees was to use Spanish. It tickled every fancy in her belly.

"It's not my fault you aren't bilingual," Santiago whispered.

"I am bilingual, jerk." Buffy scoffed at him and put her hand up in overexaggerated offense. "Talk to me when you can read three different alphabets, okay?"

"I love it when you talk dirty to me."

"Oh my God." Buffy gave up on withholding her laughter, and let it tumble forth and into the night. Santiago took her by the hand and pulled her over to the temporary dance floor in the middle of the fake grass. She was still laughing when he twirled her into his arms and took a palmful of her ass cheek at the same time.

"Santiago! Que vergüenza!" An older auntie called to him across the dance floor, before she reached down and palmed the ass of the young man she was dancing with.

The entire group burst out into laughter, dance partners mixing and mingling until Buffy found herself in Pear's arms. Buffy glared playfully at him. Pear glared back.

"Try not to break my toes, sasquatch," Pear told her.

"I'll break your whole foot then," Buffy retorted. Pear was only a few inches shorter than her.

"Only because your feet are twice the size," Pear scoffed, wincing when Santiago smacked the back of his head.

"Be nice to my wife," Santiago threatened Pear with a hard glare and continued twirling Paulina through the crowd.

"He's calling you wife now?"

"Says he's gonna marry me." Buffy shrugged.

"What do you say?"

"Yes." Buffy stared at Pear without blinking, watching the thoughts and emotions cross his face as he processed her words. "Maybe not today, but yes, I want to marry him. I want to be his wife."

Pear nodded slowly, evaluating her cooly. The dancing crowd had gained in numbers, and there wasn't enough light for Buffy to see his eyes clearly. She couldn't tell if he was understanding or getting angry. Buffy understood where he came from. Santiago was his best friend, his brother, and she had the power to break his heart.

If any of her siblings had been in love with someone who was constantly rejecting them and actively seeking out other relationships, she would be pissed too.

"I get it." Buffy spoke quieter, ensuring the conversation couldn't be overheard. "The way I treated him in the beginning...it was wrong of me. I was scared and that doesn't make it okay, and I'm still scared now but..." Buffy trailed off, looking around for Santiago. She found him whispering into the ear of the accordion player, clapping excitedly when the man nodded his understanding. "I can't live without him. That's what scares me now."

"Scares all of us, I think." Pear nodded, holding Buffy a little tighter around the waist, his hand gentling in its iron grip around her fingers. "If he's happy, then I'm happy."

Santiago appeared behind his shoulder. "I am, hermano." The two men hugged each other, reaching out and pulling Buffy into the group embrace too.

"Ew, let me go." Buffy grimaced, attempting to pull free but each of the men had an arm around her.

Suddenly, her legs were wrapped up too, Little Paulina joining the display of affection. With Paulina as the catalyst, Santiago's parents soon joined, followed by cousins and aunties and grandparents. Buffy tried not to gag at the outright display of affection.

Together, sharing an embrace, the family looked like its own solar system of brightly shining stars.

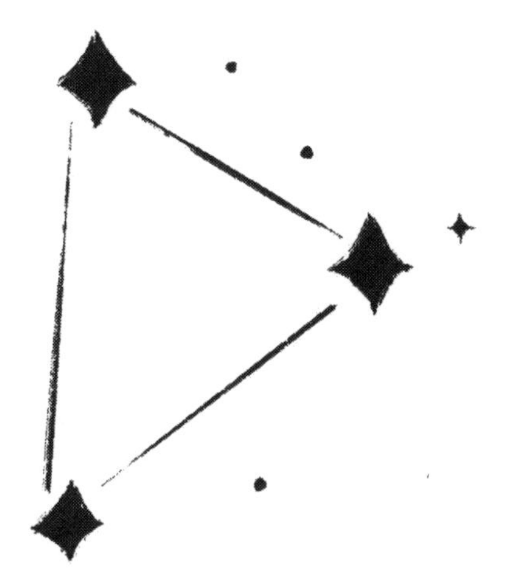

Chapter 23

The next day, Diana was awake at the crack of dawn, rushing around and waking the entire family. Once everyone was roused and dressed, she herded them into a van and took off towards the mountains. Santiago gripped a thermos of coffee, arguing with Paulina about why she couldn't have any.

Buffy fell back asleep instantly, her head bouncing gently off the wall of the car. The drive to Avi Kwa Ame, Abuela's favorite place in the world, was only about two hours but Buffy was especially prone to napping in the car. Santiago watched her sleep. She had so easily slipped into place in his life during a moment that would challenge even a long-term couple. Their cultural ways of dealing with grief were different but she was open to participating in his traditions as much as she was willing to share her own with him. Even when those traditions overlapped with Christianity. He wouldn't have blamed her if she'd wanted to stay home instead. But she hadn't. Buffy was here, with him, all in. It was a type of peace he had never experienced in a romantic relationship before.

Santiago breathed in deeply, the crisp morning desert air filling his lungs. Little Paulina slept with her head in his lap, one little hand on Buffy's knee. He smiled at the sight. Two of his most favorite women in the world. If only Abuela was here to see them together. His heart was broken, open and bleeding with sadness at his grandmother's passing. But with Buffy beside him, he felt happy. Grief and mourning hung over their heads but at the core, their relationship had moved into something that made him feel safe and happy. Buffy was his backbone. She might be unwilling to say the word 'love' out loud, but he felt it in her every touch, word, even her gaze carried the love in it.

Despite everything, Santiago felt happy. He wanted Abuela Paulina to be alive, enjoying this scene with him, but he knew that she was watching from the afterlife. That she had known Buffy loved him even before he did, likely even before Buffy realized. He could make peace with that.

Abuela Paulina wouldn't be there to watch them marry, but she was there when they fell in love. Her whispered blessing while Santiago and Buffy danced in the kitchen replayed through his mind. At the time, he had tried to ignore it in an attempt to not get his hopes up with Buffy. Now, though, he could play it over and over and over again in his head and he never tired of it.

Making a mental note to recite it for Buffy one day, he kissed her forehead and woke her up.

Diana held the simple urn against her chest. A crown of sage and cempasuchiles draped over the urn, ensuring clear and safe passage through to the spirit world. The siblings and grandchildren gathered around the urn.

Honoring his mother in Spanish, Alberto spoke evenly, with pride in his voice and love in his chest. Santiago offered Buffy a brief translation once his father was finished speaking. Diana spoke next, telling the story of their year-long engagement and the many gifts she bestowed upon Abuela Paulina. The group rumbled with laughter as she told the story, waving her hands through the air in emphasis. Uncle Rubio finished the short ceremony with a prayer Abuela Paulina had recited every day.

They ate lunch on a thickly padded outdoor blanket, the sharp bite of desert rocks poking through. Santiago examined the contents of the cooler once again. Buffy had accompanied Santiago to the grocery store the night before, wowed by the vast options. San Francisco had tiny grocery stores and Vegas had the space to spread out. She had immediately taken a liking to the large, local Mexican grocery store and their low-priced produce. It took everything in him not to buy her everything in the store. Instead, they had stuck to their list of Abuela Paulina's favorites.

Ten Mandarin Jarritos

Thirty pork tamales

Twenty buñuelos

Ten mazapan

Twenty biscochitos.

They crossed things off the list one at a time, Santiago recounting a memory for each item on the list. Buffy listened intently to him, sinking it through her skin and into her spirit.

"I hate mazapan." Santiago thumbed a broken piece of grainy peanut candy. "You're going to hate it too."

"That's alright." Buffy shrugged, "I've eaten worse things for people I love."

"Ouch." Santiago feigned hurt.

"I did not mean that." Buffy rolled her eyes and bumped her shoulder against his. "I put pineapple in all of your smoothies." She whispered the words into his ear and he shivered.

Santiago raised a devilish brow at her, raking his eyes from her head to her toes.

"Behave." Buffy murmured softly.

"Salud." Diana offered her mazapan in the middle of the blanket.

"Salud," they repeated. One by one they touched their mazapan together, holding their breath in order to be gentle and keep the candies whole.

"Vaya con dios, Mamá," Alberto said, popping the candy in his mouth.

They each placed a small piece of the leftover mazapan in their hands, gathering the rest of their set aside meal. Alberto built a small fire pit in the center of the sand, in view of the canyon and far enough from plants not to catch fire. They each dropped the contents from their palms, their final offering of the night.

The fire burned in front of them, smoke billowing out to the valley. Eventually, most of the family members returned to the city. Santiago and his parents stuck behind, Pear and Myra in tow.

White smoke reached for the moon, wrapping her in a shroud. Abuela Paulina loved painting images of the moon. Santiago hoped that now, at last, she was able to meet her greatest love.

Little Paulina nodded off in their mother's lap and they gingerly made a bed of blankets beside the fire. Santiago watched his little sister sleep, her face identical to that of their grandmother. It made him miss her. He felt guilty that he was missing her childhood by living so far away. Hadn't he missed enough time with Abuela Paulina?

And now she was gone. He let out a long breath and thanked a God he wasn't sure he believed in, for moving him to San Francisco three years ago. Otherwise, Abuela Paulina might've left them even sooner and he never would've forgiven himself. Sadness washed over him.

Santiago turned around, searching for Buffy. She wasn't there. Scanning the area, he found her at the edge of the cliff, off to one side. Seated, her feet were hanging over the edge, a tall desert bush partially obscuring her from view. Santiago could only see the tuft of her red hair bun until he got closer.

He knelt down beside her, taking a seat with his legs over the edge. Buffy didn't move. Eyes glazed over, she stared across the canyon, unseeing. Thinking over the past few days, Santiago couldn't remember hearing or seeing Buffy cry. He knew she was holding back, staying strong for him. She needed to let go.

Buffy held every emotion inside, kept them bottled up and never let them out. Santiago wanted her to feel her things: good and bad. And he wanted to be there to help her through and pick up whatever pieces fell.

"You can cry too." Santiago's voice split through the silent desert. "Crying is a show of strength, not weakness."

"I'm fine," Buffy lied.

Santiago looked at her from the corner of his eye. Buffy refused to meet his gaze.

"I was so angry the night she went into the hospital." Santiago stared at the darkening valley before them. He kicked at the dirt below their feet, a pebble scattering until it plummeted over the cliff.

"I thought that if she had told me sooner, then maybe things would've been different. Maybe she would still be alive, maybe we could've had longer together." Santiago sighed heavily. "I didn't do anything, Buffy. I was so angry with her for keeping the kidney disease a secret, it wasn't until she was gone that I realized I was angry with myself." Santiago took Buffy's hand in his. Fingertips tracing over the lines of her palm, he continued.

"How could I have let her die? Why didn't I see that she wasn't doing well? I should've done something, said anything, been anything other than complacent. If I hadn't been so focused on myself and my life and what I wanted, then maybe—"

"It's not your fault, Santiago." Buffy gripped the fingers tracing her palm. Her gaze remained on the canyon.

"It isn't yours, either." Santiago squeezed her hand, gripping it so tightly that she couldn't pull away. He watched the last sharp-edged tooth fall from the stars.

"I can't believe I missed her birthday." Buffy didn't look at him. "I'm such a horrible person. How could I do that? I didn't even call her and then she died!" Buffy's voice cracked. The floodgates ripped open and every piece of shame in her body tore through her skin. "How could I hurt her like that? I didn't even get to fix it."

Buffy stared up at the stars, tears cascading down her face and neck.

"I'm always doing shit like this, Santi. I'm not a good person," Buffy cried. "You are so selfless and so caring, and I am a heartless bitch."

Santiago couldn't help the shouting laugh that bolted from his chest. The laughter tumbled through him, infecting his every cell until he was slapping his knees and gasping for breath.

"Why are you laughing?" Buffy screeched, turning an accusing glare on him. "Are you laughing at me?" She sniffled through the tears on her face.

"Yeah." Santiago spoke the word through a giggle.

"Well, don't!" Buffy stopped crying, her confusion overpowering the aching despair. "I'm serious!"

"You are a lot of things, Buffy Yellowbird, but heartless is not one of them." Santiago finally controlled his laughter, pulling her into a tight embrace.

"I am!" Buffy argued into his neck, tucking her hands into the pockets of his jacket.

"Whatever you say." Santiago smiled into her hair. Pulling her head from his neck, Santiago wiped the tears from her cheeks and chin. Kissing each of her eyes and then her lips, Santiago rested their foreheads together.

Buffy pulled back enough to meet his gaze. Her nose and cheeks were red with cold and crying. She never looked more kissable. Santiago held her tightly to him.

"I love you," Buffy declared.

"Yeah?" Santiago raised one brow. "I love you."

"I'm well aware of that."

"Oh yeah?" Santiago laughed. "I've loved you since we met." Buffy knocked her shoulder into his and laughed.

"I'm not changing my last name," Buffy said, taking his hand into her lap.

"Mr. Yellowbird has a nice ring to it." Santiago winked.

Buffy searched for words that didn't come.

"I'll give you whatever you want, Buffy." Santiago stood and pulled her up with him. Wrapping his arms completely around Buffy, he leaned down and kissed her, his mom and dad watching from across the fire. Buffy sighed happily into his mouth.

"Mijo." Alberto called their attention when they wandered back to the group. Buffy had required sufficient time to collect herself from the unusual display of emotions. "Here." Alberto stretched his arm out towards his son.

Santiago took the thin piece of paper Alberto offered, unfolding it in his lap. Using his camping flashlight, Buffy watched Santiago read over the page.

"You're giving me the house?" Santiago dropped the paper in Buffy's lap to stand. His ears started to ring. It felt like an elephant had climbed onto his chest. He couldn't breathe.

"Well, you already live there," Diana said. "We figured you'd want it."

"I can't live there anymore," Santiago said, turning and stalking off into the darkness.

Buffy hurried after him, tucking the deed of the house into the pocket of her jacket and zipping it tightly.

She caught up to him a few feet into the brush, narrowly squeezing between two spiky Joshua trees. The desert had so many things that could hurt someone and Santiago wished she would be more careful.

Santiago faced her with wet cheeks. His voice cracked as he spoke. "I can't stay there."

"We don't have to," Buffy said.

Santiago's breath caught at her use of *we*. She was pulling out all the stops to comfort him while his resolve crumbled. "But we don't have to get rid of it, either. Maybe Pear could move in, or Myra—"

Santiago shook his head. "They wouldn't move in when she was still alive, they definitely won't be doing it now." He sighed and threw his head back to the sky. Wiping at his face with a hand, he took a shaking deep breath.

Buffy's heart squeezed in her chest. "We don't have to figure it out tonight. We have plenty of time." She stepped into his space, winding her arms around his waist.

Santiago sighed and wrapped his arms around her, letting his head fall onto her neck. Buffy held him tightly, firm enough for both of them. He breathed in time with her, clinging to her like a lifeline.

"We can stay at my place for a while, okay?" Buffy pulled his head from her shoulder. Palms on either side of his face, she held his head close to hers. "You and I both know that she will haunt us both if you give up the house. But we don't have to live there. You've got plenty of time to decide what you want to do."

Santiago nodded, kissing her once on the lips. Buffy wiped the wetness from his eyes with her thumbs.

"What if I want to move home?" Santiago whispered, his eyes pinched tightly with worry.

"I told you that I've always wanted to see the Colorado Rockies." Buffy kissed him.

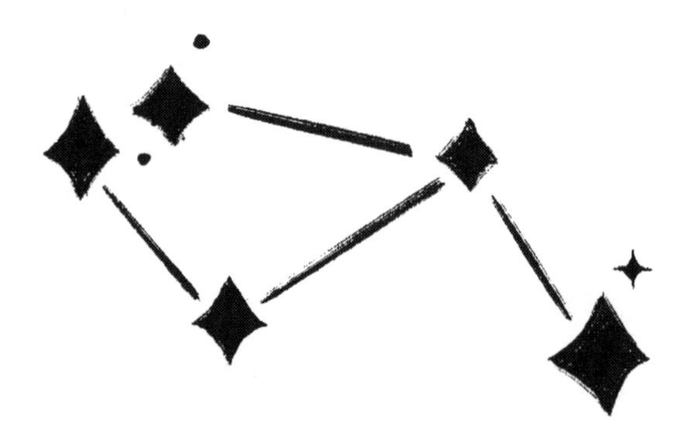

CHAPTER 24

Diana and Alberto spent the morning golfing with Alberto's siblings, leaving Little Paulina in the care of Santiago and Buffy. Paulina begged Santiago to make his world-famous churro pancakes, going so far as dropping to her knees at the side of their bed and begging her brother to wake up and save her from starvation.

Together, Santiago and Little Paulina made the batter and scooped them into small round discs on the plancha. Buffy sat at the counter and watched them with a smile. Now that the memorial was over, the house had emptied out. Only a few of the siblings and cousins remained. She felt at ease with less people around.

Santiago poured coffee, adding milk and sugar before handing it to Buffy.

"I want coffee," Paulina said.

"No," Buffy answered.

"Why not?"

"It will make you short." Santiago tapped Little Paulina on the tip of the nose, leaving a dust of cinnamon on her skin.

"I want to stay short!" Little Paulina argued.

"How will you make your own pancakes if you can't reach the flour?" Buffy raised a brow at the little girl, watching the gears in her mind turn in search of a response.

"I'll marry someone tall." Paulina stuck her finger up in the air as though she had discovered the solution to everything.

"That's what I'm planning to do." Santiago winked at Buffy, serving her and Paulina plates stacked with cinnamon-sugared pancakes.

"You're taller than me," Buffy argued.

"By like a centimeter." Santiago waved her comment off like a fly.

"You're going to get married?" Paulina sat up on her knees in her seat, clapping her tiny hands together in front of her chest.

Buffy froze, eyes wide and trained on Santiago.

"Is that why Mami gave you Abuela's ring?"

Now Santiago was the one frozen.

"A ring, huh?" Buffy peered at him, her eyes narrowed. Laughter bubbled up in her chest. She knew that Santiago wanted to marry her, but he hadn't properly asked. "You sure it will fit my giant fingers?"

"We can make it work." Santiago smiled and pulled the box from his pocket. He opened it and sat it on the counter between the three of them. The band was silver and thin, the center stone a bezel-set unfinished piece of turquoise. The blue stone was small and bumpy, the ridges and valleys numerous. Buffy had seen Abuela Paulina wear it on her pointer finger a few times before she passed.

"Buffy, will you marry me?" Santiago held her hand in his, his warm brown eyes trained on her face. There was no fear behind his eyes, no confusion, no trepidation. His confidence emboldened her.

"Yes."

Little Paulina screamed loud enough that her sunburned parents came running from the driveway, tears filling the room like a flash flood when they saw the ring.

Pulling Buffy in for a tight hug, Alberto whispered into her ear, "I had it sized the day after we met you. I could see it in his eyes." Alberto pulled away, holding Buffy by the shoulders. "And in yours." His voice cracked and Buffy swallowed to keep her own tears at bay.

"I'll convince him." Buffy nodded at Alberto, promising to warm Santiago to the idea of keeping the house. "Somehow."

"You don't have to live in it." Alberto squeezed Buffy's hand. Diana pulled Buffy into her arms, kissing both of her cheeks over and over again. Alberto wrapped his arm around his wife, squeezing Buffy with the other. "Just keep it in the family."

"Another daughter." Diana smiled and squeezed Buffy's cheeks, her eyes filling with tears.. "Welcome to the family, mija."

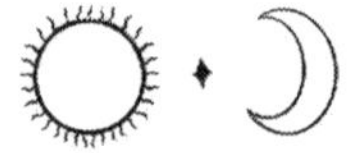

After a late family dinner from the drive-through taco spot, Buffy and Santiago watched his parents walk into the airport. His dad refused to let Diana carry either of the bags, one in each of his hands while hers held Little Paulina's. Settling into the curbside line, she watched Santiago's father tuck his mother under his chin, into his chest, away from the crowd and rain. The satisfied smile of peace on her lips brought tears to Buffy's eyes. Her own parents had been like this, once.

"Your parents are so in love." Buffy smiled at Santiago while he merged into airport traffic. They had three days before their flight home and decided to spend it on the strip with Pear and Myra. The cousins had already checked into their hotel and settled in. Excitement bubbled in Buffy's veins at the weekend ahead. She was certain they would have an incredible time together playing the slots and going to the strip shows. It would be good for the four of them to have some fun before facing reality back in San Francisco.

"I know. It's disgusting." Santiago stuck his tongue out.

"No, it isn't! Don't you want us to be like them?" Buffy asked.

"Do you?" Santiago raised his eyebrows in surprise. He merged effortlessly onto the main road of the strip, the traffic at a standstill.

"Yes." Buffy spoke with assurance, her voice as unwavering as her gaze.

"Marry me." Santiago held her gaze.

"I already said yes," Buffy scoffed.

"Right now." Santiago turned forward as traffic began to move, reaching over to take her hand in his.

Buffy laughed, kissing his cheek. Santiago glanced at her, then back at the traffic. She could see agitation coursing through his body.

He was serious.

"Can I at least change first?" Buffy glanced down at her jeans and batter-flecked T-shirt. They were only a block from their hotel.

"You have ten minutes," Santiago said.

"Ten minutes?! That isn't enough." Buffy sprang out of the car as soon as it rolled to a stop in front of the hotel entrance.

"It's all you're getting," Santiago said sternly.

Giving his keys to the valet, Santiago ran after his bride. Buffy took off through the casino to the elevator banks, squealing when Santiago caught her stepping through the opening doors. His lips were warm where they settled home in the crook of her neck, his excitement palpable in the half-moon marks left on her skin.

She wrestled his arms from around her waist once they were in their hotel room.

"We have to save that for the wedding night!" Buffy wagged a finger at him.

"It is the wedding night, Buffy." Santiago pawed at her hips woefully, dropping to his knees behind her. Leaning forward, he held her hips to him and wiggled his face into her ass cheeks, motorboating them like he would her breasts.

Buffy fell forward in an attempt to wiggle away from him, the tickle of his scruff too much to handle.

"Get off!" Buffy pushed him playfully, the two wrestling on the carpeted floor. "You're going to mess up my hair and then I won't take any photos."

"You wouldn't." Santiago evaluated the level of sincerity in her threat.

"Try me," Buffy cackled when he finally released her, sitting back on his heels he watched as she tore apart their baggage.

Her hands ghosted over the white ribbon skirt stashed at the very bottom. Buffy had it for years, part of her bridesmaid outfit for Juniper's wedding. The skirt was a beautiful and heavy white silk, the ribbons taken from their mother's original wedding gown; turquoise, orange, and red. The colors of her people, Santiago's people. In a weird way, it felt like her mother had a hand in sending Santiago to her. They were the two most stubborn and headstrong people she had ever met.

Buffy thanked herself for packing the white skirt. They came to Vegas for a funeral, for God's sake. Something in her spirit urged her to pack it and she listened.

Good thinking, Buffy.

She changed quickly, making a mental note to ask Myra for a pair of shoes. They would be a size too small, but Buffy was willing to suffer for beauty on a day like her wedding day.

Santiago was buttoning his sage-green long sleeve when she emerged.

"That's my favorite color on you." Crossing her ankles, Buffy leaned against the doorway, watching him with a heady gaze.

Santiago sucked in a breath when his eyes landed on her form. Languidly, his gaze roved over her, examining every inch. "You're the most beautiful person I've ever seen."

"I'm glad you think that."

"It's a fact," Santiago whispered.

"I love you," Buffy whispered.

"Ready?" Santiago reached a hand toward her.

"Definitely." Buffy laced their fingers together.

"Just need to grab one more thing," Santiago said.

"Oh, I need heels from Myra," Buffy said, motioning to her flat moccasins.

Santiago took her hand and pulled her into the hallway. Stopping a few doors down, he banged heavily on the door.

Pear was slightly visible in the crack, the room shrouded in darkness behind him. "Santiago, it's almost midnight in the morning. What the fuck do you want?"

"I'm getting married. Be my witness?" Santiago smiled when his cousin gasped in shock.

It was as though Santiago had thrown an entire bucket of cold water on him. Pear sprang up, his eyes darting wildly between Santiago and Buffy.

"Are you shitting me?" Pear asked.

"Not at all," Buffy answered this time.

"You went from not even saying 'I love you' to getting married?" Pear squinted at Buffy.

"I told him I loved him a few days ago." Buffy waved her hand. "Keep up, John."

Pear put his hands on his hips and stared at Buffy in challenge.

"Myra could be our witness." Buffy pushed past Pear into their dark room. Myra was asleep on the bed beside the window, sprawled on top of the covers and still in the clothes she had been wearing at breakfast earlier that day. Clearly, the two cousins had made quick work of the free drinks that came with playing slots.

Buffy clapped her hands and began turning on all the lights.

"Wake up!" Buffy and Santiago chorused, climbing onto her bed and jostling Myra awake.

"What the fuck?" Bleary-eyed, Myra squinted at them.

"I need a bridesmaid, don't I?" Buffy gestured to her white outfit.

"A bridesmaid?" Myra looked back and forth between the three of them. "For who? For what?"

"For our wedding," Santiago chuckled. Myra's eyes flashed between them in shock. Santiago took Buffy's hand and held it up in the air as though they had just won a trip around the world. He brandished her priceless turquoise ring. Tears filled her eyes and Myra blinked, throwing the covers off.

"I need to brush my teeth." Myra smoothed over her hair and ran to the bathroom.

"Hurry up!" Santiago called after her.

Pear changed into a blue-ribbon shirt and slacks. He combed gel through his dark black hair with a fine-tooth comb. Santiago fitted him with a bolo tie similar to his own when the phone rang.

"Cab is here!" Pear called, ushering the group out of the hotel room and downstairs.

They climbed into the cab, Pear sitting up front beside the driver. Myra continued asking questions with no real substance, the shock still settling in.

The chapel was bright white, bursting from the ground like an ancient tree. The interior was hot pink with red and white heart balloons scattered amongst gold and silver streamers taped to the ceiling.

"It's Vegas, baby." Santiago whistled low and kissed Buffy's cheek.

"Do you think they'd let us get married out front?" Buffy asked.

"I'll find out." Santiago took off to find the chapel owner, while Buffy assured Myra she was not under the influence.

"I'm high on life, I guess," Buffy answered her, earning a swift smack to the arm.

"This is crazy."

"I know." Buffy smiled. "Craziest thing I've ever done."

"Hey," Pear called from the back corner of the chapel. "This way."

Myra and Buffy followed Pear up a white spiral staircase to a cramped attic full of dust. Buffy started coughing instantly, hacking on the dirt in the air. With a hand, Pear guided them to step through an open window and out onto the roof.

The strip sparkled in front of them, silhouetting the mountains in every direction. The chapel's wedding planner approached with decorations, a veil, and a bouquet. Buffy stared at the items.

"I think I'm good." The wedding planner's sweet sunshiney face fell. Buffy felt like she had kicked a puppy. "What about those desert flowers out front? Could we do those and some flower petals or something?"

"Yes!" A wide smile returned to the planner's face and he scuttled through the window.

By the time her desert flower bouquet was assembled and an aisle of fake white petals was dusted across the rooftop, the sun was beginning to rise.

Buffy smiled and thanked the summer season for the early rise. She wanted to see Santiago clearly when they promised life to each other.

Standing with the sun at his back, Santiago was waiting for her wearing a literal halo of light. She smiled at the image. He was the largest star in her solar system. His warm smile set her at ease and calmed her heart rate enough that she could think freely again.

"You ready?" Santiago offered his hand, palm up.

Buffy placed her hand in his, lacing their fingers together and stepping towards him until her bouquet touched his chest.

"I'm ready."

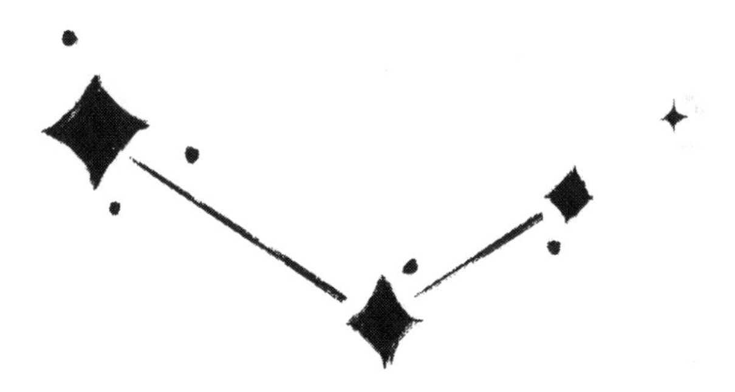

Chapter 25

"Can you believe it's our last night in California?" Buffy spoke toward the stars.

"Nope." Santiago sighed and leaned back into the pillows of the porch swing. "It feels wrong to leave." He paused and blew air out of his full cheeks. "But I can't stay here."

"I think Abuela would've been proud of you." Buffy stretched an arm around his shoulders. Abuela Paulina's easel was still standing, a half-finished painting of the moon and backyard frozen in time forever.

Buffy slid her fingers into his short hair, scratching gently at his scalp. "Using this house for transitional community members is noble, Santiago. Choosing to move home to be with your family is noble, Santi. All these choices you've made, Abuela would've been proud of you." Buffy gazed at the side of his face. "I'm proud of you."

"Yeah?" Santiago faced her. "You're proud of me?"

"The proudest."

"I'm proud of you too." Santiago snickered when Buffy dropped her gaze and looked away. "Mírame."

"No." Buffy smiled, her face pointed toward the stars.

"A husband can't be proud of his wife?"

Buffy giggled and tucked her face into his neck. "I can't believe we're married."

"Need me to remind you?" Santiago mumbled into her hair, his voice dropping low.

"I think so," Buffy squealed when he pulled her into his lap. "A daily reminder could be nice."

"How's twice a day?" Santiago spoke with his lips against her neck.

"I could do twice a day."

"Good." Santiago pulled their blanket to the ground. Wrapping his arms around Buffy, he laid her on top of the blanket. Dew spots marked the grass and seeped cold through the blanket. Buffy hissed as Santiago removed her shirt, warm skin dancing across the tiny pricks of ice.

She didn't feel the cold spots for long before Santiago was wrapping his arms completely around her, insulating her from the wet grass.

"Think the neighbors can see us?"

"Nah." Santiago brushed red hair from her eyes. "No one can see us back here."

Buffy smiled and pushed at his pants with her feet. Santiago kissed her lazily while he removed the rest of her clothing. Lips molding to hers, his tongue teased her skin and wet the edges of her lips. Once she was bare to the night sky, Santiago leaned back to admire her.

Fighting the urge to cover herself, Buffy let Santiago drag his gaze across her naked form. His eyes caressed every inch of her, his hands following close behind. He rubbed over her knees, ignoring the prickles of hair growing in from the last time she shaved. Leaning down, Santiago massaged the curve of her bicep, over her shoulder and down to her breasts. Buffy shuddered beneath him.

His touch was teasing, light - and Buffy ached for more. She fought to keep herself flat to the ground instead of arching up into his hands. They hadn't had a lot of slow sex in their time together and she couldn't bear to break Santiago's current focus on her. He was staring at her like a piece of art, something to be treasured and handled with care. Her throat tensed and she gulped.

Santiago caught the movement and met her gaze. "I love you." He didn't wait for her response before kissing down her soft belly and settling himself between her legs.

Buffy gripped the grass beside her, tearing up the blades in her worming hands. She tried to pull at his hair, but it was still too short to grip and she had nothing to grab on to except the grass. Cold prickles from the wet grass blades danced across the sensitive flesh of her arms and acted as gasoline for the fire Santiago set inside of her. Working together, his fingers and mouth brought her to explosion twice before she was able to muster the strength to flip him to his back.

Smiling up at her, Santiago's face sparkled in the night. Wetness coated his chin and neck, even reaching to the top of his cheeks and bridge of his nose. Buffy felt her face flame. Taking his hand in hers, Buffy licked his fingers clean. She felt him flex against her back. It was hard to surprise a man who knew her so well, but somehow, she continued to find a way.

Santiago wrapped his hand around the back of her neck and pulled her lips to his. Buffy rested her weight against his chest, going limp in his arms. Maneuvering their bodies, Santiago slid inside her, his tongue following suit. Gasping, Buffy let her head drop to his bare chest. Sweat was pooling on his skin despite the cool night and his scent surrounding her. Breathing deeply, Buffy inhaled the smell of his skin, the smell of Santiago.

"I love you," Buffy whispered into his neck.

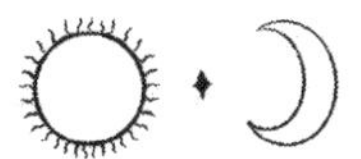

Buffy watched Santiago sign the paperwork, their names beside one another. It was eerily reminiscent of only a few months ago when they had signed their wedding license together in front of an Elvis impersonator in an unbrushed wig. That had been arguably more fun than this was.

"I can't believe you're doing this," Camila muttered, her gaze glued to the freshly inked documents. "This is insane."

"Oh my God." Buffy threw her head back in exasperation. "It's not like we gave Abuela's house to you. You're literally paying rent."

"Five hundred a month for a house in the city is *not* rent." Camila stood and leveled Buffy with a glare. "It's robbery."

"You're also paying your rent with labor," Buffy countered, pointing at Camila with the end of her pen.

"Watching after my brother and cooking a few meals is hardly work."

"Do you want me to kick you out or?" Buffy waved her hand through the air in question.

"No!" Miguel stammered, setting his hands gently overtop of Buffy's. "Camila is done asking stupid questions now." Miguel glared at his sister and offered Buffy and Santiago a smile worthy of a customer service award.

"When does the first person move in?"

"Next week." Buffy pulled out a stack of manila folders. "Now that we are using Abuela's house as temporary housing, the center should be able to serve even more people. We can house up to five clients here, along with you and Miguel. The backyard will be perfect for a little house garden to keep everyone busy. There will be one youth dinner a month and two movie nights per month. Other than that, it's all up to the two of you." Clapping her hands together in front of her face, Buffy peered at them with love in her eyes.

"Don't get too excited," Camila muttered. "I could still fuck this up. Are you sure you have to leave?"

"It's only for a few weeks!" Buffy argued.

"We will be back in the Bay before you know it." Santiago put an arm around Buffy's shoulders, pressing a kiss to her temple.

"I'm still working hybrid—technically."

"Flying out here once a quarter is hardly hybrid."

"Would you rather I work remote and stay in Colorado forever?" Buffy questioned, one brow raised.

"Of course not!" Camila squealed.

"Then be happy with what you get and expect me to fly you out from time to time, okay?"

Camila smirked at Buffy. "You'll miss me."

"Goodbye." Buffy turned to leave.

"Wait!" Camila followed Buffy out to the front porch. Santiago trailed behind them, laughing with Miguel.

Buffy waited until he was on the porch beside her, then stepped into his arms and turned to face Camila.

"What's the policy on sleepovers?" Camila wiggled her brows up and down.

"I think they should be someone you're in a relationship with. Don't you think, babe?" Buffy looked over her shoulder at Santiago.

"Definitely, someone you're committed to." Santiago nodded. "This is your place of work, after all."

"Ay dios mío, I told you I'm going to talk to Elena. You don't have to do all this." Camila wiggled her hands in the air and then threw them up in frustration. "See you in a few months."

The door clicked shut behind her.

Taking Buffy's hand in his, Santiago led her down the street. With a quick glance over her shoulder and a whispered goodbye to Abuela Paulina, Buffy tucked the unopened pink letter into her purse and stepped forward.

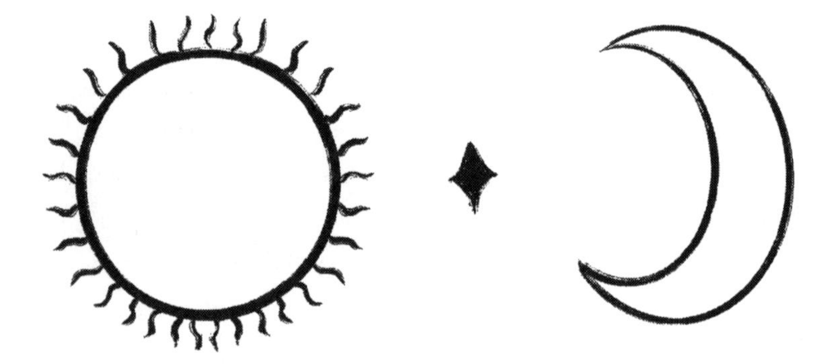

EPILOGUE

"There you are!" An excited scream echoed through the empty airport pickup, a tall brunette leaping at them from behind an old farm truck. The girl was a spitting image of Buffy. With long brown hair and golden eyes, the girl was built muscular, thick, and strong, just like his wife.

"This is Joy." Buffy stood only a hair taller than her youngest sister, who wore the same nose and smile as her.

"Did everyone agree to date Mexicans? Because I missed the memo, if that's the case." Joy glared accusingly at her sister, hugging Santiago tightly around the neck.

They piled into the truck behind Joy, stuffing the bed with their bags. With four bags between the two of them, only one was full of their clothes. The other three were full of gifts and dry foods for the Yellowbirds. Apparently, Muskwa had become a huge fan of soba noodles, so Buffy brought him a box with fifty bags. It took up an entire suitcase. Santiago melted at his wife's loving heart. She may not have been vocal about it, but she loved grandly.

Santiago swallowed the nerves in his belly. If the other Yellowbirds were anything like Buffy, he would know if they liked him immediately. Or if they hated him. With so many siblings and a single father, Santiago knew that their family bond would be so strong it was almost physical. If the family didn't accept him, this would never work.

The ride from the airport was long enough that Santiago slept through most of it, the sound of Buffy's laughter embedding itself in his dreams. He woke up on a ferry, the rocking of the waves pulling him from sleep. The night had arrived while he slept and he couldn't see anything from the car windows. There wasn't enough light to identify trees or islands or shores. All he saw was darkness.

Maybe Buffy was right and he was just a city boy. Even the Colorado country didn't look anything like this.

"Good morning, sunshine." Buffy reached into the backseat, pulling Santiago's hand forward until she could kiss his fingers. "We're almost there."

"What time is it?"

"Almost nine at night."

Santiago's eyes went wide. They had been driving for hours.

When they finally pulled up to the house, Santiago still couldn't see a thing. There was a porch light waiting for them, a light on in a barn off to the side, and smoke coming from the chimney of a small house on a far hill. Everything else might as well have been invisible.

"Are you okay?" Buffy looped an arm around Santiago's waist.

"Yeah. Yeah, I'm fine." Santiago took a deep breath, wrapping Buffy up in his arms. Inhaling her clean scent, he steeled his nerves and willed his heart to stop racing.

"Ready to meet the judges?" Joy snickered at Santiago's look of pain and led them inside.

The room erupted into noise as soon as they walked inside. Buffy disappeared almost immediately, swarmed by a large group of freakishly tall people.

Santiago turned to the side and found one other loner, like him. She was short with dark brown skin and hair so black it looked red.

"Hi." She offered a hand and Santiago took it. "I'm Xiomara."

"Santiago." He nodded at her. "You're Calehan's wife?"

"Scored myself the oldest." Xiomara threw her hair over her shoulder jokingly and turned her eyes back to the scene of flailing limbs and excited squeals. ¿Estás nervioso?"

"Claro que sí, tu sabes," Santiago answered in Spanish, glad to share his nerves with someone who was not Buffy's sibling.

"No te preocupes." Xiomara waved at a little boy who ran up to her, wrapping his arms around her thighs. "You're family already."

"You're WHAT?" a woman's voice shrieked through the room, shocking everyone into silence.

"I got married," Buffy said again, finding Santiago's eyes across the room.

He willed himself not to melt into the wallpaper and disappear from the hundred pairs of identical eyes staring at him. Every face in the room whipped toward him.

"You got married?" A younger boy stood, taller than Buffy and Santiago. He realized that Buffy wasn't lying when she called herself short. "To who?!"

"That guy." Joy pointed at Santiago, snickering at the slight step back he took.

Buffy joined him then, taking his hand in hers and standing tall beside him.

"This is my husband, Santiago. We got married when we were in Vegas a few months ago."

"In VEGAS?" the woman shrieked again. "Who *are* you?"

"Myself, just better," Buffy answered genuinely, her siblings quieting as they took in her meaning.

The back door opened then, an older man walking inside.

"Daddy!" Buffy called, pulling Santiago with her as she rushed over to the dark-haired man. "Meet Santiago."

"Hello, sir." Santiago shook Muskwa's hand, pulling it into his chest and sharing breath as he kept his eyes down.

"This is the man who convinced you to settle down?" Muskwa admired Santiago, dragging his eyes from his head to his toes.

"He loves me."

"I can tell." Muskwa stroked Buffy's cheek with his thumb, the happiness clear in his eyes. "Welcome to the family, Santiago." Muskwa hugged him and the room launched into wedding plans.

"You're going to do a ceremony, right?" Joy asked.

"You're not really married if you don't do it in ceremony," another sibling mumbled.

"Obviously we will get married in ceremony," Buffy huffed and returned to Santiago's side once again. "We just got here. Can we have five damn minutes?"

"If you wanted five minutes, then you should come home more often." Joy glared at Buffy.

"She will," Santiago answered, gazing down at her. "I promise."

Joy smiled.

They slept in the living room that first night. Spread out in front of the TV on the couch and floor, the siblings fell asleep whispering and laughing like they did as kids. Santiago felt light, seeing Buffy with her family and having them accept him felt like a sign. A sign that they had done everything right. Now he had his twin star forever.

Acknowledgements

That's a wrap on book two. I can't even believe that those words are true. Hold on, I need to say it again.

My second book is finished.

Damn, that feels good.

I have a million people to thank for making **When Stars Have Teeth** what it is. My brain can only take me so far and without my amazing friends, my books would read a lot more like a middle school journaling assignment. Thank you to my earliest readers; Robin and Tasha. You two always help me figure out who my characters are and that is priceless to me. Thank you to Paz and Lindsay, and my Mom and Nana, who have read probably as many drafts as I have. Lindsay, thank you for brainstorming with me for hours and days on end. I love you.

A million thank you's to my fantastic editor; Alexis Richoux. Your unwavering support for the story kept my head above water. All of your comments made the book and my writing so much better, all while making me laugh at the same time. You're a treasure and I am so lucky to have you by my side. Thank you to Alexis for introducing me to Bear and having them join my editing team. Bear fearlessly called me in and reminded me when I could do better – and for that I am eternally grateful. Not to mention Bear's comments had me giggling like a kid and made me feel as though I was reading my own book for the first time.

It is hard to find people who trust you enough for complete honesty and I feel proud knowing that all of you felt comfortable enough with me to be honest with your thoughts. You all had a hand in making this story, and my writing, improve.

And last, but never least, thank you to my partner in life. My Santiago. My guiding star, my moon and sun, my heart. My love. Thank you.

About the Author

Dani Trujillo is a fiction storyteller born of Pueblo and Mexican descent. The desert is her happy place and serves as inspiration for many of her works. She holds a Bachelor of Anthropology from the University of Hawai'i and a Master of Forensic Behavioral Science from Alliant International University. She currently resides on the East Coast with her husband, two spooky black cats, an elder chihuahua named after jeans, and the plethora of ghosts inhabiting her 1949 home.

Follow her on Instagram for a look behind the scenes: @dh.tujillo

Sign up to Dani's monthly newsletter for early releases and bonus content: https://www.danihtrujillo.com/

Made in the USA
Middletown, DE
14 June 2024